MY BEST BEDTIME STORYBOOK

MY BEST
BEDTIME
STORYBOOK

Written
by Zdeněk Karel Slabý
and Dagmar Lhotová

Illustrated
by Edita Plicková

Translated
by Stephen Finn

BLACK CAT

Copyright © Artia, Prague 1985
First published 1986 by Orbis Publishing Ltd
Reprinted 1987
Reprinted 1988 by Macdonald & Co (Publishers) Ltd
under the Black Cat imprint
Illustrated by Edita Plicková
Translated by Stephen Finn
Graphic design by Václav Bláha

Macdonald & Co (Publishers) Ltd,
3rd Floor, Greater London House,
Hampstead Road, London NW1 7QX
a member of Maxwell Pergamon Publishing Corporation plc

ISBN 0-7481-0170-5

Printed in Czechoslovakia by Svoboda, Prague
1/99/34/51-04

January

1 January

The Wind Elf

Up in the old attic, that smelled of dried herbs in summer and in winter tasted of frosty air, there suddenly came a sound of soft breathing. In a crevice beneath one of the beams, where the autumn wind had blown a reddish-yellow leaf, a little pixie who had just been born was taking his first timid look around him. He had opened his eyes on just one of those clear nights when your secret wishes are supposed to be granted. He crawled out of his nook, set his leaf cap on his head, and wondered what he should do next. The only living thing he could see was a butterfly, which was sleeping its winter sleep. As the pixie, starting to feel lonely and helpless, began to cry, the butterfly gently opened its wings and said, 'You should be glad to be here at all, instead of snivelling away the moment you're born. You'd do better to think about what you want to be.' 'I don't know,' the little fellow mumbled, but when he looked

at the butterfly's wings, he began to wish he could have a pair of his own and go sailing out of the window into the starlit night. And since it really was a night for magic, a voice answered his thoughts, and said: 'You can't have a pair of wings, but I will give you a magic cloak. To begin with it shall be silver, for it is a gift of the silver night, but you can learn to change its colour.' The pixie opened out his cloak, and at the touch of the cold night breeze it swelled like a pair of wings and carried him out into the night. The little pixie had become a wind elf, a wanderer in the sky.

2 January

What the World Is Like

The countryside the wind elf was flying over had a grey look about it. There was grey smoke coming from the chimneys, and the roofs of the houses were grey; even the paths and the bare trees had a veil of grey fog laid over them. 'What a sad sort of world this is!' the sky traveller thought to himself, and he glided down into one of the grey streets. Minny the cat was sitting beside the gutter. For the time being her

mouth was busy yawning, but it quite fancied something to sink its teeth into. 'No point in getting eaten when you've only just been born,' thought the elf, and he spread his cloak again and landed on the nearest window-ledge. The world wasn't a bit grey on the other side of the glass. There, in a gay little room, Julie was merrily playing away. The little girl was holding some sort of fête or gala, and the wind elf blinked at the sight of all those bits of coloured paper, trailing and flapping about. Suddenly, Julie opened the window and peeped outside. She probably thought some frozen little bird had landed on the ledge. As soon as she saw the elf in his cloak, she snatched off her paper hat and — pop! the world wasn't grey any more, nor coloured. It was quite, quite black. It was as dark as dark can be. And the wind elf was caught like a bird in a cage.

3 January

What the World Is Like

In the darkness beneath the hat the wind elf began to whine: 'Just when I had decided what I wanted to do, I can't do anything any more. Now I *know* what I want to be. I shall be a great explorer.' He started to cry like anything. But after a while a little crack of light appeared at the bottom of the hat. That was little Julie, peeking curiously inside. She got a good look at the elf for the first time. He looked like a big butterfly, with a reddish-yellow leaf on his head. His dark cloak was lined with silver moonbeams that shone more beautifully than anything Julie had ever seen. 'If you give me a little piece of your cloak,' she said, 'I will let you go.' The little sky traveller was not too sure if he was supposed to give away bits of his magic cloak, but in the end he agreed. 'All right then, but only the teeniest piece.' Julie touched a corner of the silver cloak, and some of the silver rubbed off on her finger, and that was enough for her. She gave the elf some bits of coloured

paper in return. He hung them on one half of his cloak. 'How marvellous the world is!' he called out, and off he flew.

4 January

The Boy Who Was Always Painting

It was snowing a little, so that the world was now half grey, half white, and in between the snowflakes the bits of coloured paper on the wind elf's cloak flitted like little flying flames. It was a pity no one noticed them. The sky traveller landed on another window ledge, where he saw a small boy on the other side of the panes. His name was Chrissie, and he had a crayon in his hand. On the table were some paints and coloured chalks, and there were painted sheets of paper lying all around. His mother had already given him all the paper and exercise-books, all the wrappers and the backs of old letters to draw on, but it wasn't enough for Chrissie. He had started to paint on the walls, then on the cupboards and chairs and tables, and on the white lace curtains, until his mother began to shout:

'Call the doctor! I can't stop him! That boy is painting mad!' When Chrissie got to the window, he painted the glass and the frame, then he opened the window and saw the dark side of the wind elf's silver cloak. He would have started painting that, too, but just then he saw the little elf. 'Who are you?' he asked, and a tiny voice replied: 'I'm a great explorer.' 'Then you must tell me about everything you've seen and heard and come across!' The sky traveller wasn't sure he knew how, and he hadn't seen all that much of the world just yet, but he did his best. Chrissie forgot all about his painting for a while, and his mother said: 'Just look how quiet he is — that little fellow has cured him!' When the wind elf had told him everything he knew, he flew off again with a whirrr! I suppose he went to tell the other children what he had seen.

The Proud Cat

Because little Margie wanted a cat so very, very much, and because you weren't allowed to have real live animals in the flats where she lived, her mummy crocheted one from bits of wool. And since the wool was pretty, three-coloured and angora, the cat was pretty, three-coloured and angora, too. But she turned out to be terribly proud and quarrelsome as well, and Margie began to wish she had never wanted a cat at all. Most of all, Angora liked to make bets. Every night she would say to Margie: 'Bet you can't find me tomorrow!' They would bet a bun, or a toffee, or an ice-cream — Angora didn't mind what, since she always won and ate everything. Margie was annoyed at how good the cat's hiding-places were, and at how big-headed the creature was becoming. She knew she would have to find Angora once at least, if the cat were not to become quite impossible. Then she had an idea. That evening, before Angora had a chance to say as usual in her crocheted little voice: 'What will you bet me you can't find me in the morning?', Margie secretly untied the little knot at the back of the cat's neck and unravelled a stitch or two. Angora swaggered out of the door and had

no idea that Margie was holding the end of her fur. This time the cat got found right enough. And afterwards she always had a zig-zag pattern across her fur where the wool had unravelled. That's how you can tell it's Angora, because she isn't a bit proud any more.

6 January

The Tale of a Giraffe

Amanda the giraffe was very proud of her neck, and it truly was very nearly the longest of all the long necks in the giraffe pen. But very nearly wasn't nearly enough for Amanda, so she decided she would stretch her neck and wear high collars, until her neck had become the longest of all and they had put her in the Guinness Book of Records. From that moment on she always had her nose in the air, and she became most disagreeable. Her starched collars pinched terribly, so that she was always sighing out loud. And then she kept trying to find special sorts of vegetables and grass that made you grow more quickly, and was always boasting how famous she would be, and telling everyone that her name would be in the papers. The foolish giraffe was really expecting the reporters and photographers to come soon, because her neck had indeed begun to get longer. It grew so much that in the end she had her head in the clouds, and she could almost talk to the moon. But she had lost all her friends, and had no one to complain to, which was what she liked doing best of all. She forgot all about the record books and the reporters, and just cried all the time. Now, when people cry, they don't stretch their necks at all, in fact they hang their head instead. So Amanda hung her head until she suddenly found herself back among her friends again. How pleased she was!

7 January

The Snow Maiden

The midwinter frost was as keen as a honed sickle. The old folk were saying they couldn't remember a January like it, that it was only as cold as that once in two hundred years. The children were wearing warm woollen mittens and scarves, and were busy building snowmen. In front of the cottage where the old couple lived there were seven snowmen with black coals for eyes and leaky pans on top of their round heads. Grandad was remembering his boyhood. 'Grandma, what if we were to build a snowman, too?' 'Don't be a silly Grandad,' laughed Grandma. 'You'd better go and chop some firewood to warm the parlour.' But Grandad was not to be put

the baby girl a drink of goat's milk, wrapped her up warmly, and rocked her to sleep. And when Grandad began to muse over what they should call the child, Grandma had an answer ready at once: 'What else can we call her but Snegourka, since she is made of snow?' Snegourka grew, and grew, as if each passing week was a year. Before very long she had grown into a pretty girl with skin like snow, raven hair, and eyes the colour of a summer sky. Because she was good and kind, she was not only a comfort to her parents, but also the favourite of children for miles around. Every day they would call at the cottage, and take Snegourka to play in the snow, where they snowballed and slid and tobogganed all day long. 'Take your pullover, or you'll catch a cold!' Grandma would tell her anxiously, but Snegourka would only laugh. She could go out in frosty weather with only the lightest of clothes on, and she never felt the cold, never caught a chill, and never had the 'flu. And there was nothing she liked better than to play in the snow.

off, and he gave Grandma no peace until she agreed. 'All right, Grandad,' she said in the end, 'if it will make you happy. But I'll tell you what. We won't make an ordinary snowman. Since we are all on our own here, we'll make ourselves a snow child.' And so it was. They rolled a big ball of snow and carved a little body, arms, legs and a head out of it. When they had given the little snow girl eyes and a nose, a chill wind swept past the cottage, and a faint whine was heard. Was it the wind? The frost stroked the snow child and it blushed, blinked, and began to cry.

8 January

The Snow Maiden

As the snow child started to cry, Grandad's mouth fell open. 'Grandma, a miracle has happened. A snow girl has been born to us!' Grandma hurriedly picked the child up and took her into the cottage. There she gave

9 January

The Snow Maiden

All through the winter Snegourka spent more time outside than inside at home, and she loved even the fiercest of blizzards, the sort you wouldn't turn a dog out in. Nor would she sleep in the cottage parlour, where the roaring stove was much too hot, but only in the freezing scullery. All the same, the sun began to get hotter and hotter, and soon all that was left of the seven snowmen outside the cottage was just so many blackened stumps. The icicles under the roof had cried themselves away, and the snow thawed until it was altogether gone. Spring had come. Snegourka would wander off by herself into the deep forest, looking for what was left of the snowdrifts. She was sad to find them getting smaller day by day. She sought the shade of spreading trees, and one day she heard a deep sigh from the thicket, and thought it was a deer pushing through the branches. It wasn't, though. It was the icy wind, fleeing the glare of the sun. Winter was over.

10 January

The Snow Maiden

Everything was in flower. The grass grew green again, and the air was warm. But Snegourka grew sadder day by day. She shut herself up at home, as if she were afraid of the bright sunshine, and the other girls would wait in vain outside the cottage for her to come out and play. Just once in a while she would play with her best friends, Anna and Natasha, but only in the cottage hallway, which was the coolest place she could find. 'How pale you are!' Grandma would say. 'If only you would go out in the sun sometimes!' Snegourka did not answer, but the old woman fancied she saw the glint of a tear in the young girl's eye. 'Whatever is wrong with the child?' she would wonder. Snegourka only cheered up once, and that was the day a hailstorm came, and the little white balls of ice were scattered everywhere. But the hail soon melted away, and the snow maiden was sadder than ever. 'What are we to do, Grandad?' the old woman asked, anxiously. But the old man could say nothing to cheer her up. He was thinking only that what winter had given them, summer would take away, and that soon the two of them would be all alone again.

of the window at the sunny summer's day. But Anna and Natasha pleaded and begged, and promised to look after Snegourka, until at last Grandma agreed. 'Off you go, my child,' she said. 'It might cheer you up, at least. What must be,' she was thinking, 'must be, sooner or later.'

12 January

The Snow Maiden

So Snegourka went with Anna and Natasha. The rest of the girls greeted her joyfully, wove her a garland of wild flowers for her hair, and drew her into the circle for a dance. She danced and sang with the others, but still she didn't smile. Then the boys lit a bonfire, and the girls got ready to jump over it, as was the custom on that day. Anna and Natasha stood on either side of her, and Natasha whispered in her ear: 'Don't worry: you jump after me, and Anna will watch out for you and help you if you

11 January

The Snow Maiden

It was Midsummer's Eve, and the revels had begun. The young folk were celebrating the feast of the good fairies. In the woodland groves the girls were weaving garlands of flowers, and singing and dancing. This time no one came for Snegourka: her friends knew she never left the house. 'She's probably ill,' they would say. But in the middle of a merry song, her best friends Anna and Natasha suddenly caught each other's eye. They felt sorry for Snegourka, all alone at home. They were sure she would like to join in their fun. Without having to say a word, the pair of them set off for the cottage at a run. Grandma didn't want to let Snegourka go, and the snow girl herself grew quite afraid as she looked out

can't manage it.' So Snegourka jumped over the flames, but, as she did so, she vanished before Anna's very eyes, and she and the other boys and girls heard only a mournful sigh. Everyone fell silent, their gaiety instantly gone. Had Snegourka melted like snow in the flames? But there was nothing to fear. What seemed like a warm breeze wafted by, and all at once Snegourka was standing there with the rest of them, her cheeks rosy and smiling. Maybe it was because she wasn't afraid of the fire, or maybe it was the work of the Midsummer fairies, but either way the snow maiden had become like all the other girls. When the next winter came she wore gloves and a woolly jumper, just as they did, to keep out the cold. But she still loved the snow as much as ever.

13 January

The Start of the Tale of a Cupboard

In a mysterious room in a mysterious house, there once stood a mysterious cupboard. And if you want to know more, you'll have to wait until February 13.

14 January

The Fox Settles a Quarrel

Two breadrolls were arguing over which of them was the prettier and the tastier. 'See how golden brown I am, how many poppy seeds I have on me, and how appetising I smell,' cried one of them. 'Who wants to be brown?' scoffed the other. 'See how wonderfully pale I am, the same on both sides, and sprinkled with crystal salt. I look as if I am studded with precious stones!' 'Huh!' replied the first. 'How can a skinny thing like you consider himself handsome? Just look at *me*! I am as round and plump as a pigeon's crop!' 'Who are you calling skinny?' the other snapped back. 'How much better to be slim like I am, than to be a fatty like you!' The pair of them went on boasting, each raising his voice a little more as the argument continued. It would probably have come to a fight, if a fox had not happened to pass by. He peeped in at the window, then jumped up on to the table. 'I'll soon settle the matter,' he said, opening his hungry jaws, and he ate them at one gulp. 'Both equally delicious,' he congratulated himself, and trotted back to the woods.

15 January

The Laughing Queen

There was once a queen who was always laughing. And how she would laugh, loud and long, till the plates fell from the dressers and the pictures from the walls! The slightest thing would set her off, and the noise was so terrible that the courtiers and the servants in the castle, and even those subjects who lived beneath the castle walls, had to stop up their ears when it began. They used their fingers at first, but in the end they had to make themselves earplugs so that they could get some work done. No one knew what the queen's real name was, since she was called Her Merry Majesty by everyone. She roared with laughter when the Chancellor told her the kingdom was going bankrupt, had a fit of giggles when she fell downstairs and broke her leg, and when an earthquake came and left the palace in ruins, she just laughed until her sides ached. All the famous doctors came to try and cure her, but she would only dismiss them with a wave of her hand. 'Laughing is healthy,' she would insist, chuckling till the

tears came streaming down her face. 'But, Your Majesty,' the Chancellor dared at last to object, 'laughter is one of the spices of life, and spices should be used sparingly.' Now, if there was one thing the queen didn't like it was having people disagree with her, so she had the Chancellor put to death. She thought this was so funny that this time she really couldn't stop laughing, even to catch her breath, and by and by she choked to death with laughter. At last the courtiers and the citizens were able to enjoy some peace and quiet.

16 January

The Cruel Fairy

There was once an old fairy who was very lonely. None of the other fairies would speak to her because of all the cruel catastrophies she had brought upon fairytale folk. It was she who had once declared that Sleeping Beauty should prick her finger and sleep for a hundred years. Indeed, she might have slept for ever if she had not been kissed by a passing prince. And it was she who made them send Bobbikin floating down the river in a frail wicker basket, caused the sea fairy to be shut up in a glass castle, and saw to it that Red Riding Hood was eaten by the wolf. There was no end to the ill-fortune she had spread through her spells. And when at last she retired from her work of spinning the webs of fate, she was quite friendless, and soon grew very sad. She trudged up and down fairyland, bemoaning her own cruel fate and complaining that it was not her fault she had been so wicked, that it had been *her* fairy godmother who had stood over *her* cradle and decreed that she must spend her whole life doing all those evil deeds. But it turned out all right in the end, thanks to the good fairies, who granted her a happy ending. For who knows what would have become of the cruel fairy, if it hadn't been for a certain young lad who heard of her plight. Because he was fond of

doing good deeds, he decided to help the fairy. He visited her regularly, and they would sit and talk for hours. By and by his warm breath melted the ice that surrounded the cruel fairy's heart, and in the end she turned into a kind old granny who liked nothing better than to roam the world, telling the nicest fairy tales she knew.

17 January

How Princess Wilhelmina Got Married

King Frederick the Fainthearted of Utterfalia had a huge kingdom, a daughter called Wilhelmina, and a headache. His headache was due to the fact that the royal treasury was as empty as a beggar's larder, and that his neighbour, King Knot I, had drawn up his armies on the border between their lands. Since Utterfalia had no army of its own, and had an empty treasury as well, there was no hope of raising one, so

Frederick thought his neighbour's terms seemed very reasonable. All he was asking for was Wilhelmina's hand in marriage. The only real difficulty was that the princess flatly refused to marry King Knot. 'Grumpy old tyrant,' she said. 'Oh, Daddy, how *can* you expect me to agree?' What she didn't say was that she was madly in love with her father's armourer, who was called Harold. It was better not to mention it, for though he was a clever young man, and as brave as any, his blood was hardly what you might have called blue. He kept the royal suits of armour and weapons as clean as new pins, even if there was no royal army to use them any more. He didn't mind that he got no pay, as long as he could be near the princess. But when a messenger arrived from King Knot to say that if the princess did not change her mind within three days he would seize the throne of Utterfalia and shut Frederick up in his own dungeon, that did it. 'Wilhelmina,' Frederick said, sternly, 'you will have to get married, whether you like it or not. I am certainly not going to move to the dungeons on your account, the royal chambers are quite damp enough!'

their heads and get a closer look at this funny, friendly dragon. The mayor, who took his job seriously and, even though he had never actually come across a dragon before, supposed that it must be a mayor's job to deal with one, said a little grandly, 'How might we be of assistance?' 'I'm looking for a home,' said the dragon, politely. After thinking for a moment, the mayor replied, 'I think we might have just the thing.' And he had a pen built in one of the city parks, where the dragon went on show to all who were willing to pay a modest entrance fee. By and by people got used to the dragon, so the clever mayor added some elephants, lions, hippopotamuses, baboons and other animals, and that is how the first zoo in the world was started.

21 January

The Three Dragons

When the dragon brothers B and C grew a little bigger, their mountain lair got overcrowded again. 'Why go on bumping into each other all the time?' said Dragon B. 'It's time I went out into the world as well.' As he left the lair, he accidentally stepped onto a loose boulder, and both dragon and boulder rolled right down the mountain and across the plain, and ended up at the foot of the royal city walls. King Montague the Gloomy himself came out onto the battlements to see what was going on. He blew his nose majestically with his royal handkerchief, and said: 'Most esteemed dragon, I bid you welcome. You may take Princess Ermintrude the minute her bags are packed.' 'Why should I do that?' the puzzled dragon enquired. 'Because it is the age-old custom that dragons carry off princesses,' explained the king, a trifle severely. He didn't say anything about Ermintrude's being rude, quarrelsome, plain, grumpy and bad-tempered, so that all the marriageable princes in the neighbourhood

gave his kingdom a wide detour. 'In that case,' replied the dragon, anxious to please, 'I should be delighted to take her.' There was great relief and rejoicing in the royal city, and a magnificent wedding was celebrated. Ermintrude became a dragon princess. At first she nagged poor old Dragon B terribly, scolding him and slapping him, but when the kindly dragon just bore it all patiently, she didn't enjoy it any more, and in the end she treated him kindly. Believe it or not, she started to look quite pretty in the end.

22 January

The Three Dragons

Dragon C had the lair all to himself now, but he soon got bored up there on his own. He decided to go in search of his brothers, but he got mixed up, and instead of setting out south to follow Brother A, or west after Brother B, he headed east. Since he was more timid than the other two, he decided to go on foot, so it was a long time even by dragon standards before he finally reached the town of Cloutcaster. He strode straight into the market-place, where the children from the local nursery-school were just setting off for their afternoon walk. 'Look at that!' said Harry, 'I bet it's an advert for something!' 'Bet it's not,' said Linda. 'It's prob'ly a film!' And before long the dragon was surrounded by stroking, patting and tickling little children, who kept saying: 'Good dragon — there's a good dragon!' 'I *am* a good dragon,' he agreed, deciding he liked being stroked, and he stayed with the nursery-school children. They let him live in the school garden, where he gave the children rides and let them climb on him and slide down the smooth bits of his scaly skin. He enjoyed that no end and, as you can imagine, the children did, too.

23 January

A Feast

Down by the lake lived a young stork, and in the nearby woods a fox. 'We are neighbours,' they said to themselves, 'so we ought to invite each other to a feast.' The first to issue an invitation was the fox. He greeted the stork just a little bit too politely, and led him back to his den. Then he set out all manner of goodies on plates beneath a low wide shelf, and told the stork to take his pick. The stork, with his long beak, was unable to pick anything up, and the fox ate everything himself. 'Just you wait,' thought the stork, and the next day he returned the compliment. When the fox arrived at the stork's feast, all the food was served in jars with narrow necks. The stork invited his neighbour to take his pick, saying he would eat what was left. But the fox couldn't get his snout beyond the narrow necks of the jars, and he didn't get a bite to eat. The stork had to eat everything himself, and that was the last time the two neighbours invited each other to a meal.

24 January

The Beauty Queen

Once a year, on January 24th, there is a great council of witches and sorceresses from all over the world. The occasion is also attended by all manner of other hags and bad fairies of lower rank, and they all

do their best to think up better ways of making people miserable. But there is always some special sort of entertainment to round the meeting off. Once it was a mixed choir of hullabaloos and frogs, another time some fairies danced a poor traveller off his feet. And then there was the beauty contest. What an affair that was! The competitors, some of the younger women, that is those under a hundred and fifty years old, dressed themselves up, combed their hair with their fingernails, daubed their faces with their favourite make-up, and then paraded up and down on the stage. A jury of specially invited wizards was given the task of choosing Miss Underworld. After throwing a little fire and brimstone at each other, they managed to agree on a winner, a bewitching creature from Nether Styxia. The only thing was that her victory went completely to her head, and before they knew it she had entered a human beauty contest. She came last, of course, and when the people laughed at her warty nose, hairy chin and crooked back, she lost her temper. Out of spite, she turned all the other competitors into toads. The jury had to admit that she came closer to what the rulebook said a beauty queen should look like than a troop of toads, and so they had to reverse their decision. It was only after they had presented her with her sash that she turned the toads back into young ladies. She still proudly wears that sash at all the black magic congresses.

25 January

The Wicked Stepmother and the Twelve Young Men

Mrs. Mallet had two daughters, Rosie and Jane. She fed the first on roast chicken and stuffed pigeon, while the second scarcely got enough to eat. The first didn't have to lift a finger, while the second had to toil away from morning till night, doing all the housework, and without so much as a word of thanks. The first daughter went about in silk and velvet, while the second wore only a rough linen smock, in summer and winter. And why was that? Because Rosie was Mrs. Mallet's own daughter, while Jane's mother had been Mr. Mallet's first wife. Mr. Mallet was mostly away anyway, looking for work, and when he was at home he was always too tired to take any notice of the way Jane was treated. It was January, and the midwinter frosts bit hard. The snow outside glistened as if it were inlaid with diamonds. Everybody was glad to snuggle down in front of a fire. Only the snowmen were pleased that the winter was a good one, but

even they had a ruddy patch on their carrot noses. Mrs. Mallet stuck her chin out of the door for an instant, but she soon popped it back in again in case she got a chilblain on the end of it. She decided she would put paid to her stepdaughter once and for all. 'Jane, dear,' she said, in a kindly voice, 'go into the forest and pick me a bunch of lilies-of-the-valley. I should like to put them in a vase and smell them.' 'But Mother,' the girl replied in surprise, 'how am I to find lilies-of-the-valley in January? Not even the snowdrops are out yet.' But her stepmother flung the door open, pushed the poor child outside into the bitter cold, and called after her: 'Don't you dare come back without them, or it will be the worse for you!'

26 January

The Wicked Stepmother and the Twelve Young Men

Jane waded through the snowdrifts as best she could, until she reached the forest. There she met twelve young men like sturdy ash trees. The funny thing was that some of them were dressed in summer clothes, as if it were July or August. They all began to ask the girl where she was going in such frosty weather without a coat, and Jane told them the whole story. 'What if you were to tell us which of the months you like best?' suggested one of the youths, who was dressed in a sheepskin coat. Jane thought for a while, but then she said: 'I like all of them, for each of them brings something pleasant, whether it be snow, flowers, fruit, rain, or whatever.' The young men looked at each other and nodded, and one of them took a bunch of lilies-of-the-valley out of his pocket and handed it to the astonished girl. Jane thanked them, and hurried home. Suddenly, she wasn't even cold. Her stepmother was annoyed, but there were the sweet-scented lilies-of-the-valley

standing in the vase, so she had no reason to scold her stepdaughter.

27 January

The Wicked Stepmother and the Twelve Young Men

The next day Mrs. Mallet gave her stepdaughter a smile as if butter wouldn't melt in her mouth, and said: 'Dearest Jane, bring me a basket of strawberries from the forest, I have such a fancy for them!' 'But, Mother, strawberries don't grow in January,' protested the girl, almost in tears. 'Be quiet!' yelled her stepmother. 'If you can bring me lilies-of-the-valley, then you can bring strawberries, too!' And she slammed the door behind Jane's back. The poor child was

up to her knees in snow, and the cold wind cut through her thin clothes, but she managed to reach the forest, where she met the twelve young men again. She told them what her stepmother wanted this time. The young men frowned, and the one in the sheepskin coat said: 'You shall have your strawberries, but that stepmother of yours had better watch her step.' He made a sign to a youth in a white smock, who reached into his satchel and filled Jane's basket with delicious-looking strawberries. Then the youth in the fur coat breathed on them a little. 'Perhaps that will cure her,' he said. Jane thanked them and hurried home. She felt quite warm. Her stepmother frowned fit to turn milk sour, when she saw that Jane had again brought back what she had been told to. The strawberries looked inviting, so Mrs. Mallet sat down with the basket, and she and Rosie gobbled up the lot. They did not even offer one to Jane. But the pair of them moaned and groaned all night long and felt as if they had eaten a basketful of hailstones.

28 January

The Wicked Stepmother and the Twelve Young Men

The next morning Rosie and her mother felt a little better, and Mrs. Mallet was soon busy trying to think up another dirty trick to

play on her stepdaughter. In the end she said, in a voice dripping with honey, 'Jane, dear little Jane, take a rucksack down to the orchard on the other side of the forest, and fill it with apples for me. But make sure they are all Worcester Pearmains, for they are my favourites.' This time Jane did not even bother to object. She said nothing at all, just sighed a little, put the rucksack on her back, and went outside. She slipped and slid on the icy snow, and three times she fell down and cut her knees before she reached the forest. There she found the twelve young men, as if they had been waiting for her. The one in the sheepskin coat, who had spoken to her before, again asked her what she was doing there, and why she had come out once more in the cold. When Jane told him, he laughed grimly. 'So,' he said, 'your stepmother has taken a fancy to apples. And they must be Worcester Pearmains!' He took the rucksack and placed it in front of a youth wearing a short tunic, who reached inside a basket and took out one apple after another. They were Worcester Pearmains, each of them perfect, and the young man filled the rucksack with them. 'I don't suppose your stepmother will enjoy them very much,' said the young man in the sheepskin coat. And he breathed three times into the rucksack, until a cold vapour began to rise from it. 'Don't even touch the apples,'

said the young man. 'And tell your stepsister not to eat them.' Jane thanked them and set off back home. The rucksack on her back seemed as light as a feather, and she walked across the icy snow as if it was a bed of soft moss.

29 January

The Wicked Stepmother and the Twelve Young Men

Jane's stepmother couldn't believe her eyes this time. But she didn't ask the child how she had managed to complete her impossible task. She just bit into the apples with enthusiasm. 'Sister, don't eat them,' Jane whispered to Rosie, but her stepsister pushed her aside and began to tuck in. But when both mother and daughter had gobbled up ten of the Worcesters, they began to clutch their stomachs and to cry out that the pain would tear them into a thousand pieces, and that the ungrateful Jane had set a trap for them, because she was in league with the devil. But it didn't tear them into a thousand pieces. They just flew out through the chimney like witches on broomsticks, shot through the air like

rockets, and landed in a snowdrift somewhere a long way away, so that they never found their way home. Jane lived on happily in the cottage with Mr. Mallet, until she found herself a good husband. Then all three of them lived there, more happily than ever. And the twelve youths? Perhaps they were the twelve months. Jane never saw them again. I suppose she didn't need them any more.

30 January

Grandma and the Doughnut

Grandma Bailey was well over eighty, but she still liked a nice bit of something to eat. She had a sweet tooth, and there was nothing she liked better than doughnuts. One January day she made a batch of doughnuts that came out especially well. Grandma stood back and admired them. Suddenly, the most golden and plumpest of them all began to speak, or rather to sing, 'This doughnut's a singer, a singer all right. He's rather more nutty than doughy, but still pretty light.'
'What's going on?' shrieked Grandma Bailey. 'I could have sworn that doughnut was singing!' 'Cut the hysterics, Granny,' said the doughnut, rudely. 'You bet I can sing. You ain't never heard a singing doughnut before? What I wanna know, Grandmamma, is what you got lined up for

me in the way of engagements? I got talent, you unnerstan me? Mebbe I even oughta go to opera school.' Grandma Bailey was speechless at first, but then she grew angry, and said, 'Just you keep a civil tongue in your head, and remember that doughnuts are made for eating, not singing, and you're no exception . . .' And she reached out to grab the cheeky doughnut. Only he managed to jump out of the dish, off the table and through the open door. Grandma Bailey set off after him, but there was no sign of the singing doughnut anywhere. He had disappeared at the end of the street. Where did he get to? Well . . . maybe he'll reappear in February.

31 January

Enough is as Good as a Feast

Gimlet the woodworm, known to his friends as Gimmy, lived in an old cupboard. He was the laziest woodworm that ever lived, and probably the sleepiest, too. He would sleep for hours, days and weeks on end, waking up occasionally to nibble a bit of timber and bore a little hole, so that a tiny pile of sawdust would appear on the floor. But it really wasn't too often, and in the end all his relations moved out, saying they weren't going to do all the work for a lazybones like that. Gimmy was left in the cupboard by himself. The furniture all around, trunks, tables, chairs, echoed with the crunching and munching of woodworms, but inside the cupboard there was silence. It was beginning to look as if Gimmy was going to laze around like that till doomsday. Then suddenly, one day, somebody bought his cupboard. Woodworms are not the least bit fond of moving house, but as it happened Gimmy found himself in a family that suited him to a tee. They played quiet, sleepy music all the time, and everything would have been fine, if only the mistress of the house hadn't said: 'I don't want that cupboard! It's not even eaten away by woodworm, so it can't be a proper antique. It'll have to go!' 'Oh, no!' shrieked Gimmy, who didn't want to leave his peaceful new home. And he gnawed away so busily that before long he had eaten the roof over his head. Which only goes to show that one can always have too much of a good thing.

February

the window pane, and through a crack in the frame he breathed: 'Wait here! First I'll bring you some of the big orange and the silver roll to taste.' Before long he was back again with a silver ice cube in one hand and an orange ember in the other. Which is how he managed to save the sun and the moon for us all.

2 February

The Bell

When twilight falls, then a sleepy peace falls on all the people and the houses and trees and cats and dogs, because the day is getting ready to take a rest. But once upon a time, somewhere between here and nowhere, a little girl got lost just as evening was on its way. She must have gone astray in the park. And that was the end of the twilight peace. Mother wept and wailed, Nurse wrung her hands, Father rushed hither and thither, and the neighbours all tut-tutted their sympathy. In the end they all set out for the park to look for her. But she didn't answer their calls. She must have gone to sleep somewhere, which was just what Mother was afraid of. 'Oh dear, Julie'll freeze to death before we find her!' As it happened, the wind elf had just been thinking about how little Julie had given him a handful of coloured paper and had set

1 February

The Sun and the Moon

The wind elf glided across a country where the sun went to bed early and didn't rise again until it was nearly lunchtime. Since it was winter, no one was surprised at this, and they simply welcomed the sun all the more, when it did come out. Except for one little boy, that is, because he wasn't grateful for anything. It's very easy to see why, because he had everything he could ever wish for. He had so many things all around him that he spent all his time looking at them, and was too busy to look up at the sky. But one afternoon he happened to look out of the window and see the sun going down. 'I want that big orange!' he shouted, and his father gave orders for the sun to be brought at once. His servants hurried out into the town square with a long ladder, but by the time they had climbed up it, the sun was gone and the moon was out. 'I want that silver breadroll!' cried the spoilt child, stamping his foot. Just then the wind elf came flying by, and he thought to himself that it would be a great shame if the servants were to climb up the ladder to the first cloud and then sail along to the moon and take it down. So he hurriedly rapped on

him free, and he was on his way to visit her. But he found only a crowd of sad faces in the park, and a weeping mother. He landed gingerly on her shoulder and whispered quietly in her ear, so as not to give her a start. 'Walk along the side-paths ringing a bell. I've seen them looking for lost sheep like that. Julie will wake up, you'll see.' Mother had no idea who it was who had whispered this advice to her, but she followed it anyway. And it wasn't long before she was hugging her dear Julie in her arms again. You can see how much wiser the sky traveller had become. Well, he was a month older, after all. And a month is like ten years to a wind elf.

3 February

Chrissie's Piano Lessons

Chrissie, the little boy who was so fond of painting that he upset everyone, had been given a piano. They thought it would be a good thing for him to have something else to do besides mess about with brushes and paints. Daddy brought along a music teacher, and the music teacher sat Chrissie down on one of those round stools you can spin up and down on a screw. Chrissie, of course, found the stool much more exciting than all those notes and scales, and having to listen to the music teacher. But, like it or not, they laid his hands on the keyboard, and he had to play. 'He'll never manage to learn!' Mummy sighed, but the music teacher said gravely: 'That's what I'm here for.' Then Daddy's birthday came along, and Chrissie had to play a new tune all the way through without making a mistake. But it was just then that the wind elf came visiting, and he sat down on the keyboard so awkwardly that Chrissie got the black notes mixed up with the white ones and made a mistake. Then he made another, and another, as the elf jumped about on the keys in complete confusion. That was that, as far as the great performance was concerned.

Instead of celebrations and congratulations there was only a telling-off, and the music teacher sighed: 'He'll never make a musician!'

4 February

Chrissie's Piano Lessons

When the wind elf saw what a mess he had made of things at Chrissie's house, he began to wonder how he might put things right. Then he flew down to the sea shore, found a nice shell that was nearly as big as he was, and hurried back to Chrissie with it. When the boy put the shell to his ear, he could not only hear the waves and the seagulls, but also various other birds, and the wind, and churchbells, and sirens and gales, and horses' hooves, and the hum of an aeroplane, and the patter of the rain. The shell had learnt all those new noises on its way from the sea, and now it taught

Chrissie to understand the music of the world, even without a piano. Then he sat down at the piano and tried to repeat everything the shell had taught him. Just then, his music teacher arrived. He listened for a while, and then said to Mummy, 'Can you hear? I told you I could make a musician of him!'

5 February

A Poorly Little Girl

Beneath the ground a little pip had woken up. It had dropped out of Helen's apple one autumn day, and had fallen asleep in the grass. Then it had tumbled into a mousehole and wandered along an underground maze, until it had fallen asleep once more. It didn't even know it had ended up under the floor of Helen's house. Helen was lying in bed with a temperature. None of the doctors

knew what was wrong with her, not until one of them said: 'I think Helen is summersick. She wants the sun to shine again.' The pip under the floor heard what the doctor said, and from then on he had no peace. He felt he must grow, and blossom, and become green. He wanted to so much, that in the end it happened. A little green flame appeared in the cellar, and out of it a trunk grew up. When it reached the ceiling, it burst through, pushed up the carpet, and stood in the middle of Helen's room. Helen took a deep breath, and felt better at once. The trunk quickly grew some branches and began to blossom. Then green leaves appeared, and finally red apples grew and ripened. As soon as Helen ate one, her cheeks grew rosy again, and she wasn't poorly any more. And what about that tree in her room? Did it stay there? I don't really know. Maybe she just imagined it, but the important thing is that she got better.

6 February

Amanda and her Brother

Amanda was a poor girl, but she had a fairy godmother, and for her birthday, which was in February, her godmother once gave her a pot which filled itself with delicious stew whenever you told it, 'Pot, cook stew!' Now Amanda's silly brother, Bertie, couldn't make out how the pot managed to keep making stew when no one ever put anything into it, so one day he decided to try it for himself. The moment Amanda had left the cottage, he called out, 'Pot, cook stew!' The stew began to bubble and boil louder and louder, until at last it boiled right over onto the stove. From the stove it spilled over onto the floor, and before long it had filled the whole parlour, and swept Bertie through the door and into the street. People began to shout at him, 'What have you done? Stop the stew, quickly, or there'll be trouble!' But it was too late now. The avalanche of stew carried away everything that stood in its path, horses, carts, market stalls, and passers-by. Bertie had no idea how to stop it. He just kept screaming, 'I don't want any more stew, I don't want any

more stew!' Luckily, Amanda came home, and she saw what had happened at once. 'Pot, enough!' she shouted, and the river of stew stopped streaming forth. The whole of that day, and the whole of the next, and the whole of the one after that, and for a long time afterwards, people had to eat their way in and out of their houses. All because of Bertie's inquisitiveness.

7 February

Amanda and her Brother

For her next birthday Amanda's fairy godmother gave her a hand-organ. When you told it, 'Hand-organ, play!' it began to play a magic tune that everyone had to dance to. As soon as Amanda left the house, her brother Bertie wanted to try it for himself, and he said: 'Hand-organ, play!' Before he knew what was happening, the organ was playing such a merry tune that Bertie couldn't help dancing. He caught hold of the hand-organ and danced out into the yard. All the chickens started to dance, then the cat and the dog, and the neighbour's wife, who had just come out to

hang out her washing. She caught hold of a starched shirt and danced out into the path, just as Uncle Ernest was walking by. Before he knew it, he was dancing, too. Soon there were more dancers, and everyone who passed by had to join in the whooping and prancing. But after one hour, and then two hours, their legs began to ache terribly. They were all limping, but they had to go on dancing, because the hand-organ went on playing. 'You've done it again, Bertie!' cried the neighbours, angrily. 'Hurry up and stop the music, or it will be the death of us!' But Bertie didn't know how to turn it off. He just kept shouting, 'I don't want any more music, I don't want any more music!' And that didn't do any good at all. They had to wait until Amanda arrived. She called out 'Hand-organ, enough!' and the music stopped. For days on end the villagers soaked their feet in mustard baths, and rubbed their legs with liniment, and they got well and truly behind with their work. All because of Bertie's inquisitiveness.

8 February

Amanda and her Brother

When Amanda's birthday came round again, her fairy godmother gave her a broom. Now this was no ordinary broom such as you would use to sweep the floor. It could do something quite different, but only

Amanda knew what. She was especially careful not to tell her brother Bertie. All she was willing to say was that you told it what to do by saying, 'Broom, jump!' When she left the cottage, she locked Bertie in, just to make sure he didn't bother the neighbours again. But she didn't go away, but watched secretly through the window, to see what would happen. Bertie lost no time at all. The moment the door was closed, he picked up the broom and examined it closely. Then he gave it its orders. The words had scarcely left his lips, when the broom leapt up in the air, landed on Bertie's back, and began to give him such a hiding as he had never had in his life before. And the broom did not take the slightest notice when Bertie shouted, 'Stop it! Stop it! Just you wait!' and other things of that sort. As soon as Amanda saw that her brother had learnt his lesson and was almost in tears, she burst into the parlour and called out: 'Broom, enough!' In no time at all beating had stopped and the broom was standing in the corner, as if nothing had happened at all. But something had happened. Bertie was quite, quite cured of his inquisitiveness.

9 February

Princess Josephine

Good king Willibald had an only daughter, who was the apple of his eye. Her name was Josephine, and she was really very beautiful, but she was the biggest slowcoach you ever saw. Wherever King Willibald left her, he was sure to find her there when he returned. It wasn't that she was all that lazy, it was just that she didn't seem to be interested in anything, excited about anything, or impressed by anything. She just looked at everyone with a serene smile, as if to say, 'Nothing ever surprises me.' Willibald would worry from time to time that the princess was so spiritless, but he would always tell himself that when she got married she would snap out of it. So as soon as

Josephine's eighteenth birthday came along, he announced that the palace was seeking a husband for her, and kings and princes gathered at the royal court from far and wide. All of them liked the look of Josephine, and they competed with each other, showering her with gifts, each trying to outdo the rest in wooing her. Each evening the king would ask her, 'Which of your suitors do you like best, my dear?' But she would only shrug her shoulders and reply, 'I really don't know, Father.' 'What about King Rufus? He's a widower, of course, but his treasury's full. You wouldn't go far wrong there.' 'I really don't know, Father.' 'Or how about Prince Ivor? Now *there's* a fine figure of a man, and an excellent swordsman, too. Think what a good general he would make.' 'I really don't know, Father,' Josephine kept saying, and so it went on.

10 February

Princess Josephine

King Willibald was at his wits' end. He had a courtful of impatient suitors to feed and keep amused, several chambers full of presents that Josephine couldn't even be bothered to unwrap, and no wedding in sight. Every time he asked the princess what she thought of King This or Prince That, she would only say over and over again: 'I really don't know, Father.' 'Have I to put the names in a hat, then?' he asked in the end, beginning to lose his royal temper. 'I really don't know, Father,' was all Josephine would say. She greeted each of her suitors with an enchanting smile, but without the slightest interest. All their compliments just went in one ear and out the other. King Willibald couldn't take any more, so he slipped down to the tavern to drown his sorrows. There he happened to take a seat beside Dusty the miller, and when he had downed a couple of pints of ale, he told his companion of his troubles. 'Do you know,' the miller told him, 'I don't blame her. They're just a bunch of smooth-talking tailor's dummies, if you ask me. You can't really expect Josephine to be able to choose between them. I mean, it's six of one and half a dozen of the other, isn't it?' 'Then what am I to do?' asked the king. 'I'd haf thought that was easy enough to work out, Yer Majisty,' replied the miller. 'You'll just have to find your little princess a bridegroom she can really take a fancy to!' 'That's all very well,' said the king, sadly, 'but where am I to lay my hands on one of those?' 'Don't you worry, old Sire,' said the miller. 'I'll send you one along tomorrow.'

11 February

Princess Josephine

The next day, a fine, strapping young mill-hand appeared among the princess's suitors, dressed in a white smock, with his hair uncombed, and hatless. The others turned their noses up at him. 'What's the like of him doing here?' they asked, and made it quite clear what they thought of the intruder. The mill-hand took no notice of their insulting remarks. He just stepped forward and let his eyes pass over the princess from head to foot. Though he fell in love with her at once, he pretended to be dissatisfied. 'I expected you to be prettier, Josephine,' he said. 'I beg your pardon!' said the princess, getting upset for the first time in her life. 'Do you realize to whom you are speaking?' 'You bet,' replied the mill-hand. 'To a certain young lady everyone says is a real lazybones, princess or not. Now, I'm a mill-hand, and a mill-hand's son, but I'm not afraid of a little hard work. So what do you think of that?' 'I think I shall have you boiled in oil, that's what I think,' said Josephine, stamping her foot angrily. 'You'd better apologize right away!' 'Well now,' replied the mill-hand, 'and they do say that nothing hurts like the truth! But you, my dear princess, will just get uglier and fatter and sillier, because all you ever do is sit and stare.' Josephine glanced round to see if the others had heard, and then she started to cry. 'I don't want to be ugly and fat and silly,' she said. 'Why hasn't anyone ever told me that that is what will become of me? What am I to do?' 'I'll tell you that tomorrow,' said the mill-hand, and he left the castle.

12 February

Princess Josephine

That evening Princess Josephine tried to get the king to tell her who the young man in the smock was. 'I really don't know, my dear,' fibbed His sly Majesty. 'I expect it was some common fellow who somehow managed to get past the sentries. If he turns up again I'll have him thrown out.' 'Oh, no, don't do that, Father,' she said. 'Not that I like him, of course, but I should rather like to speak to him again.' 'Very well, my dear,' said the king, playfully, 'speak to him you shall, but then you must decide which of the

The king gave his consent, because the princess was the apple of his eye, and at the wedding feast Josephine leaned over and whispered in her husband's ear, 'I quite forgot to ask your name!'

13 February

A Bit More of the Tale of a Cupboard

In a mysterious room in a mysterious house, there once stood a mysterious cupboard. It was positively the only thing in the room. And if you want to know more, you'll have to wait until March 13.

kings and princes you will marry.' The next day all the suitors gathered again, and began to shower the princess with compliments, but she only gazed at the door all the time, waiting for the mill-hand to arrive. 'Sorry, Josephine,' he said, when he did at last arrive, 'but our cow was calving, and I almost forgot.' 'You think more of a cow than you do of me?' asked the princess, sadly. 'Don't you like me just a little bit?' The mill-hand wanted to shout out, 'Yes, a lot.' But instead he told her, 'I must say I have quite a different notion of what a wife should be like. She must be lively, hard-working, clever . . .' Josephine was hooked. She wasn't the least bit interested in all the dandies who were paying court to her. The only one she wanted was the mill-hand, and he was the only one who didn't want her. 'What if I were to mend my ways?' she asked, in a whisper. 'Well, if you were to promise . . .' began the mill-hand. 'Then?' asked the princess. 'Then we might be married at once,' replied the mill-hand. And they were.

14 February

The Magician

A strange old man would walk the streets of a certain town, and on his back he carried a bundle, whose contents were even stranger than he was. He would stop beside the fountain in the market-place, or under one of the arches, and then he would call out to the passers-by that he had things for

sale that no one else could offer, and that he would exchange them for a kind word or a good deed. But the townspeople would only call out in reply, 'We've heard that one before!' or 'Be off with you. What money can't buy isn't worth having!' In short, they didn't believe the old man, and after all, there were plenty of tricksters around as well. But one little boy called Jimmy and his friend Jane decided to wait for the old man one day. As soon as he came into the market-place with his bundle on his back, they ran towards him calling out: 'Hey, wait a minute, we'll help you with that!' As soon as the old man heard this, he slipped the bundle off his back and gave the children a present. A little bead. But the children were cross. An ordinary bead, for offering to help an old man with such a load? They threw the bead away and strode off, without even looking round. But the bead came bouncing after them, and everywhere it touched the ground it left a halfpenny in a little hole. The children tried to catch the bead, but it disappeared from sight. 'How silly we were,' they said to themselves. 'We could have picked up enough halfpennies to buy some ice-cream. We won't make that mistake again!'

The Magician

It isn't all that easy to make friends again with an old man who has a bundle of strange things that he gives away in return for a kind word. You really have to *mean* that kind word, before it counts. Jimmy and Jane were afraid to go back to the old man, even though they were as curious as could be. In the end they couldn't resist, and came running up to him again. Each of them had a slice of bread and butter with apricot jam, which was the nicest thing they fancied to eat. They ate one slice between them, and offered the other to the old man. He winked his little eyes, smiled at them and, taking his bundle down from his shoulders, spread out his wares. This time he gave the children an old haversack that had definitely seen better days. But it was just the same as last time. Jane quite forgot her previous mistake, and said, 'I'm not carrying that thing around. Everyone will laugh at us!' At the very moment she said this, the haversack suddenly became filled with oranges, dates, bananas, figs, apples, and even fresh apricots. But it was too late. When they tried to take them out, everything disappeared, without leaving even a pip or a stone behind.

the strange lenses passed in front of Jimmy's nose, he saw out of the corner of one eye that on the other side of the glasses was a wonderful world such as no one had ever seen. Well, Jimmy wasn't going to see it either. The old man packed up his bundle and was gone. 'I'll be cleverer tomorrow,' Jimmy said to himself. 'I'll take the ugliest thing in the old man's bundle, if he offers it to me.'

17 February

The Magician

The moment Jane opened her eyes the next morning, she ran to ask Jimmy if he had met the old man with the bundle, and he told her all about the magic glasses. 'There you are,' she told him. 'You weren't the least bit cleverer than I was. But we must get the most magical thing in the whole of the old man's bundle. Then it will keep us amused for ever and ever, and we'll never be bored again.' Jimmy agreed. They had long since run out of things to play, so these days they just hung about in their rooms or down in the market-place, and it wasn't a bit exciting. So off they went. But the old man was nowhere to be seen. He wasn't by the fountain or under the arches. 'We'll have to look for him somewhere else,' said Jimmy, so they put some proper shoes on and set off out of town. They found a hill with a slide on it, which they tried out at once. They found fields with trees, whose snowy tops looked like fairytale old men with white beards. They found some icicles down by the stream, and played a tune on them. They saw the wintry woods, looking as though they were enchanted. They discovered one wonderful thing after another. 'We haven't found the old man,' said Jimmy, 'but don't you think we've found

16 February

The Magician

Jimmy was angry with Jane for having too much to say for herself, and because she had spoilt everything. He decided to go and see the old man by himself, and spent the whole day wondering what good deed he might perform that would please him. But he couldn't think of anything, so that in the end he went out into the streets without any clear idea of what he should do. But he saw that the old man's shoes were covered in mud, so he took a handful of the snow which had been falling, and scraped the old man's shoes clean. The old man was pleased, because his shoes had been getting heavy. He thanked Jimmy kindly, took down his bundle, and spread out his wares. Jimmy would have liked to choose something for himself, but the old man wouldn't let him. Instead he gave him a pair of glasses. 'A fine present that is!' Jimmy grumbled. 'No one wears glasses if they don't have to, especially not ones with a thick frame like that. Anyway, they're quite black!' 'You don't have to take them if you don't want,' said the old man, and he put them back with the rest of the things. But as

a magic present? This is where we'll come and play!' So you see, when you think about it, they really didn't even need magic glasses!

18 February

The Fan

One day Princess Proud was driving through the forest, on her way home from a ball in the neighbouring kingdom, when she lost her most beautiful fan. It was interwoven with gold thread and decorated with turquoise, and everyone said it was the most beautiful fan in the world. But now it was lost, and the princess gave an order to her ten servants. 'Search high and low, until you find it, and bring it back to me here at the palace, whatever you do!' The servants ran off through the forest in all directions. Nine of them came back empty-handed, while the tenth returned with news for the princess. 'I have found your fan,' he said, 'but a peacock is carrying it.' Since then peacocks' tails have really looked like fans, and peacocks have walked around looking just like Princess Proud.

The Ghost in the Old Mill

The old mill on the far side of the pond was supposed to be haunted. No one knew who haunted it, or how, or why, but the part of the village which lay on that side of the water was quite deserted. Everyone had moved out. People would still walk that way in the daytime, but at night no one dared go anywhere near. The people who had once lived there were sorry that their cottages were empty and abandoned. They persuaded the blacksmith's son Peter, a big, strong fellow who wasn't afraid of anything, to try and drive the ghost away, so that they could go back to their homes. That's how it is. If you happen to be born brave, you have to keep on showing everyone just how courageous you are. Peter walked round the pond, and it was quite dark by the time he reached the old mill. 'How am I supposed to find a ghost, when it's pitch dark?' he muttered crossly, but the moment he entered the mill he bumped into something hairy and horned. 'A devil!' he cried and, taking it by the horns, he threw it across his shoulders and hurried back to the blacksmith's workshop. All the villagers were waiting there to see if he would return safely. As soon as they saw him, they burst out laughing. The ghost they were all so afraid of, which they had seen or heard in the old mill from time to time, turned out to be nothing more than an old ram. Well, they do say that fear has big eyes!

Clever Jack

The snow still lay in the fields and meadows when Jack decided it was time for him to go and seek his fortune. 'Mother, I am going out into the world,' he said. His mother wrung her hands and cried: 'But Jack, what will become of you on your own? Everyone will take advantage of you. You are too kindhearted by far. And there's something wrong with the oven today, so I can't even bake you any cakes to take with you. Wait till tomorrow.' She thought that, if Jack slept on it, he might forget all about the big, wide world and stay at home. But Jack had wasted enough time already. 'Cakes or no cakes,' he said, 'I must be on my way. I shall manage without them well enough. And I feel strong enough to face up to the devil himself.' 'Strength isn't everything,' his mother told him. 'You need to have your wits about you to get by in the world.' 'I know,' said Jack, 'but I haven't spent all these years by the kitchen stove for nothing. I've done a good deal of thinking, and I dare say I'll get by well enough.' What was she to do with him? She couldn't stand in the way of her son's happiness. So she made the sign of the cross on his forehead, and off he went, without a single cake. But he had courage enough for two.

21 February

Clever Jack
Jack wandered through far-off lands, working at this and that. Sometimes he needed his strength, sometimes it was his common sense that saw him through. In short, when he set off home again, he had thirty silver pieces sewn into the lining of his coat. That was quite a sum in those days. And he had something else, something that money can't buy. He had learnt how to deal with rogues and scoundrels. Along a track leading through the fields he came across a soldier. He was on his way back from some war or other, and thought he was the cat's whiskers. He sang a boastful ditty as he marched along. 'We are the soldiers of the king. What we don't know don't mean

a thing.' Jack was annoyed at the soldier's bragging. 'And what have you done to be able to boast like that, soldier?' he asked. The soldier looked at the lad, with his nose in the air: 'Me, young fellow? Why, I have fought, and killed, and won. I have earned myself a full thirty silver pieces!' 'There you are, then,' Jack replied. 'I haven't fought anywhere, killed anyone or won anything, and I, too, have earned just thirty silver pieces, with these two hands and this head.'

22 February

Clever Jack
The soldier's eyes lit up when he heard how much money Jack had, and he began at

once to think of how to relieve him of it. 'Sixty silver pieces is better than thirty,' he thought. 'It shouldn't be too difficult to get the other thirty off a country bumpkin like him. He surely didn't get any second helpings when they were giving out the brains!' 'I'll tell you what,' he spoke aloud to Jack, with a cunning smirk. 'We'll have a little contest. Whoever wins gives the other his money.' 'Very well,' Jack replied. 'You decide what we'll do.' The soldier had noticed that Jack was only wearing a pair of light shoes, while he himself had his heavy army boots on. 'You see these two flat stones?' he asked. 'Whoever stamps on his the harder will win all the silver pieces.' And he brought his steel-tipped heel down on one of the stones so hard that sparks flew in all directions. But Jack had not been idle in the meantime, and had poured a little water from his bottle under his stone, without the soldier noticing anything. 'That's nothing,' said Jack, with a wave of his hand. 'When I stamp on my stone, water will spurt out of it.' The soldier laughed, until his sides ached, at the idea of a stripling like Jack stamping water out of a stone with the heel of his dainty shoe. But Jack brought his foot down, and the soldier got a soaking.

23 February

Clever Jack

The soldier scratched his ear. 'Wait a minute, young man,' he said. 'That's not all. Now we shall see who can throw a stone higher.' 'And who, pray, is going to measure it for us?' asked Jack. 'We'll count how long they take to come down. He whose stone stays up longer is the winner.' The soldier picked up a stone and drew back his arm. He had the strength of three bears, and it was a wonder his stone didn't go sailing through the clouds. 'Twenty-two, twenty-three, twenty-four ...' they counted together. Then thud! The stone came to earth about three paces away, driving itself deep into the ground. The soldier gave a contemptuous wave of his hand, certain that Jack was unable to beat him. 'That's nothing,' Jack grinned. 'It'll take twenty-four days for mine to come down.' And he picked up a stone and threw it. Actually he pretended to throw it, for in fact he had secretly dropped it into his knapsack. The soldier stood staring upwards, and counted:

'A hundred and twenty-two, a hundred and twenty-three ...' Then he sat down, and went on counting: 'Three hundred and twenty-two, three hundred and twenty-three ...' He looked at Jack suspiciously. What if the lad really were such a muscleman? Perhaps it wouldn't be such a good idea to get into a fight with him!

24 February

Clever Jack

'Hang on a minute, my friend,' said the soldier, seeing that Jack was already holding out his hand for the silver. 'Good and bad things come in threes. Whichever of us can whistle the louder, shall have the money.' The soldier had a whistle, while Jack had only his lips and teeth. And the soldier was short of breath. He blew once, twice, thrice. He whistled so loud that they raised the alarm in the barracks three miles

away, and the troops came charging out to attack the enemy. They all had their leave stopped for a month after that, because, of course, they failed to find any enemy, which was considered to be an act of cowardice. 'Not bad,' said Jack to the soldier. 'You whistle very well, really, only not quite loud enough. When I whistle, you will go deaf and blind.' At this the soldier took fright, and thrust his purse into Jack's hands. He hadn't come out of all those battles in one piece only to go deaf and blind on a quiet country path!

25 February

Clever Jack

'But I haven't won yet,' objected Jack, when the soldier pressed the money on him,

though he pocketed the purse to be on the safe side. 'You are entitled to hear me whistle. Only bind your eyes and ears as tightly as you can. That way nothing will happen to you, and at least you can be sure that you didn't give me your money for nothing.' The soldier wrapped three scarves round his eyes and ears, so as not to take any risks. Jack picked up a stout stick and beat him about the head until the poor fellow's ears rang in spite of the scarves. 'Enough!' shrieked the soldier, tearing the scarves from his head, and running off so fast that wild horses couldn't have caught him. He didn't even look round. And Jack? He went home to his mother. Sixty silver pieces was enough to set their little farm to rights, and they were doing very nicely thank you by the time Jack married little Rosie from down the road. And wasn't that the reason he had gone out into the world, anyway?

26 February

The Crow, the Fox and the Dog

The crow had stolen a piece of cheese from the grocer's shop. She flew into the willow tree to enjoy her meal in peace. But a hungry fox caught sight of her, and ran to the foot of the tree. 'Mother Crow,' he said, 'they say you are the cleverest of all the birds. Is that so?' The crow nodded her head, but held on tight to the cheese. 'Indeed,' the fox continued his flattery, 'I daresay you are the cleverest of all the animals. What do you think?' The crow puffed herself up like a turtle dove, but still her greed for the cheese was greater than her conceit. So she just nodded her head, and didn't make a sound. Then the fox had an idea. 'They say you sing very beautifully, but I shan't believe that until I hear it.' This

time the crow very nearly started cawing, but at the last moment she realized she would lose her cheese. So she just shook her head in silence. The fox had had enough, and slunk off. Then the crow, pleased with her cleverness, called out. 'That stupid fox can't fool me!' When she opened her beak to say this, the cheese fell to the ground, and was gobbled up by a dog that was following the fox's scent. 'A lump of cheese in the stomach is better than a fox in the undergrowth,' he said, and trotted off home. The crow watched him open-beaked.

27 February

The Doughnut and the Baker

Do you remember the doughnut we met in January? Well, he wandered about the neighbourhood until he was quite exhausted, and then he stopped to rest on the pavement in front of a shop window. But he didn't notice it was a baker's shop, and that there was a whole bowl of doughnuts in the window. The baker happened to step outside for a breath of fresh air, and he caught sight of the

doughnut lying on the pavement. 'Now, how did that get out here?' he thought, and quickly put it back in the bowl. But it made all the rest of the doughnuts look pale and sickly and rather skinny, while our doughnut was plump and brown, as if he had a healthy tan. So the baker decided to take it out of the window again, because otherwise no one would want to buy the other doughnuts. He wondered what he should do with it. In the end he decided he would slip it in with whatever the next customer bought. The first to arrive was Mrs. Marple, who was as round and as plump as a doughnut herself. She asked for a dozen doughnuts, and the twelfth one she got was our little friend. The baker put him right on top. As soon as Mrs. Marple went out of the shop, the doughnut squeezed out of the paper bag, jumped down from the shopping-bag, and made off as fast as his legs could carry him. Where did he go? Somewhere into March. He never even found out how Mrs. Marple quarrelled with the baker for selling her one doughnut short.

How the Rhinoceros Got into a Story

All of a sudden, out of nowhere, a rhinoceros arrived. Where did it arrive? Here, in this book of fairy tales. No one was expecting him. He was quite out of breath, and he apologized: 'Sorry I'm so late, but you know how it is. Whenever you're in a hurry, some visitor comes along to delay you. Well, my cousin from the London Zoo arrived. Now, you can't send her away, can you, so I made a nice cup of tea, 'cause there's nothing my London cousin likes better than a nice cup of tea. Then the 'phone rang. That was Grandad from the Paris Zoo, calling to ask after my health. Well, he went on for half an hour, but he didn't talk about anything except *his* health. And it went on like that. Before I managed to do anything at all it was evening, and then it was the next evening, and before I knew it a whole week had gone by, then a month, and of course a rhinoceros gets older, so who knows? Perhaps I'd never get into a fairy tale at all, and ...' We had to interrupt. 'But we weren't going to have a story about a rhinoceros. You don't belong here at all. It must be some sort of mistake. Who told you to come?' The rhinoceros grinned. 'No one did. That's why I came of my own accord. No one ever thinks of rhinoceroses, you see, so we have to think of ourselves. And now you've got a rhinoceros story anyway. You're not going to leave it out, are you?' So we've left it in the book. Why not, if it'll make a rhinoceros happy?

March

1 March

A Birthday Concert

The wind elf flew in at the first open window he came to. It had just started to rain, and he was afraid of getting his new hat wet. It was a black one, which was quite natural, since the Night gave it to him as a present for his birthday. The sky wanderer has a birthday on the first of every month, which is like once every ten years to a wind elf, as we know. 'I'd like today's birthday to be especially beautiful,' thought the wind elf, as he landed on a table, beside a velvet jacket sleeve. It so happened that that velvet sleeve belonged to the composer and conductor, Mr. Albert Eggro, who had just laid his head on a sheet of paper covered in lines and musical notes and gone to sleep. He had been composing a symphony all night, and he just couldn't get the last few notes right. It wasn't until morning, when he heard the sound of the rain and the rustle of the wind elf's cloak, which sounded like the swish of wings, that he managed to finish the piece. The sky wanderer flitted about the room from one object to the next, until at last he alighted on a gramophone record. It was black and shiny, like his new hat. The little elf put his head beneath his cloak and began to dream. He dreamed of a wonderful birthday. He wanted something very special to happen . . .

2 March

A Birthday Concert

The wind elf woke up with a start as the gramophone record he was sitting on began to turn. At first it made him dizzy, but when he got used to it, it seemed to him that he was on the most wonderful roundabout, filled with music. The composer, Albert Eggro, was listening to his favourite piece of soothing music. It was nearly evening, so long had the sky traveller lain there dreaming, with his head under his cloak. The room was in twilight again. The only bright thing was the composer's white shirt, which he had just put on because he was conducting a concert of his own works that night. He was just about to leave, when he realized he hadn't got his bow-tie, which he had put down somewhere, but couldn't remember where. The wind elf saw how upset the poor fellow was, and thought he would help him in return for the nice ride on the roundabout. He landed on the composer's shirt and spread his cloak, so that no one could tell the difference between him and the most elegant of bow-ties. When they stepped out onto the platform, the sky traveller did not regret his good deed in the least. He had the best birthday treat he could imagine. The music thundered all around him, then lulled him gently, and it seemed that all the musicians were playing just for him. When the concert was over, and Eggro bowed to the applause, the wind elf felt the same pleasure as the conductor. Then he flew up to one of the lights, and he had the feeling the people were clapping for him as well.

3 March

The Restless Needle
Just as a carpenter likes to have a proper chisel and a blacksmith a good hammer, so,

of course, a seamstress is never quite content without a nifty little needle. Mandy had a needle with a tiny little eye, but it was terribly inquisitive just the same. It always listened carefully when Mandy told her little sister fairy tales. And it listened more carefully than ever when Mandy turned the radio on. One day there was a travel programme, where they said that everyone who is good at something can always find work to do in the world. 'I'm a good stitcher,' the needle whispered to itself, 'Mandy always says so. Maybe I can find my fortune in the world.' The next day it secretly hid itself in Mandy's coat. Mandy went into a food shop, and at once the needle set to work. It wanted to embroider its mistress's signature on a bag of flour, but a stream of white powder poured out onto the floor, and Mandy got a good telling off, as if she had been the one who caused the trouble. 'Perhaps I'm not all that good at signatures,' the needle whispered to itself. 'But never mind, I'll do better next time.'

4 March

The Restless Needle
Mandy walked down the street, and the needle in her coat said to itself, 'I don't suppose there's anyone better at sewing things together than I am. Even when I only tack things, they hold together like glue.' Mandy got on a bus that was full of people. Some of them were sitting, some of them were standing, all next to each other. As the needle was watching them, it suddenly had an idea. It got down to work and, quick as lightning, it sewed Mandy's coat to the lady's next to her, and then that lady's coat to that of an old man. It sewed the old man's coat to someone's sweater, and the sweater to a trouser leg. The trouser leg it sewed to a skirt, and the skirt to the sleeve of a sports jacket. It worked so hard that by the time they got to the first stop all the passengers were sewn together, and no one could go

anywhere without everyone else. So they all
had to get off together, and if they hadn't
been clever enough to slip off their coats
and sweaters and unpick the stitches, then
they would probably be standing there to
this day, because Mandy's little needle really
was good at its job. I wonder if anyone
praised its work?

5 March

The SS Olympic and
the Sea Monster

The sea was calm, and everyone aboard the
steamer Olympic was in a good mood.
Captain Downes walked up and down
among the passengers in his Sunday
uniform, cracking jokes. The sun was
shining and the water clear. The Olympic
was making full steam, and her prow cut
a white vee through the blue of the ocean.
'Rocks ahead, Captain!' called the lookout
in the crow's-nest. 'Not much of them

showing above water, but it looks like there's a lot more under it!' 'What's that?' asked the Captain in amazement. 'I've been sailing these waters for a year or two now, and I don't know of any small rocks hereabouts, let alone big ones!' And he hurried to the bridge, to take a look through his telescope, to see whether his lookout had just been drinking too much rum. But it was too late. The steamer hit the rocks at full steam, and the rocks weren't rocks at all, but the sea monster Lotsmorbilow, who wasn't the least bit pleased, because he had just been having a quiet nap. 'Either I smash your stupid little washtub to smithereens with a blow of my three-hundred-foot tail,' he growled angrily, 'or, or . . .' And he thought the matter over carefully.

6 March

The SS Olympic and the Sea Monster

Thinking the creature had gone to sleep, Captain Downes gave orders to sail round the obstacle. Strangely enough, the collision had left the Olympic's bows undamaged, so that the manoeuvre might well have succeeded, if there hadn't been a roar of 'Stop!' from the monster. 'I haven't finished speaking yet,' he added. 'Or,' the monster continued where it had left off, 'you bring all the women you have on board on deck so I can choose one. You see, I get very bored here on my own, and I need someone to talk to. And women are best at that.' 'Better to sacrifice one woman,' said the first mate, who was known to have a grudge against women, 'than for us all to go down with the ship. Just look at the size of the monster,' he added, turning to the captain. True, Lotsmorbilow was not a pretty sight, and looked well able to do as he had threatened. So the captain ordered all the women to be brought on deck. Only one stayed behind, and that was Miss Esther,

whom he was to marry when they reached port. The monster stretched out his long neck until his egg-shaped head was right beside the ship, and began to consider the assembled women, some of whom were sobbing, some looking away from the creature's gaze. 'Don't like any of them,' the monster said at last. 'Either I smash your tub to pieces with my enormous tail, or . . .' And he fell into deep thought again.

7 March

The SS Olympic and the Sea Monster

This time Captain Downes supposed that the monster had not fallen asleep, so he thought it best to wait quietly until he had done his thinking. 'Or,' said Lotsmorbilow at last, 'you are hiding some little beauty from me, and that wouldn't do at all.' Before anyone had time to deny it, Esther herself stepped up on deck. She was so beautiful that the whole crew and the sea monster gave one great sigh of admiration. 'That's the one I want!' cried the monster triumphantly, reaching out his long claws towards Esther. 'And you, Captain, can take

back down on the deck. And Lotsmorbilow was crying, or better to say sobbing his heart out, with great teardrops rolling down his neck, until the sea all around was so oversalted that even the fishes' eyes began to smart. 'Take her, Captain,' gulped the monster, in between enormous sobs, 'but look after her like a jewel...' And he disappeared beneath the waves. 'How did you manage that, Esther?' asked the astonished captain. 'I told him I had to marry you, John,' she replied, 'or you would make an end of my mother.' 'But I don't even know your mother,' said Downes with a smile, as he climbed out of his diving gear. 'And I still don't see why *that* should make such an impression on the sea monster.' 'Well,' said Esther, 'I told him that my mother, Junokentheweenessie, was a relative of his.' 'My, but you know how to spin a good yarn, and no mistake,' said the captain, admiringly. 'But it's true, John,' said Esther. 'Junokentheweenessie really is my mother, and a cousin of Lotsmorbilow's. I don't look a bit like the rest of my family, it's true, but maybe our children...' But the captain wasn't listening any more. He had fallen into a dead faint, and the first mate had to take command aboard the Olympic.

this tub of yours wherever you please!' Lotsmorbilow held Esther at arm's length and looked her up and down carefully. 'What are you waiting for?' the first mate asked the captain nervously. 'Call out *Woman Overboard!* and sail away, just like the nice monster says! He might change his mind!' But the captain had other ideas. He hurriedly changed into a diving suit and began looking for a harpoon. He looked like an ant getting ready to fight an elephant.

8 March

The SS Olympic and the Sea Monster

'I'll settle that ill-mannered monster's cheek,' growled the captain through his teeth. 'I'll tear it apart, I'll wring its oversized neck, I'll...' Suddenly, he stopped in his tracks. The monster was heading back for the ship, where he set Esther gently

Terence by the hand and started to dance. He quite enjoyed it at first, but they began to dance faster and faster, until he was quite out of breath. He tried to break out of the circle, but bony hands gripped him tightly from both sides, forcing him to prance about more wildly all the time. Suddenly, the alarm clock went off, and the bony dancers vanished like the spirits that they were. Terence lay down in an empty coffin beside the churchyard wall, and he was so exhausted that he went straight to sleep. The next morning the gravedigger woke him up and asked him what he had been doing in the churchyard at night. 'You were lucky,' he said, when he heard Terence's story. 'There've been two travellers danced to death in my time alone.' 'Lucky?' said Terence, with a shrug of his shoulders. 'Maybe. But it was mostly the alarm clock. It rang at half past twelve — half an hour early!'

9 March

Saved by the Bell

Terence the tramp had only one possession in the whole world, an alarm clock that gained half an hour a day. If anyone ever asked him why he didn't get it regulated, he would reply, 'What for? That way it always wakes me up half an hour sooner than I set it, and so at least I shan't sleep so much of my life away.' One night, on his travels, Terence came to a lonely churchyard. It was just on midnight, and a couple of ghosts came up to him at the gate. 'Come and dance with us!' they told him. 'We've got an hour, but we have to keep an eye on the time, because we mustn't stay a minute after one o'clock!' 'Don't worry about that!' grinned the tramp. 'What do you think I've got an alarm clock for?' The ghosts took

10 March

King Pugnatius

King Pugnatius had always liked fighting, ever since he was a little boy. When he grew into a young prince, he thought there was no finer sport than taking part in all sorts of tournaments, where he would enjoy the sword-fencing or jousting on horseback with wooden lances. As soon as he became king, he got married, but he would leave his lovely wife Maud alone in the royal castle for many a long month, because he never missed a chance to fight in some battle or other. If the fighting was going on somewhere nearby, he would tell Maud, 'Before you've slept ten times, I'll be back with you again.' But if it was a war in distant lands, he would shake his head and say, 'I hope you won't get bored without me for a couple of months.' And off he would ride on his charger, without even turning to look up at the window where his wife was

waving him farewell with a white scarf. Pugnatius would hurry away to his skirmishes, and Queen Maud would be left behind to twiddle her thumbs. It was a lucky thing that the chief legal clerk was around, since he knew how to read. He would sit and read books to his mistress, and she got so used to his company that she didn't even miss her husband any more.

11 March

King Pugnatius

The belligerence of King Pugnatius began to try the nerves of the neighbouring rulers, so the three next-door kings finally got together and signed a treaty to say that they would teach Pugnatius a lesson. Pugnatius got hold of some allies of his own, and marched off to battle at the head of a good-sized army. He knew it was going to

be no joke this time, so when he said farewell to his wife, he told her: 'If I should not return within a year and a day, I shall no longer be in the land of the living, and you may consider yourself free to remarry.' Maud was surprised to hear such grim words, but in any case she thought of her husband as some sort of casual visitor by now, while she would sit with the chief legal clerk late into the night and listen to him talking. The legal clerk had already got through the handful of books Pugnatius' father had left in the castle library, half a dozen times, and now he used to make up stories of his own. A year and a day went by, and there was no sign of Pugnatius. Queen Maud sent for the chief legal clerk. 'You know what my husband told me before he left,' she said. 'And you know, too, that you are more dear to me than a dozen warriors such as Pugnatius. The year and a day has passed, and the king is no longer alive. What if I were to ask you for your hand in marriage?' 'I should be most honoured, Your Majesty,' replied the legal clerk, 'and I will not try to pretend a lack of affection for your person. However, I am only a commoner, and it may be that His Majesty is held captive in some distant land. Wait for another year and a day and then decide.'

12 March

King Pugnatius

Pugnatius had not been killed in battle. He had been wounded and taken prisoner by King Littlegorm, who locked him up for a couple of years, and then sent for him. 'I hope you are cured of your warmongering, Pugnatius,' said Littlegorm. 'Next time I shall not be so generous, and if I should once more happen to nab you on the battlefield, you shall lose your head. But now I am going to set you free.' Littlegorm kept his rival's charger as a fine, so Pugnatius had to walk home. When he

13 March

The Tale of a Cupboard Goes On

In a mysterious room in a mysterious house, there once stood a mysterious cupboard. It was positively the only thing in the room. There were no chairs and no tables, not even a settee. And anyone who wants to find out more about it will have to wait until April 13.

finally arrived back at his castle, he found that a wedding was being prepared, since the second year and a day had passed. The queen had taken to heart what the chief legal clerk had said, so she had raised him to aristocratic rank and made him the Royal Steward, so that he would be worthy of her. They held a great celebration, which was attended by royalty and gentry from far and wide. Among those who congratulated Queen Maud was King Littlegorm, but he didn't say anything about Pugnatius, only giving a mysterious little smile. No one took much notice of the ragged tramp who arrived at the castle towards the end of the wedding feast. Nobody recognized the king without his sword and his warhorse. Pugnatius shed a bitter tear. 'I've lost everything on account of my wars,' he whimpered, 'kingdom, riches, even my wife! I'm finished.' When he had eaten the chicken leg which they gave him in the servants' quarters, he wiped his mouth and his eyes, and set off again, to no one knows where. At least he was never seen again in his old kingdom.

14 March

The Golden Fish

Old Vasil went down to the sea to have a look at what he had caught in his nets. When he spread them out, what did he see but a golden fish. As soon as he caught hold of it, the fish said, 'If you put me back in the sea, I will grant your every wish.' Old Vasil thought for a moment, then said: 'Very well, you shall go back into the sea. But I do not know what to wish for. I must go and ask my wife.' He went home and told his wife what had happened. The old woman scolded him. 'Go back at once and ask for some fine new clothes for me to wear.

The Two Mice

Two mice tiptoed into the pantry and found a piece of cheese on one of the shelves. They talked it over, and the older one said, 'We shall share it, but since I am older, I should have the larger portion.' 'Oh, no,' replied the younger mouse. 'I should have a bigger piece. I must eat more, so that I may grow to be as big as you are.' They argued for a while, but then they decided to think it over until the next day. In the morning they met again in the pantry, and this time the older mouse said, 'You were right. We shall divide the cheese up as you suggested.' 'Oh, no,' replied the other, '*you* were right, and we shall share the cheese so that you get more, for that is indeed fairer.' Again they spent some time arguing, but in the end they agreed to sleep on it again. The next day they met in the pantry again, and

I have only this torn old blouse.' As soon as the old man returned with the new clothes, she sent him back again, telling him to drive back and pick her up in a golden coach, because she had never ridden in one before. Old Vasil was soon back again with a golden coach, but even that was not enough for the old woman. Now she wanted a beautiful castle by the sea shore, with great gardens and a host of servants. But even that did not satisfy her. In the end she had a strange idea. She wanted the golden fish to come and serve her. The moment the fish heard this, it grew angry, and took away all its gifts. The old woman was soon standing in front of their tumbledown cottage again, wearing her torn old blouse and mending nets. There you are, then! If you try to get too much, you may end up with nothing at all.

this time they both called out at once, 'I know what! We shall share the cheese equally between us!' But when they got to the cheese, they found it had gone mouldy. 'I dare say we shouldn't have thought about it so much,' said the older mouse.

16 March

The Sad Jester

A certain faraway kingdom was ruled over by a certain King Vulgarian II. But what a miserable kingdom it was! No one knew how to laugh, make merry or enjoy himself. Everyone was always serious, and people quarrelled over every trifle and even envied each other the air they breathed. Vulgarian pondered how he might make his subjects a little more gay, and finally decided to employ a court jester. Now, you might well ask how that would help his subjects, but the king said to himself, 'If I am sad, then there is no wonder the whole kingdom is sad. As soon as I am happy again, everyone in the realm will rejoice, and everything will be all right again.' Which only goes to show how some rulers think altogether rather too

much of themselves. So Vulgarian had it proclaimed throughout the land that the next Sunday a great competition was to be held in the palace gardens, to find the jester who was going to be lucky enough to follow the king around wherever he went. But, alas! there wasn't much choice, as it turned out, since the only one to turn up for the contest was one solitary, sad subject. So the king had to employ him. Only the new jester was so sad that the courtiers all burst into tears whenever they saw him. 'Why on earth do you keep a jester like him?' they asked the king. And the king replied, 'So that I can see that someone at least is sadder than I am.' And tears came to his eyes.

17 March

The Sad Jester

The sad jester did not succeed in cheering the king up, but he did tell him a lot about the people of his kingdom, and why they were so sad. 'You can't make me happy, so you're trying to make me angry instead,' the king told him. 'My subjects are quite

contented. All my counsellors say so!' 'Then why don't you dress up in disguise and go and see for yourself?' suggested the jester. 'That way you'll soon find out what they really think.' Vulgarian liked the jester's idea. He was looking forward to hearing his subjects praise him, and to taking off his disguise and revealing that it was really him they were praising all the time. When he left the palace the next morning, not even the queen herself would have recognized him. He asked everyone he met how they were getting on. But they all replied, 'You must be a stranger here! Otherwise you would know that our king thinks only of himself, while his counsellors rob his treasure chests and his subjects, as well! And if anyone tries to oppose them, he gets thrown in jail.' 'How do you come to be telling me all this?' asked the king, incredulously. 'We're not afraid of you,' the people told him. 'You are

a poor man like ourselves, so you won't have us thrown in prison.' Vulgarian returned to the palace sadder than ever. For three days he sat by himself in his study, and no one was allowed in to see him. Then he sent for his jester, handed him his crown and sceptre, and told him, 'I've decided. Better for a jester to rule the kingdom than a king like me!'

18 March

The Sad Jester

As soon as the jester had the sceptre in his hand and the crown on his head, he began to smile. 'Do you remember your younger brother, Vulgarian?' he asked. 'Why do you wish to make me sadder than ever?' asked the ex-king, hanging his head. 'You know he has been dead for years. When I succeeded to my father's throne, an old fortune teller told me that one day I should hand over my crown and sceptre to my younger brother. So I ordered my chief counsellor to have the two of them put to death. I can't tell you how much I have regretted it.' 'Well, there you are, then,' said the new king. 'But the fortune teller had enough money to bribe the chief counsellor, and he set them both free.' 'How do you know?' gasped Vulgarian, and the jester replied. 'I lived with the fortune teller, who hid in a mountain cave for many years. For I am your brother, and the prophecy has been fulfilled. You have handed me your crown and sceptre.' 'What are you going to do with me?' asked Vulgarian, anxiously. 'Don't worry,' replied his brother, 'I shan't have you put to death. From now on I appoint you court jester. We shall simply exchange our jobs.' 'But I shall be an even sadder jester than you have been,' warned Vulgarian. 'We shall see,' the king told him. 'When I have got rid of the corrupt counsellors, and when the people of this kingdom have learned to be merry again, perhaps they will find your sadness funny.' And he rang the bell. But

that wasn't the end of the tale of the two royal brothers, it was just the beginning.

19 March

The Two Bars of Chocolate

Ellen got two great big bars of chocolate for her birthday. One of them was milk chocolate, the other one bitter chocolate. Ellen bit a piece of each of them, and said to her mummy, 'The milk one's nothing special, but the bitter one's ever so nice.' The milk chocolate would have turned green with envy, if it hadn't been far too brown for that sort of thing. Why should it be nothing special? What was so special about bitter chocolate anyway? But she imagined it was easy enough to do something about *that*. Becoming bitter was no problem, really. So the milk chocolate tried very, very hard to grow bitter, and thought to itself: 'I'm going to be bitterer than *that* other bar! Who does it think it is?' The next time Ellen came along to take a bite, the bitter milk chocolate was shivering with excitement. How the little girl would smack her lips! Ellen broke a piece off and put it into her mouth, but she spat it out again. 'Ugh!' she said. 'This chocolate was all right yesterday,

but it's gone right off!' 'What doesn't she like this time?' thought the chocolate to itself, and waited to see what Ellen's mother would say. 'You're right,' said Mummy, when she had tried a piece. 'It's turned quite bitter. We'll have to throw it away.' Then the chocolate bar had lots of time to think about the different ways there are of being bitter.

20 March

The Boy Who Didn't Want to be Naughty

There was once a little boy whose real name was Tim, but his mummy and daddy called him Timmy. It seemed to them that he was terribly quiet, for he just sat about like the hole in a doorway. 'Whatever will

become of him?' asked his daddy, anxiously. And he kept on playing tricks on Timmy, like putting drawing-pins on his chair, or a wet sponge in his bed, and all sorts of other practical jokes. But it didn't have any effect. Timmy would just look at books or draw pictures. His mother and father, instead of being pleased, got quite upset. 'He hasn't got any friends,' sighed his mother. 'Except Benjy the monkey!' Now Benjy was a little blue fur-fabric monkey that made a soft 'waaah' sound when you pressed his tummy. It was the only noise Timmy liked to hear. 'That boy is seriously ill,' declared Daddy one day, and Mummy clicked her lips in sad agreement. 'He's no trouble, and he's never naughty, so it's about time we took him to the magician doctor to have him cured!' They opened the newspaper and went throught the advertisements until they found the one they were looking for. Then they quietly put on their coats, and slipped outside without Timmy noticing them. They couldn't wait to get the magician's help.

21 March

The Boy Who Didn't Want to be Naughty

On the magician doctor's door it said in big letters, 'A. B. Cadabra, Doctor of Clinical Magics'. For a while Timmy's parents argued about why it said 'magics' instead of 'magic', but then they decided it didn't make any difference, because it sounded very grand, even if they didn't know what 'clinical' meant anyway, and they knocked on the door. A voice said, 'Reveal yourselves!' and the door opened of its own accord. That wasn't really all that surprising, since it was, after all, a magic surgery. When Timmy's mummy and daddy had told the magician doctor the trouble, he was surprised that they hadn't brought the boy with them. 'We didn't want to upset him, you know,' said Mummy. 'He's very sensitive, you see.' 'But we've brought Benjy his monkey instead,' Daddy went on. 'And we've got an idea. It's our Timmy's best friend, you see, and he's very fond of it. We thought perhaps that if the monkey was alive and merry and running about all over the place, Timmy might pick it up as well, sort of catch it off the monkey, then he

might be more like other kids.' The magician doctor thought it was a good idea, and before long Daddy was carrying a squealing Benjy under his coat, and they were on their way home.

22 March

The Boy Who Didn't Want to be Naughty

As soon as Mummy and Daddy got home

23 March

Fearless Bertha and Nick the Devil

Bertha wasn't afraid of anything. Not that she was a big, strong lass with biceps like a blacksmith, or anything like that. No, she was quite a pretty young girl, about the right age to be getting married. But she wasn't afraid of anyone. And she loved to dance. Wherever there was a dance or a ball, there you would find Bertha, worrying about whether she would have enough partners. Actually, there were *always* enough partners, but if any of them dared to ask for a kiss, it was wham and bam, and he got such a slap in the face that it made his head swim. So by and by the number of young men who wanted to dance with her grew smaller and smaller. One night she was making her way home across

and set the monkey down on the floor, it jumped up onto the table, and from the table to the cupboard, and from the cupboard to the light, where it swung back and forth until the whole lot came crashing down. Little Timmy shouted 'waaah!', and then it began. Before long they had turned the whole house upside down. There wasn't a single piece of furniture left in its place. Curtains were pulled down, books torn to pieces, and there were clothes-lines hanging all over the place, with Timmy and Benjy taking turns to swing on them. They made such a din that the neighbours came round to complain, and then they threatened to call the police, or the fire brigade. Soon Mummy and Daddy were hurrying back to the magician doctor, with Benjy the monkey tied up in a shopping-bag, and they begged him to change the creature back into a good little soft-toy monkey again. He did as they asked, but Timmy stayed the way he was. Once again Daddy went round saying, 'Whatever will become of him?' And Mummy said, 'I don't think we should ever have gone to see that doctor in the first place . . .' What do you think?

the fields from some dance or other, without a young man to see her home, as usual. It was pitch dark, and an owl was hooting eerily, but Bertha strode along the path as though it was broad daylight. Suddenly three young lads jumped out in front of her. She couldn't tell who they were in the dark, but they were out to give her a fright, and no mistake! They'd picked the wrong one in Bertha, though. She tripped the first one flat on his face, shoved the second over backwards, and gave the third such a backhander with her left hand that he went spinning round in circles. 'I'm not even scared of the devil,' she said scornfully, 'let alone a bunch of silly kids like you!'

24 March

Fearless Bertha and Nick the Devil

Bertha drove the three youths who had ambushed her back into the village like a little flock of sheep. There they turned out to be three dancing partners, who had all at some time or another had a taste of one of Bertha's slaps. Now they were in real disgrace, when everyone found out how

they had tried to get their own back. But the next time there was a dance not even the village idiot asked her to dance. All the menfolk were afraid of her. 'I'd dance with the devil himself if he were to ask me!' said Bertha out loud, when she had spent half the evening standing in a corner with the rest of the wallflowers. Down below the dance floor, a long, long way below it, Lucifer stamped his hoof until sparks began to fly. 'There she goes, taking our name in vain again!' he said. 'First she's not scared of the devil, then she says she'd dance with him . . .' He rolled his eyes. 'Well, Bertha, we'll see, we'll see.' And he sent for young Nick. He ordered him to pretend to be a dashing young huntsman with a feather in his hat, and to go and dance Bertha off her feet, then carry her straight off to hell for her boasting. Hardly had Lucifer said this, when Nick the young huntsman was standing in front of Bertha, with his horns hidden beneath his hat and a hoof on one foot instead of a shoe. 'May you have the pleasure?' smiled Bertha, when he asked. 'Why, young man, I've been waiting for you all along!' And she danced one dance after another with this fellow who smelt a little of fire and brimstone.

25 March

Fearless Bertha and Nick the Devil

Nick was a fine figure of a devil, no weakling to be sure, but after the twentieth dance with Bertha he was quite exhausted, his long red tongue hanging out like that of a breathless cocker spaniel. His hat had fallen off, and two small horns stuck out from his black curly hair. Now everyone could see where Bertha's partner had come from. They all left the dance-floor and stood watching from a safe distance waiting to see Bertha come, as they supposed, to a sticky end. The musicians would have liked to have packed up and gone home, but

Fearless Bertha and Nick the Devil

Nick was at the end of his strength before he finally brought Bertha in front of Lucifer's throne. The Prince of Darkness drew himself up to his full height, and there was a flash of lightning and a roll of thunder. 'Oo, that was *very good,* Mr. Satan,' said Bertha, full of praise. 'Your lightning is *so* much better than our amateur dramatic society's. Mind you, I *would* say that their thunder has the edge on yours. You could do with a bit more of a rumble and a bit less of a bang, if you see what I mean.' 'Amateur dramatic society!' Lucifer roared, beside himself with rage. 'You're not at the theatre now, my girl, you're in hell! And you're going to pay for your insults!' 'You're quite right, you know,' Bertha agreed. 'In any case I was thinking that there aren't any

Bertha was in her element, and she ordered them to play a solo. 'I . . . I think that's maybe enough!' gasped poor Nick, but Bertha whirled him around the room, as if it was her first dance of the evening. The young devil could scarcely stand. Suddenly a devilish little fly, sent by Lucifer, flew into his ear. 'Nick,' it buzzed. 'It's high time you brought Bertha downstairs. We've lit the fire under the cauldron!' Nick was caught between the devil and the deep blue sea. He knew he must obey Lucifer's orders, but he was scared stiff of Bertha. When their solo came to an end, he said hesitantly, 'Bertha, would you . . . I mean, do you think you might like to . . . to come home with me, that is down there . . . ?' He closed his eyes, ready for the almighty slap he was sure would come. But Bertha began to laugh. 'To hell, you mean? Why not, you devil! I've never been there, it's true.' And she jumped up on the panting demon's back.

husbands worth having up there. There's no point in beating about the bush. I like Nick, and Nick likes me, so there's nothing for it but for you to hold a wedding feast, Mr. Satan, is there?' Lucifer was beginning to wonder if he wasn't imagining the whole thing, but he took a hold on himself and stammered to his henchman, 'N-N-Nick, the w-w-water's boiling in number three-five-eight. T-T-Take Bertha along, will you, and . . . and . . . well, you know what to do, don't you?' Nick knew exactly what to do, but he stood there for a moment, wondering how he might explain to his master that Bertha was more than just another victim to him . . . But Lucifer didn't give him the chance. '169827 Fallen Angel Nicholas!' he screamed, 'carry out your orders immediately!'

27 March

Fearless Bertha and Nick the Devil

Nick took Bertha by the hand and led her

off to cauldron number three hundred and fifty-eight. 'You see this cauldron, Bertha,' he said. 'Well, you . . . that is — er — you'll have to . . .' 'I know, I know,' said Bertha soothingly. 'Then go and get me seven pounds of potatoes, some parsnips, carrots, celeriac, onions, garlic, butter, caraway seed and marjoram. And if you should happen to have any dried mushrooms, so much the better.' 'But Bertha, you don't understand . . .' the devil tried to explain. 'That's as may be,' Bertha interrupted him with a stamp of her foot, 'but do as I ask, and leave the rest to me.' With a helpless shrug of his shoulders, Nick trudged off to fetch what Bertha wanted. Then she set to work, and before long there was such a delicious smell coming from the cauldron that in no time at all a little knot of demons had arrived to see what was cooking, and even the sinners in the other cauldrons popped out their heads to have a look. All of a sudden Lucifer arrived on the scene, scowling darkly. 'What's going on?' he shouted. 'I'll not have any shirking in *my* torture-chamber! Why have those cauldrons been left unattended? Where is the chief tormentor?' But Bertha cut him short. She took a ladleful of soup out of the cauldron and pressed it to the arch fiend's lips. Before he knew it he had taken a sip, then another, then another, and his frown was gone. A smile spread over his face, and there was a faraway look in his eyes. 'I've not eaten potato soup like that since I don't know when,' he said, and he remembered the good old days, when devils really meant something. 'Bertha,' he said, 'I appoint you chief cook of hell and purgatory, and grant you a full pardon!'

28 March

Fearless Bertha and Nick the Devil

For a week, then a fortnight, then a month, Bertha boiled, baked and fried for that

couldn't take any more of it. 'All right, all right,' he said. 'I see I shall have to do something I hate to. You can't get married in hell, my dear, but . . .' And he whispered the rest in her ear, so that not even the other devils could hear what he was saying, let alone you or I.

29 March

Fearless Bertha and Nick the Devil

Do you know, within a week of her heart-to-heart with Lucifer, Bertha was married. Not in church, mind you, just in the registry office, but she didn't mind that. And who did she get married to? Why, Nick the devil, or just plain Nicholas, as he was by then. He no longer had his tail, or his horns, or his hooves; now he was just a good-looking young man, well-built, with curly black hair. Lucifer settled the whole affair the only way he could. Nick was banished from hell. And since you can't have a devil without hell, he turned into an

infernal crowd, and all the devils, including Lucifer himself, licked their lips before meals and their fingers after. But one day the chief cook of hell and purgatory came to see Lucifer, arms outstretched, and said, 'I've had enough!' 'What seems to be the trouble?' asked Lucifer. 'Don't we praise your meals to high heaven? Er, that is, well, you know what I mean.' 'But I want to get married,' said Bertha, firmly, 'and I haven't seen hide nor hair of my husband-to-be all month.' 'Nothing to get upset about, my dear,' Satan tried to soothe her feelings. 'He's away on business.' 'And who *sent* him away on business?' asked Bertha, with a frown. 'Just you see to it that he comes back again, and make ready for our wedding!' Lucifer scratched the base of his right horn. 'Bertha,' he said, 'you must understand that a devil can't really marry a human-being like you. If you don't like it here, you can go back up there, though we'll be sorry to lose you.' That was more than Bertha could bear. Now she really gave Lucifer a piece of her mind. 'What do you take me for? Do you think I could possibly put up with all that gossip if I went back without a husband?' In a while Satan

ordinary young man, and became Bertha's husband. As it happened, the job of gamekeeper had just come vacant in the nearby woods, so the newly-weds moved into the gamekeeper's lodge. Folk used to say that the former devil was well and truly hen-pecked, but if anyone said anything of the sort in front of him, the new gamekeeper would give a wave of his hand and say: 'I'm out in the woods all day, anyway, and after being in hell the fresh air is amazing!' He didn't seem to be the least bit homesick for hell. He did as Bertha told him, but there was one thing he refused to do, and that was to go dancing with her again!

30 March

The Doughnut and the Fox

Do you remember the doughnut you last met in February? Well, by and by he came to a woodland clearing, where he met a fox. 'My, you're a welcome visitor,' said the fox, licking its lips. 'I've been expecting you.' 'How could you know I was coming?' asked the doughnut. 'I didn't even know myself where I was going.' 'I know everything,'

boasted the fox. 'I even know that you would like to ride on my tail.' 'How come?' asked the doughnut. 'It never even occurred to me.' 'Just try it,' the fox told him. 'You'll soon see how fine it is to ride on a fox's tail!' 'I don't mind trying,' said the doughnut, and up he jumped. The fox started running, and the doughnut squealed with delight. But the fox stopped suddenly, and the doughnut went flying through the air and, before he knew what was happening, landed in the fox's jaws. He saw at once that he had been tricked. 'If you know everything,' he said, 'then you surely know how much I have been looking forward to your eating me.' 'Really?' asked the fox, setting the doughnut down. 'Certainly. Only I should like you to grant me one last wish.' 'Why not?' said the fox. 'What is it to be?' 'I should like to play hide-and-seek with you. I'll hide, and you look for me. When you've found me, you shall eat me.' The fox agreed, closed its eyes, and began to count to fifty. It's still looking for the doughnut, all around the clearing. Because the doughnut didn't hide at all, of course. He went running off into April.

31 March

The Persian Carpet

Mr. Finch bought himself a beautiful coloured carpet and took it home. He unrolled it on the floor, but then he heard a voice say, 'I'm a Persian carpet, and I'll take you to a Persian market if you sit on me. It's a wonderful sight, such as you'll not see the like of round here.' Mr. Finch agreed, and he sat on the carpet and took off. Before long the carpet landed in a perfectly ordinary market-place. Mr. Finch knew dozens like it. 'Oh, no,' the carpet told him. 'This is a *Persian* market, 'cos I'm a Persian carpet. And now you must sell me to someone else so that I can get to know a bit more of the world, and meet some new people.' 'And how am I supposed to get back home?' asked Mr. Finch. 'Why, by car, or by train, or by aeroplane, or helicopter!' replied the carpet, laughing at him. 'You don't suppose people still go flying around on carpets these days, do you?' So Mr. Finch sold the carpet to someone else, and as he was setting off for the station, he heard the carpet telling its new owner, 'I'm a Persian carpet, and I'll take you to a Persian market if you sit on me . . .'

April

1 April

The Twins Make Themselves Useful

Milly and Molly the twins were as restless as a couple of frisky lambs, and Mother had her work cut out with them. One day, just as she was wondering how to keep them busy, she heard the pips on the radio, and the announcer's voice said it was time for Woman's Hour. 'That's an idea,' thought Mother. 'It's time they learned a bit about housekeeping.' So she sat the pair of them down in front of the radio, and set off to do her shopping with a light heart. But no sooner had the door closed behind her, than the lady on the wireless said she was going to read out a recipe for a delicious pudding.

'Hurrah!' shouted Milly, reaching for her apron. Molly ran off to get all the ingredients ready, but instead of corn flakes she brought a packet of soap flakes. And when, in a little while, the lady said it was time for the washing tip of the week, things really started to go wrong. Before long the soap pudding was frothing away in the oven, while bits of gooey breakfast cereal were sloshing about in the washing-machine with the clothes. Who knows what would have happened if the wind elf hadn't chanced to fly past, and knocked against the switch on the radio? A pity he didn't turn it off sooner, wasn't it?

2 April

The Flowerpot That Didn't Know What It Was For

The wind elf, sky traveller, flew out of the town and into the countryside, where he landed in a garden. There was a row of flowerpots beside the path, and in each of them a little seed was sprouting, sticking out its little green tongue. Seeds are allowed to stick their tongues out, and actually gardeners like them to. The wind elf stood looking at the flowerpots for a while, and then he noticed that one of them was empty. They must have forgotten to fill it with earth, which was a good enough reason for it to feel grumpy. 'There's nothing worse than not knowing what one is for, like me!' The wind elf felt sorry for it, and went around asking everyone what should be done about the matter, but no one was able to tell him. It was only when he met a hedgehog that he had an idea. This prickly fellow would make a fine cactus if he would only sit in the flowerpot! The hedgehog took a lot of persuading to climb into it, and he hadn't been a cactus for long before he started to complain. 'I must say, I feel a real ninny. I don't know the first

drew his silvery black cloak over the snowy-white egg, so that it had feathers and leaves underneath it and a wind-lined cloak to cover it. Then the elf took a deep breath, and breathed on the egg like a warm spring breeze scented with sunshine. This was just what the egg needed, or rather the little cock inside it. And now, shhhh! We'd better not disturb them.

thing about flowering, and I can't even sit still enough to be a plant. But I know how to find grubs and catch flies.' And out he crawled. 'Dear me,' said the wind elf, wrinkling his nose. 'What now?' But he soon had another idea. He found a bead on a piece of string, and he had soon turned the flowerpot into a fine bell, the sort you ring at the end of fairy tales.

3 April

The Egg

At the beginning of April, the wind elf's wanderings took him into a pantry where there was a basket of eggs. He heard a scratching and piping coming from inside one of them. 'What's the matter?' he asked, knocking on the shell. 'What's going on?' And a voice from inside said, 'I want to hatch out and grow up, and crow, and strut up and down some farmyard among the hens!' These words sounded so mournful to the sky traveller that he asked again, 'And how can *I* help you?' 'That's easy,' said the egg, with a little wobble. 'Take me to a warm place and look after me until it's time for chickens to hatch out of eggs.' 'All right, then,' sighed the wind elf, who really liked doing good deeds. He made a snug little bed among the jars of bottled fruit and

4 April

The Storyteller and the Boy Who Could Only Moo

The storyteller was sitting behind his typewriter at a table in the garden, writing

bleated. And so it went on. The boy only mooed, bleated and gaggled, but he couldn't say a word. What was even worse, the same thing happened at school the next day, every time he was supposed to do a sum or recite a poem. You have to admit that,

'Moo, moo, moo!
Baa, baa, baa!
Gaa, gaa, gaa!'

isn't the sort of poem that teachers like to hear. Tommy was sent to see the headmaster, and when he mooed at him as well, his mummy and daddy had to come and collect him.

5 April

The Storyteller and the Boy Who Could Only Moo

Tommy's parents called the doctor, but he could only shake his head and say, 'I know it's incredible in the Twentieth Century, when there aren't even many children left who believe in magic, but somebody must have cast a spell on your son.' 'Ah!' cried Mother and Father, both at once. 'Why

one of his fairy tales. But little Tommy, the neighbours' naughty child, decided he wasn't going to let him have any peace. He kept on making noises, lowing, bleating and gaggling away on the other side of the fence like a farmyard of animals. In the end the storyteller snatched the piece of paper out of his typewriter and went inside. He was well and truly annoyed, because it's not very nice having to carry an unfinished story around in your head, when it's trying to get out all the time. Not having anyone to annoy any more, Tommy went inside to beg a biscuit or two. But all he could say was, 'Moo!' 'Don't mess about,' his mother told him, 'and speak properly.' Tommy wanted to say that he wasn't messing about and that he was hungry, but this time he just didn't *we* think of that? It must have been that neighbour of ours. He's always writing fairy stories, and he must have learnt a little magic off all those witches and wizards.' They hurried off to visit the storyteller, and demanded that he lift the spell from their son. They asked him quite gently at first, then they started to get stern, and in the end they were rather rude, but it was all no good, since their neighbour kept on repeating that he didn't know the first thing about magic spells, and that he never would. When Tommy's mummy and daddy were quite hoarse with shouting, a beautiful woman appeared in the storyteller's sitting-room. 'I shall get a headache from all this din,' she said in a soft voice. 'It was I who cast a spell on your little rascal. I was sorry for the storyteller here, because the lad wouldn't give him a moment's peace to get on with his fairy tales. But if Tommy promises not to annoy people any more, I shall give him back the gift of speech.' Tommy nodded his head to show that he promised, and the fairy, because, of course, that is who she was, lifted the spell, and everything was all right again. Except that Tommy's mummy went round whispering to all the neighbours that there was a queer sort of woman in that fellow's house, 'you know, the one that's always writing those stories', and what a carry-on it all was!

6 April

Rosy the Worm

One day, Miss Forgetful left a tube of pink toothpaste open on the bathroom shelf. She just unscrewed the top, and then completely forgot that she had been going to clean her teeth. She forgot about the soap and comb as well, and left the bathroom without washing or combing her hair. The toothpaste tube said, 'Well, I never!' and bent its back a little. A pink worm slid out of it, soft and shiny and smelling sweetly. 'Dear me!' cried the toothpaste tube, when

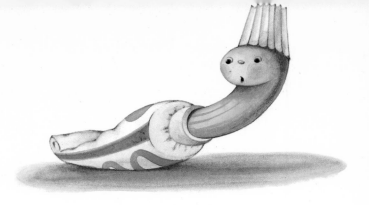

it saw that some of its toothpaste had been squeezed out, and there wasn't a single tooth in sight. But Rosy the worm was out of the tube, and she looked around the pink bathroom. 'How lovely it is here!' she said, trembling with excitement, and suddenly she began to feel hungry. She tasted a piece of pink soap, washed it down with a drink of water, and went sliding along the bath as if she was on a toboggan. Then she slid out of the door. It wasn't pink at all on the other side. Instead of the pink tiles there was patterned wallpaper, and the chairs had colourful covers. 'I don't like this at all!' she shouted. 'I want the world to be like me! I'm going to change it!' And she got down to work at once.

7 April

Rosy the Worm

Rosy the toothpaste worm was only the size of a little, little finger, but she made as much racket as half a dozen children. She decided she would take charge of the house. So as to grow fatter and seem more powerful, she began to eat one bar of pink soap after another. When she had eaten all the soap she could find in her own bathroom, she went and ate the neighbours' as well, and then crawled around all the bathrooms in the neighbourhood guzzling soap. True, she left a pleasant smell everywhere she went, and people liked that. So when Madame the

Pink Worm (that's what she called herself now) told them they should make everything pink, they took her advice. Everyone was so busy decorating and tidying up that they didn't have time for anything else. They even washed all their books in pink soap flakes. The books were

pink and smelled very nice but you couldn't read the print any more. But no one had any time for novels or fairy stories any more, since in any case they were all dashing around with dusters and scrubbing brushes, washing and cleaning, until they were all soapy and scented themselves. But soon they were tired and cross, too, and had had quite enough of all the running about. But they weren't allowed to stop, because Madame the Pink Worm was by now the undisputed ruler of the whole town. 'Now I am famous!' she congratulated herself.

8 April

Rosy the Worm

That pink worm which had once been no more than a couple of centimetres long now insisted that everyone call her Madame Rose, the Great Fat Pink Worm. And she had really grown so fat that she was first like a hippopotamus, then more like a big, pink train that kept getting more and more carriages added to it. The real trains couldn't keep up with the demand for pink soap. They couldn't bring it into the town fast enough, because not only Rosy the Worm was feeding on it now, but even the townspeople had started eating it for breakfast, lunch and dinner. In the end the grocers' shops and supermarkets had nothing but shelf upon shelf full of pink soap and soap flakes. People were so crazy about soap that they began to greet each other with the words 'How's suds?', and when they parted they would say 'Must be lathering along now'. Things went from bad to worse in the town, even though everything was spotlessly clean, and the children were always soapy and never got dirty at all. It was only then that little Miss Forgetful, who was the cause of it all, realized what she had done, and began to say to herself, 'How can I put things right?'

9 April

Rosy the Worm

'Madame Rose the Great Fat Pink Worm will just have to forget how famous and hungry she is,' said Miss Forgetful to herself, 'and I shall have to teach her to forget. But how?' She thought for a little while, then she mixed up some soapy water in the washing-up-bowl and began to blow bubbles for Rosy the Worm to see. When she caught sight of the bubbles, Rosy was quite carried away with delight. 'Oh, how lovely they are! How pinky rainbowy! I've never seen anything so wonderful in all my life!' she cried. From then on she could think of nothing else but blowing bubbles of her own, and trying to blow the biggest and the rosiest in the world. She was so busy playing her new game that she quite forgot all about soap, and the cleanliness of the town. She forgot to eat, and started to get thinner. By and by she was back down to the size she had been to begin with. 'At last!'

sighed Miss Forgetful, and she opened the tube and shoved Rosy back inside. The next day she used Rosy the Worm to brush her teeth with, and everything returned to normal. They sent a couple of train loads of pink soap back to the warehouse, and Miss Forgetful said to herself, 'I shall have to see about getting my name changed, just in case.'

10 April

Plain Patricia

Patricia was fat, and quite ugly, when she was a little girl. She managed to grow out of being fat altogether, but she stayed as plain as can be, even when she was a big girl. None of the young men stopped by her window, and at the local dances she would just sit in a corner and watch the other girls as they danced. After a while she stopped going to dances, and she would work in the fields all day and read books when she got home. One day a young doctor arrived in the village on holiday. He happened to knock on the door of the cottage Patricia lived in, looking for eggs and milk. Patricia told him he could go there every day, and

she added a slice of home-baked bread and some freshly churned butter for good measure. Patricia had a pleasant voice, and the doctor was very short-sighted, and had come without his glasses. He took a fancy to the lass, and she took a fancy to him. People laughed at the idea of such an educated fellow from the town falling for a plain thing like that, but after a day or two their laughter died away. Patricia had suddenly started to be pretty. 'Something funny's going on,' the villagers began to say, when they saw the change. And it was. Patricia was in love, and they do say that love can work miracles.

11 April

The Miller and His Son

Allen the miller had an only son called William, and he had looked upon him as his successor since he was in the cradle. 'When you grow up, you shall take over a fine mill,' he would say, 'like I took it over from my father, and carry on the miller's trade. The Allens have been millers as long as anyone can remember.' But William liked to work with wood, and ever since he had been able to hold a knife in his hand he had carved things. When he grew up, he decided that he wanted to be a woodcarver and nothing else. His father threatened to disinherit him. When that didn't have any effect, he promised the lad heaven and earth, but all to no avail. William's love for carving was stronger than his wish to please his father, stronger even than his father's will. When he got nowhere by threats or persuasion, Allen threw his son out of the mill. 'You'll learn, in the wide world!' he shouted after him. And off William went. There was wood to be found in the world, just as in his native village, and he and his knife would get along somehow. But from that day on, old Allen never seemed to be able to work as he could before. All of a sudden he didn't see any reason to work hard and save. By

and by, the farmers stopped bringing him their grain, because there was a better miller down the way. Allen started drinking, and the mill went to rack and ruin. In the end the miller set off into the world himself, with a staff and a linen bag.

12 April

The Miller and His Son

Allen the miller wandered the world, but couldn't seem to find any work, anyway. His linen bag was always empty, and his staff

became a beggar's stick. He ate when folk were generous, and lived from hand to mouth. By and by he reached the capital city. As he was asking around to see if he could find work, he happened on a large woodcarver's workshop, where the owner carved all manner of beautiful objects, and employed a large number of workmen and apprentices. It seemed that their work was much in demand, since the business was prospering. The owner looked at the old man who was willing to sweep the floors in return for a crust of bread, and tears came to his eyes. He flung his arms wide. 'But, Father, don't you recognize me?' he asked. 'Why, you are at home here!' It was only then that Allen realized he was standing in front of his own son. 'Aren't you angry with me, William?' he asked. 'Did I not turn you from my door?' 'That is all a long time ago,' replied his son. 'But you must forgive me, too. I believe that a man should do the work he loves. Only then can he do it really well.' 'But what am I to do here?' the old man asked, sadly. 'You will have work enough,' replied the woodcarver. 'I have three sons, and you have three grandsons. Perhaps you'll make a miller of one of them.'

13 April

The Tale of a Cupboard Goes On a Little More

In a mysterious room in a mysterious house, there once stood a mysterious cupboard. It was positively the only thing in the room. There were no chairs and no tables, not even a settee. And no one lived in the house. And if you want to find out more, you'll have to wait until 13 May.

14 April

A Prophecy Comes True

Sometimes fairytale fairies, standing over babies' cradles, predict the first thing that comes into their heads. So it happened that, when a baby prince was born to a certain powerful king, and the old magician who was in charge of prophecies and forecasts was asked to attend, she made the following strange pronouncement. 'You shall be a charming child, and a delight to your parents, but on your fifteenth birthday a wave will wash you out to sea.' 'Rubbish!' the king burst out, and he had the magician thrown out of the palace. He and the queen had a good laugh about it afterwards, because their kingdom was a land of forests and mountains, and the nearest sea was miles away, right on the opposite side of the world. What had they to worry about? They forgot all about the prophecy, and for a whole fifteen years they rejoiced in their growing son. It wasn't until the eve of his fifteenth birthday that the queen remembered the magician's prediction, and began to feel uneasy. 'No problem,' said the king. 'We'll put the prince in a room up in the tallest tower, where no wave could reach even if the sea were to make the journey half way across the world to our kingdom!' 'Very well,' said the queen, with a sigh of relief, and she went to bed with a light heart.

15 April

A Prophecy Comes True

The prince from the mountain kingdom had hoped for quite a different sort of birthday. Instead of sitting with his parents in the banqueting hall and receiving presents, there he was, stuck in a little chamber up at the top of the tallest tower, sighing with disappointment. He looked out through the narrow window at the high mountains, from which a sudden strong wind was blowing storm clouds, and thunder and lightning. One of the flashes of lightning split the tower in half, and a black cloud carried the startled child away. It took him over field and forest and mountain peak, right across to the sea, where it set the lad down for a wave to wash away, just as the prophecy had foretold. It was a long time before the the storm died down and the sun came out again. But the prince did not see it even then. He had mixed with the waters of the sea as the dew mixes with the soil, and had plunged down into the depths. Back in the palace the queen wept, and wept, and there was no comforting her. The king stroked her head and tried to cheer her up. 'You know very well I threw the magician out before she finished her prophecy,' he reminded her. 'She was going to say more, and the ending is sure to be a happy one. We'll find her again, and she'll tell us what will happen in the end.'

16 April

A Prophecy Comes True

But the magician couldn't tell the royal family anything, because no one could find her. No one even knew if she was still alive. Now that the queen had lost her last hope, her grief was greater than all the mountains in her kingdom put together, and her sorrowful tears ran down in streams, and the streams mixed with the mountain brooks, and ran down into rivers, and the rivers made their winding way down to the sea. So it was that the queen's grief joined the grief of her lost son. The current carried the prince to the surface, and the wind sent him scurrying across the sea as a fluffy white cloud, and back to his homeland. There he became a rain cloud, and when the

and that he didn't own any white paint, anyway, and they threw him in gaol. 'Fancy that,' thought Alfred to himself miserably. 'There I am, making my way peacefully from Little Saltham to Saltham-on-the-Marsh, and all of a sudden, for no reason at all, I end up in prison.' At that moment, the door opened, and the gaoler's daughter Lizzie brought him his supper. Alfred couldn't take his eyes off Lizzie. He had no idea what he was eating, but he began to take more kindly to the idea of being in prison. Lizzie used to bring him his breakfast, lunch and supper, and by and by she spent more and more time sitting in his cell. Whereas at first she only waited for the prisoner to finish his food before taking his empty plate, she soon started to sit and talk for a while after meals, and it wasn't long

rain fell it lay sparkling on the grass of the royal gardens. Then the sun touched the beads of rain with its life-giving rays, and the prince appeared. 'There you are!' said the king, leaping up and down with joy. 'I knew everything would be all right in the end. A storm carried our son off, and a storm has brought him back again. There was no need for you to cry so.' But this time the king was wrong. If the queen hadn't cried so much . . . But you know all that, don't you?

17 April

How Alfred Got Put in Prison

Someone in the town of Fogleton had painted 'THE MAYOR IS A PIG' on the mayor's gate in white paint. The constables received strict instructions that all leave was cancelled until they arrested the culprit. The constables caught Alfred red-handed as he was reading the sign with some amusement. They refused to listen when he explained that he was only passing through Fogleton,

before the two of them found they were rather fond of each other. In the meantime, the chief constable had discovered that it was the town clerk who had written 'THE MAYOR IS A PIG', because he had ideas of being mayor himself, and hadn't quite made it. The whole thing was quickly hushed up, and the chief constable himself went to see Alfred, who was sitting in gaol for no good reason at all.

18 April

How Alfred Got Put in Prison

The chief constable was an expert beater-about-the-bush, and he went on about how these things happen and how the policeman's lot is not a happy one, and so on — anything so as not to admit having made a foolish mistake. After going on like that for ages and ages, he finally suggested to Alfred that the prison doors would be left open that evening, and that if he cared to step outside he might escape without any trouble at all, for no one would try to stop him. 'Dear me,' said Alfred, stubbornly. 'That won't do at all. I couldn't *escape* from prison. No, you arrested me in broad daylight, and you shall let me go the same way, so that all may see my innocence.' He didn't like to say that he was quite content in prison, so long as Lizzie kept visiting him three times a day. 'But that would mean getting the town clerk mixed up in the affair,' sighed the chief constable, 'and that would never do. The town clerk is an aristocrat, you see, and we can't go nabbing no snobs, now, can we? Not to mention the fact that chief constables is also snobs, and we snobs 'ave got to stick together, you know.' 'That's up to you,' said Alfred, with a shrug of his shoulders. 'Only I'm not going to run away from gaol like a common thief, and that's that. You and the other snobs can sort it out among yourselves.'

19 April

How Alfred Got Put in Prison

After that Lizzie was not the only daily visitor to Alfred's cell. The chief constable kept coming back to try and persuade his contented prisoner to escape. But Alfred wouldn't hear of it, and he said he was staying where he was. Only the chief constable hadn't got where he was by being completely stupid, and he soon noticed what was going on between Alfred and Lizzie. 'There's something I ought to tell you,' he said to Alfred, in a confidential whisper. 'Lizzie's father doesn't want you to get married. He'll try to stop you.' 'That's not surprising,' Alfred replied, 'when I am still a prisoner whom no one has declared

innocent.' 'That's not the reason at all,' the chief constable told him, with a knowing wink. 'He wouldn't want you for a son-in-law even if you'd never been accused of anything. You see, he wants Lizzie to marry the town clerk's boy!' This time Alfred hung his head. 'The only way out of it,' the chief constable went on, 'is for you to elope with her in the night. I promise we'll chase after you in the direction of Little Saltham, and you can safely make for Saltham-on-the Marsh.' This time Alfred agreed. And in the end everyone was contented. Alfred and Lizzie, who were in Saltham-on-the-Marsh together, the chief constable, who had got rid of his unwanted prisoner at last, and the town clerk, who was glad no one had ever had to find out who really wrote 'THE MAYOR IS A PIG'. Only the gaoler was upset, but he soon got over it, and came to visit Lizzie in Saltham-on-the-Marsh the week after.

20 April

The Wonderful Doctor

Mark's mother had died when he was a small boy. He and his father, the chemist, lived together, and they got on well with each other. Mark liked to sit in his father's shop, which smelt of herbs and ointments, and he read the Latin labels and often asked what the different medicines were for. But one day his father fell ill, and it was a waste of time Mark asking him which powder he was to mix, or which tea to brew. 'There is no cure for my illness,' the old man told him. 'And my only comfort is that you will take the chemist's shop over, and continue to help those in need, without a thought for yourself.' 'That I promise, father,' Mark replied. Then he burst into a flood of tears, for he saw that his father could no longer hear him. Mark was all on his own. The day after the funeral he opened the doors of the shop to carry on his father's work, just as he had promised. It wasn't long before the bell over the door began to tinkle, and in walked two women with veils over their faces. The boy had never seen them in town before. 'May I be of service?' he asked, politely. 'You are my first customers, so I am glad to see you, and you can have your medicines free of charge.' 'Your words have won our hearts, my boy,' said the woman in the blue veil. And the woman in the black veil added, 'We have not been greeted so kindly in all our lives. You shall be rewarded for that.'

21 April

The Wonderful Doctor

The two visitors drew back their veils, and Mark found himself looking into the feverish faces of a pair of repulsive women. The one with the black veil in particular was all skin and bones, with hideous sunken eyes. But Mark had seen many horrors in the time he had spent sitting in the shop, and he did not flinch. 'I am Disease,' said the first of the women, letting her blue veil fall back across her face. 'And I am Death,' announced the other, covering herself with her black veil. 'I'm not sure if I have the right medicines for you,' Mark admitted. 'We don't want medicines,' Disease told him. 'We are looking for someone to help.' 'Everyone hates us,' Death explained, 'so we are trying to find at least one human being who might be grateful to us. Now we have found you.' 'As soon as anyone falls ill,' Disease went on, 'you must go to him. If you see me standing at his head, give him the most ordinary medicine you know, and he will be cured. But we have one condition, which you must follow. You must charge as much as possible for your cures. We want

you to become rich.' 'Mind you well, though,' said Death. 'If you should see me standing beside the patient's head, he will not recover, even if you were to give him all the medicines in the world. You will not be able to help him, and you must go away.' 'Won't other people see you?' asked Mark, surprised. 'Of course not,' replied Disease. 'We are invisible, and we shall appear only to you.' So Mark agreed to give this healing business a try.

22 April

The Wonderful Doctor

Mark closed the chemist's shop, putting only a few pills and herbal teas in his bag, and set off into the town walking wherever his feet happened to take him. Suddenly he heard the sound of weeping coming from one of the windows. He went inside and saw a young boy, in tears, standing beside his mother's sickbed. The woman in the blue veil was standing at the head of the bed. 'If you like,' Mark told the boy, 'I shall cure your mother. But my treatment costs money.' The boy brought a pot containing coins of all kinds. 'These are our savings,' he said. 'If you make my mother well again, they are yours.' Mark noticed that Disease nodded her agreement. So he brewed some peppermint tea and gave it to the sick woman. Then he motioned to Disease to go away. In a few moments the boy's mother was as right as rain. 'This is all we own,' said

the boy, handing Mark the money. Mark would have liked to refuse it, but then he remembered that the women had made it a condition, so he took the pot and went his way. He cured many more people in this way, until the fame of this wonderful doctor spread throughout the land. Wonderful, yes, but the doctor was also known to be expensive, for Mark had become greedy. He would take a look around each house he visited, and he knew at once how much to ask. And he never made exceptions. 'If you can't pay the doctor, you have an alternative,' he would say, jokingly. 'You can die for free.' He didn't even know himself where his greed had come from. He made the excuse that it was Disease and Death who had decreed that it should be so, that he should grow rich.

23 April

The Wonderful Doctor

Whenever Mark went into some house and saw that the woman in the black veil was standing at the patient's head, he always left immediately. The relatives would offer him the most precious gifts, but without success. He would not even answer them. So it came to be said that he whom the miraculous doctor refused to treat would die for certain. Mark had by now made such

a fortune that he was able to build himself a palace to match that of the king. He had silver plates and gold ornaments, and he rode to visit the sick in a fine carriage drawn by a foursome of black horses. He could choose his patients, since there was always a row of humble people, begging for treatment, in front of his palace gates. No one dared to knock at the gates, but only waited for the doctor to step outside and hear what he was being offered, so that he might decide the order in which he made his visits. Mark was satisfied with the services of Disease and Death, and they were satisfied with him. Then, one day in April, someone came knocking on the door of his palace, and when the servant went to open it, a man in a nobleman's dress came in. 'Who dares disturb me like this?' cried Mark. 'By order of the king,' the aristocrat replied. 'The princess is gravely ill, and I am to return with you at once. You may choose your own reward, afterwards. Only now you must hurry!' Mark was flattered to be called to the royal court, and surely his reward would also be a royal one.

24 April

The Wonderful Doctor

'Where is the princess?' Mark asked, as he stepped down from his carriage in the courtyard of the king's castle. 'First you must go before the king,' the nobleman told him, and he led the famous doctor to the throne room. 'We have heard much of your powers,' the king told him, 'and you are our only hope. But we also know that you sometimes refuse to treat the sick, and that they always die. We have therefore decided to set the following conditions. If you cure our princess, beloved above all things, you may name your own reward. But if the princess does not recover, then you will be shorter by a head!' Then four of the royal guards took up positions on both sides of the doctor, and marched him off to the

flushed with fever. She breathed heavily and jerkily. It suddenly seemed to Mark that he had known her all his life, and that he couldn't live without her. But then he remembered that he wasn't going to, and suddenly he was filled with a new determination. He was not going to let the princess die without a struggle. There was still some of his father's skill and patience left in him, and he began to study the princess's illness to see how it might be treated. He read learned books on medicine, and reminded himself of the uses of different herbs. The princess woke up from her feverish sleep and whispered, 'Help me . . .' 'I shall try,' he answered. 'We'll see who is the more powerful,' hissed Death, drawing aside her veil. 'We shall indeed,' Mark replied, sourly, and he summoned the chamber-maids. He told one of them which tea to prepare, another what sort of bandage to apply, and a third what the princess was to drink with the powder he gave her. For three days and nights he never left the bedside, and it seemed that the sickness was losing its hold over her. But on the third night he saw Death reaching out her bony fingers towards the princess. Had his struggle been a waste of time?

sick-room. Mark felt as if they were leading him to the gallows. But when he reached the bed on which the princess lay, he gasped with horror, for standing beside her head was the woman in the black veil. 'I must be left alone with her,' Mark said, miserably. When the others had left the chamber, he turned to Death and said, 'I must cure her. Go away, I beg you!' But Death replied, 'The terms of our bargain are clear. Where you find me, you have no power.' 'Just this once,' Mark beseeched her. 'My own life is bound up with hers.' 'It's no use,' said the woman in the black veil. 'I couldn't help you, even if I wanted.'

25 April

The Wonderful Doctor

Mark hung his head, repeating to himself, 'My own life is bound up with hers . . .' Then his glance fell on the princess, and his heart almost stopped beating. His patient was sleeping fitfully, and her cheeks were

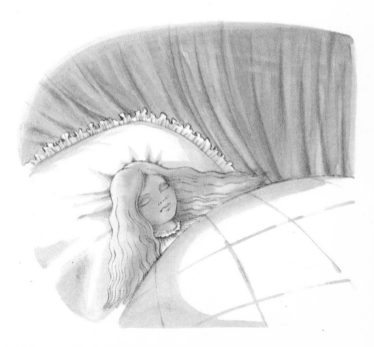

shoulders!' 'But Father,' said the princess, appearing at Mark's side. 'Don't be so old-fashioned. To be the wife of a wonderful doctor is not unsuitable for a princess.' 'A doctor, yes,' Mark told her, 'but a wonderful one no more, though I have a chemist shop filled with medicines. If a man wants to gain something, then he must sacrifice something else.' 'See, Father! How wisely he speaks!' said the princess, proudly. 'I will marry him, even if it means going to live in his chemist's shop!' But since that was the last thing the king wanted, he had a great wedding prepared instead.

26 April

The Wonderful Doctor

Mark was fearfully tired. His arms and legs felt like lead, and his eyelids were drooping. But when he saw what Death had in mind, he leaped up and grabbed her bony hand in his. 'Do not interfere with my work,' Death snarled, 'or you will pay dearly for your impudence!' But Mark refused to give in, and after a long struggle he managed to push the woman in the black veil out of the door. 'Very well,' said Death, in an icy voice that sent a chill through the room. 'Have it your own way. But you will never see either Disease or myself again. And all the riches you have amassed with our help are gone, from this moment!' Death vanished from sight. Had Mark taken in what she said? He heard it well enough, but he no longer cared whether he had a palace, or riches. The important thing was that the princess was now breathing easily, and smiling. 'What do you ask in return for my daughter's cure?' asked the king. 'The only reward I will accept,' the doctor replied, 'is her hand in marriage.' 'What impudence is this?' thundered the king. 'Get out of my sight, you no-good doctor, and think yourself lucky you still have a head on your

27 April

Horace the Mole and the Worm

The most important place in a mole's burrow is the larder, which contains all sorts of goodies, and a comfortable bed as well. Horace the mole had a bed made of dry clover, wild thyme and peppermint. That was because peppermint tea makes a good night-cap, four-leaved clover is for good luck, and wild thyme is supposed to tell fairy tales before you go to sleep. Horace could hear the thyme telling stories, anyway. One day, as he was listening, he wished something special would happen to him. And, do you know, his wish was granted. It all started when he met a very clever worm. This worm knew how to play chess, draughts and dominoes, and had read a lot of learned books. No wonder! It lived in a flower-bed beside which the gardener would sit after work, reading aloud to his wife, or playing board games. The worm had always watched carefully, and now knew all there was to know about chess, it could checkmate the gardener in no time at all, and could read almost as well. It would have been a pity if Horace the mole had eaten such a well-educated worm the very first time they met, now wouldn't it? 'Listen,'

Horace the Mole and the Worm

The next day the worm said to the mole, 'What will you bet that I can't make such a maze of underground passages that you can't find your way out of it? I've read lots of puzzle books, you know, and there's no one can make a better labyrinth than I.' 'Then what's the point of betting?' asked the mole, sadly. He didn't know what a labyrinth was, and he wondered why the worm kept saying 'I' instead of 'me'. He was beginning to feel ignorant. At least, that's how he would have felt if he had known what *that* meant. So he went to see the gardener to ask if he would teach him to read and play chess and so on. Only the gardener was busy, and didn't have much time for the mole. 'I've got work to do,' he said. 'It's spring, and I have to turn the soil over, and plant the peas and beans, and sow the carrots and radishes. Don't get in my way!' That's life! Some are lucky, others are

the worm had said to him, 'if you swallow me, you'll miss an awful lot. I know so much about the world, I could be a schoolteacher if I wanted!' Horace didn't know what schools were, but he agreed to leave the worm alone. In the end he even promised to become a vegetarian, and give up eating worms altogether. But as soon as he changed his eating habits, he turned into quite a different mole.

not. The worm had got an education without even trying. Not only that, but it was useful, and moles were pests. 'Get your own back!' called another mole from a neighbouring garden, scurrying over to show him how. He turned up a pile of earth right in the middle of the gardener's seed-bed, until the little round peas went rolling in all directions. Then he made another pile, then another, all in a neat little row. He thought he'd teach Horace how it was done. But Horace went and got a rake and before long the seed-bed was back how it was before. The pair of moles were at it with all their might when the gardener came along and said, 'My, you're a good helper! Do you want a job?' The mole was happy to agree, at least he would be useful. He was just a little angry when the worm came along and said, 'We can't all be schoolteachers, you know!'

29 April

The Doughnut and the Doughnut

Do you still remember the doughnut we last saw in March? Well, he rolled along the road, down into another town, and there, right in front of the school, he bumped into another doughnut. It was lying on the ground, crying. If it hadn't been for the

tears, our doughnut would have thought it was looking in a mirror. The second doughnut was exactly the same. 'What are you lying here for?' asked the wandering doughnut. 'Judy dropped me,' sniffed the other. 'She says she doesn't fancy me. And her mummy was so careful to make me nice.' 'You should be pleased,' our doughnut comforted him. 'Forget all about your choosy little girl, and come travelling with me!' 'I'm not the travelling sort,' the other doughnut told him. 'I'm lazy, you see, and I'm looking forward to being eaten.' 'Hmm,' said our doughnut, 'I see you and I are quite different. But if all you want is to get into someone's tummy, we'll soon put that right!' He had spotted Bonzo the hungry dog, sniffing along the street looking for something to eat. 'Here you are!' he called, pointing to his companion. Bonzo must have misunderstood, because he made straight for our friend, the singing doughnut. The doughnut had to run away yet again, off into May somewhere.

30 April

The Clever Tortoise

A certain hare tripped over a tortoise's shell one day, and began to scold the creature. 'Why do you have to stand here in the middle of the path, when there's plenty of room everywhere else?' The tortoise stuck its head out and, thinking up an excuse quickly, said, 'I was just having a race with my friend, but he's so slow that I decided to take a little nap until he catches me up.' 'Poppycock,' replied the hare, standing on his hind feet. 'I don't believe a word of it. You'll be telling me you can catch *me* next!' He drew a line across the path in front of him. 'Ready, steady, go!' he called, and off he ran. The tortoise knew he didn't stand a chance of winning, but he had a smart head on his shoulders. He saw that the path led downhill, so he looked around for a round stone, and sent it rolling after the hare. As the stone passed the hare, the tortoise called out, 'There you are, you see! I've caught you!' The stone threw up a lot of dust as it went by, so that the hare really did think the tortoise had overtaken him, and gave up the race. The tortoise just stood at the top of the hill and smiled. He had won the race without going anywhere!

May

1 May

The World Outside

A certain little kitten liked nothing better than sausages. If they gave him anything else he would hiss and sulk, so in the end they had to place a running order with the butcher. The kitten didn't even want to go outside, and he was so lazy and fat that he wasn't at all nice. He never took the slightest notice of mice, either. 'What a stupid kitten we've landed ourselves with,' his master said one day. But a moment later he changed his mind. 'Stupid, my foot!' he said. 'It's too clever by half. I know what, though! Tomorrow I'll let him go hungry.' But the cat's mistress, who was herself as round as a melon, said that it was cruel to torment cats, and anyway, it might be enchanted. She kept hoping the kitten would get over his taste for sausages somehow, even though all the others laughed at her. Now it so happened that the wind elf came flying into that house. The cat sniffed at this strange creature and mewed. 'You smell funny, like nothing I've ever smelt before. I think I shall eat you!' 'Wait a minute,' the wind elf yelled at him. 'There's something I must tell you first. I smell of wind and sun, and earth and smoke, and

grass and rain and . . .' 'I don't know any of those,' said the cat in wonder. 'Tell me where I can find them. I think I might like them better than sausages.' 'All you have to do is go outside,' the wind elf told him. 'You'll find it all there.' So the cat jumped out of the window. It was so pleasant outside that he forgot to eat the wind elf, and his sausages as well. And when he had had his first taste of hunting, he began to wonder how he could have spent so long lounging in front of the fire.

2 May

Horace the Mole Helps Out

'Well what would you like me to do today?' Horace the mole would ask the gardener every morning. He wanted to be in on everything. He liked to help, and most of all he liked being praised. But one day he pulled up the carrots instead of the dandelions when the gardener told him to do some weeding, and he got a good telling off. 'I should have known, shouldn't I? Moles spend most of their lives

underground, and they can't see too well, can they? Well, my lad, you'll have to get yourself some glasses if you want to keep your job, and that's flat!' 'But where?' thought Horace, peering enviously at the gold-rimmed spectacles balanced on the gardener's nose. From that moment on he longed to have a pair like those. Only the more he thought about his glasses, the more mistakes he made, so that he was always being told off instead of praised. Then, one day, before sunrise, he was getting ready for work when he sighed so unhappily that the wind caught up his sigh and carried it over hills and valleys until it reached the sky traveller (the wind elf). The next day the wind elf came flying into the garden, and went straight up to the mole. Under his cloak he carried a pair of borrowed glasses. They had exactly the same gold rims as the gardener's. Horace put them on at once, but what was this? The blades of grass were no longer soft and friendly. A spider's web looked like a rough fishing net, and everything was so huge that the mole felt small and helpless. 'I don't want any glasses,' he told the wind elf. 'And I've had enough of gardening, too.' And off he went to do his own sort of digging, and to annoy the gardeners again.

3 May

The Forgotten Street

There are corners of every town that don't look nice at all. They are so dirty and untidy that you can't see what they looked like before. In a street like that, tucked away out of sight, the wind elf found a window that was half blind. He blew away a little of the dust and peered inside, to where an old man dressed in black was sitting at a table. He looked almost as if he wasn't breathing, as though he had left this world behind him. But his heart was still beating, only it was beating as sadly as could be. He was sad because no one came to see him, sad for his

dog, which had died, and sad for his cat, which had gone astray. He longed to have a fire burning in the stove, a clean cloth on the table, and heaven knows what else. The wind elf clasped his hands in dismay. 'I've never seen so much sadness and longing,' he cried, and shed a sympathetic tear. Then he leaned on the window, so that it opened a little, and the sun shone into the old man's eyes. The wind elf greeted him out loud. Then he looked around and dropped his tear into a glass that was standing on the table. And because he wanted to give him another present as well, he added a little leaf that had somehow got stuck to his cloak. The little dry leaf at once turned green, and it began to grow and to flower, until it decorated the whole window. The neighbours stopped to see it, and asked what this wonderful plant might be. They wouldn't believe it had grown out of a little salt water, the wind elf's tear. He had long since departed on his travels again. Perhaps he didn't even know that the ugly little street had become pretty again. Flowers blossomed in every window, and once again people started to notice each other, and to talk to each other.

4 May

Little Billy

Five little baby birds hatched out from the five little spotted eggs snuggled together in the warmly lined nest. Their mother and father fed them night and day, seeing to it that those skinny little creatures grew into fluffy balls of feathers. In time the baby birds had grown so much that there wasn't enough room in the nest any more. 'As soon as your wings get a bit stronger,' their mother told them, 'you'll learn how to fly. Your father and I have had quite enough of all this rushing to and fro to bring food for five hungry mouths. You'll have to learn to look after yourselves!' So one fine day she told her five fully-fledged songsters: 'Ready, steady, go!' But only four of them flew to a branch further down the tree. Then they flew back up to the nest, then back down again, and so on. But little Billy, the youngest, just closed his eyes, so as not to see that fearful drop below him, and

shivered with fear. His mother tried to persuade him, and his father shouted at him, but it was no use. A piping little voice up there kept repeating, 'I'm scared!' and there was no sign of the flutter of little Billy's wings.

5 May

Little Billy

Days went by, and little Billy's brothers and sisters were already able to look after themselves, but he still sat there fearfully in the nest, not even daring to look down. Then Daddy had an idea. 'The only thing that will make Billy forget how afraid he is of flying is to make him even more afraid of something else,' he said. He was just wondering how he might make Billy more frightened than he already was, when he saw a cat crawling along the tree. It had known for a long time that they were feeding Billy up nicely, ready for some clever cat to come along and eat him. 'It will be no trouble at all. Doesn't the stupid child just sit there, waiting to be gobbled up?' But the cat had miscalculated. The sight of the sharp teeth, long claws and big yellow eyes was enough to send the youngest of the bird family sailing down from the edge of the nest, and Billy was flying before he knew

what had happened. Not only did he save himself, but he also found out how nice it was to fly. 'What a fool I have been,' he thought to himself as he flitted from branch to branch, just as deftly as his brothers and sisters. It was a thousand times better than crouching there in the nest.

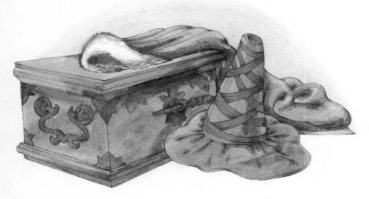

6 May

The Magic Box

A certain wizard, whose name was Rigmeroll, lived in an old castle beyond nine forests and nine rivers. There was not a living soul for many a mile around. Rigmeroll was a solitary sort of fellow, and not too friendly, so he wasn't particularly fond of company anyway. Well he may not have needed any company, but where, you may wonder, did he do his shopping? Did he have to walk through nine forests and swim across nine rivers every time he wanted a loaf of bread or a bottle of beer? Not a bit of it. He had a box. It was no ordinary box, but a magic one. He would close the lid, tap it gently, and say, 'Abracadabra, give me a sugar-loaf, fiddle-de-dee!' When he opened the lid again, there would be a sugar-loaf inside, or whatever else he happened to fancy. But you mustn't suppose the box was just for doing his shopping. Dear me, no! He could conjure anything he liked out of it. Since the box was a big one, he could tap on the lid and say, 'Abracadabra, give me a camel, fiddle-de-dee!' And inside the box would be his camel, one hump or two, whichever he wanted. That was the sort of box it was.

7 May

The Magic Box

The magic box was very old. It had been passed down from father to son in the Rigmeroll family for countless generations. Even the wizard himself had no idea just how many. Perhaps it was so old that it should have seen a box-doctor now and again. Why? You'll see in a minute. It all started quite harmlessly. One day Rigmeroll tapped on the lid and said, 'Abracadabra, give me some bread and butter, fiddle-de-dee!' But when he lifted the lid, the wizard found, instead of bread and butter, a tin of caviar and a bottle of brandy. He could scarcely believe his eyes. And when he had drunk the bottle of brandy, he couldn't believe his eyes at all, because he kept seeing two magic boxes instead of one. The box behaved itself for a while, then it suddenly presented him with a tortoise instead of a white horse. He did try sitting on it, in case it was a magic tortoise that travelled at the speed of light, but he soon found out that it went about as fast as a lame snail. After that the box would sometimes give him what he asked for, and sometimes not. But by and by, the times it didn't got to be more frequent than the times it did. It seemed that the ancient box was getting very absent-minded.

8 May

The Magic Box

I daresay Rigmeroll would have got used to his magic box's strange ways, by and by, and would simply have filled his attic with the white elephants and plain junk that the forgetful, or maybe mischievous, box kept churning out. After all, he still got what he asked for now and then, and the two of them might well have gone on like that, if ... well, if the box hadn't produced a newspaper one day when the magician asked for apple turnover. Instead of throwing it in the attic, Rigmeroll began to read, and his eye was caught by a picture of a beautiful girl on the society page. He read at once what was written underneath it, and learned that all suitors wishing to win the hand of Princess Olivia were to report at Castle Tumbling at such-and-such a time on the whateveritwas of the month. 'Gracious,' thought the wizard, because the paper was a week old, and the day and hour in question had just arrived. At that very moment the would-be husbands were lining up to seek the royal approval. 'I'll have to put a stop to that!' cried the unsociable wizard, who had taken a great liking to the girl in the picture. Tapping on the lid of the magic box, he said: 'Abracadabra, give me Princess Olivia from Castle Tumbling, fiddle-de-dee!' And he flung the lid open again. A young prince stepped out, looking just as surprised as Rigmeroll himself. He had a moment ago been standing in front of Olivia, and was just about to tell her his name was Galligad, when everything had suddenly gone blurred and the next thing he knew he was standing in the wizard's box.

9 May

The Magic Box

Rigmeroll invited Prince Galligad to take a seat, and tapped the box again, repeating his order: 'Abracadabra, give me Princess Olivia from Castle Tumbling, fiddle-de-dee!' But the box turned out to contain another of Olivia's would-be husbands, a certain Prince Lililiver. But the wizard refused to give up even when Galligad and Lililiver were joined by Rustihelm, Bandilex, Glumiface and another ninety-five princes. As the growing crowd of hopeful bridegrooms filled the room and gradually spilled over into the corridors and overflowed downstairs into the dining-hall and the dungeons, and into every scrap of space that wasn't already taken up by the box's previous mishaps, the wizard just went on and on demanding that Princess Olivia be brought to him. 'How many more suitors can there be in Castle Tumbling?' he cried in exasperation, as another one appeared in the box. 'None at all,' Prince Nobblinee assured him. 'I'm the last.' 'Now!' cried the wizard. 'This time it must be the princess.' His finger was very sore by now, but he tapped on the box once more, asked

it for Princess Olivia, and opened the lid impatiently. 'Botheration!' he called out, angrily. The box contained an axe. The axe lifted itself up and smashed the box into little pieces. Rigmeroll didn't have a magic box any more. What he did have was a whole regiment of princes to look after. And poor Olivia, back at Castle Tumbling, was left with not even one possible husband.

10 May

How Petrof Played and Didn't Play

In the house of a certain old lady there lived a piano called Petrof. His name was written inside the lid in gold letters. The old lady often sat in front of him on a round stool, playing the loveliest pieces of music she knew. Her slim fingers struck the black and white keys, now softly, now with stormy excitement, her foot working the pedal to release the notes with their full force. Petrof was pleased when the lady played, because music was the great love of his life. Only one day she didn't come, nor the next. Then, on the third day, the room was filled with mournful faces, black clothes and sad bunches of flowers. Petrof discovered that

his mistress had died. Not that he knew what it meant to die, but he understood that she would never again sit down to bring his keyboard to life with the most beautiful music he had ever heard. That night Petrof played it all over again, but quietly, for himself, on his own special strings somewhere deep inside him. Then he fell silent. And he remained silent when the removal men came and took him away to a store-room for OAPs, old and ancient pianos. Petrof missed his lady, whose hands had breathed life into his wood and metal. Now it seemed to him that he was quite useless.

11 May

How Petrof Didn't Play and Played

The home for old and ancient pianos in which Petrof found himself was part of the store-rooms of a shop for retired musical instruments, where there were second-hand guitars, saxophones, trumpets, trombones, and so on. Customers would often walk through the store-rooms, where they would tap a drum or strum a mandoline. Then, sometimes, one of the instruments would

disappear. Petrof didn't notice this at first, but then, by and by, he started to wish that someone would come and run their finger along his keyboard, to see what he sounded like. At last it happened! A father and mother arrived with a little girl, and the little girl picked out a simple little tune on Petrof's white keys. What an insult! He, whose strings had vibrated with the world's great masterpieces, was to play childish melodies like that? The idea put him quite out of tune. The little girl's father noticed at once, and he said, 'We'll have to have it tuned.' They bought Petrof, and the next day the removal men were to come and take him away. Beside him stood a battered old double-bass, and it saw that Petrof was miserable. The double-bass was not very talkative, but it said to him, 'Your old mistress was once a little girl who plonked out children's songs on a piano. Everyone has to learn sometime.' And Petrof was ashamed of himself, and when he got to his new home he did his best to make the little girl's simple tunes sound like the most wonderful works of the masters.

12 May

The Princess and the Pea

King Guzlemede's castle was miles away from anywhere, and it wasn't often they had visitors. Which is why Prince Pettrifyde couldn't find himself a bride. One miserable evening the wind was whistling through the battlements and icy raindrops were whipping against the windows. The royal family was snug in front of a blazing fire, when they suddenly heard a banging on the gate. In a while a half-frozen girl dressed in rags was brought before them. She said she was a princess, that a band of robbers had murdered her parents and sacked their royal palace. The queen didn't much like the look of her, thinking she seemed more like a beggar-girl than a princess, but the prince kept muttering, 'How beautiful she is, how beautiful she is!' His mother didn't want to refuse the wanderer a bed for the night, but she decided to test her. She placed nine eiderdowns for the girl to sleep on, and underneath the bottom one she put a dried pea. 'If she really is a princess, as she claims to be,' the queen explained, 'she will feel the pea pressing on her back.' In the morning the girl woke up, and when the queen asked her how she had slept, she replied, 'Very poorly indeed. I seemed to be lying on a boulder or something, but I was too tired

to take it out of the bed.' 'She is indeed a princess, and you shall marry her, Pettrifyde!' the queen cried joyfully. The prince jumped for joy, and hurried to the bedroom where the princess had slept. There he removed from the bed the large stone he had put there the night before, just to make sure.

13 May

On and On Goes the Tale of a Cupboard

In a mysterious room in a mysterious house, there once stood a mysterious cupboard. It was positively the only thing in the room. There were no chairs and no tables, not even a settee. And no one lived in the house. It was empty, except for that one mysterious cupboard. And if you want to hear more about it, you'll have to wait until 13 June.

14 May

Forget-Me-Not and Recall-Me-Not

In one particular grove of one special forest, in a certain larch-tree house, lived a couple of fairies called Forget-Me-Not and Recall-Me-Not. Were they good fairies or wicked ones? Well, it's difficult to say for sure. They were just forest fairies, whom no

one would ever have known about if they had been content to stay in their larch-tree house. But one day Recall-Me-Not got tired of their woodland grove, where there were only birds and butterflies and beetles, and she decided to take a trip to the town which lay a mile or two beyond the forest. Forget-Me-Not tried to persuade her to stay at home, saying that the town was no place for fairies, but Recall-Me-Not had made up her mind, and off she went. She took with her the only thing she had in the whole world, and that was the sneezing-powder of forgetfulness. She offered some to the first person she met, who happened to be the watchman. He had a fit of sneezing, and forgot to sound the hour of midnight. The mayor wanted to punish the watchman for his carelessness, but when he, too, had taken a pinch of the powder he forgot not only about the watchman but also that he was supposed to call a meeting of the town council. Housewives forgot their geese and cakes in the oven and the children forgot to do their homework. That didn't matter too much, because the teacher forgot to go to school. But lovers forgot to sigh for their loved ones, the baker forgot to bake his rolls, and everyone just went around sneezing and forgetting to do things. Recall-Me-Not thought it was all very funny, and went around laughing her head off.

15 May

Forget-Me-Not and Recall-Me-Not

Recall-Me-Not enjoyed seeing people sneezing and forgetting things, so much so that she tipped the rest of her sneezing-powder out in the streets and parks and went about blowing it in through peoples' windows. The townsfolk sneezed, and sneezed. Now they even forgot to get washed or to clean their teeth, to eat or to sleep. They staggered around from one sneeze to the next, and from one house to another, since no one could remember where he lived any more. They kept on

saying, 'Now, what was I going to do? What did I come here for? I'm sure there was something I wanted . . .' But they could never remember. Meanwhile, back in the forest, Forget-Me-Not decided she had better go and see what her treemate was up to. When she arrived in town and saw what was going on, she was horrified. 'Dear me,' she said, 'but I haven't got a powder to make people remember, or even to stop them sneezing!' But she found in her pocket lots of little seeds from some sort of flower. She quickly spread them around the town, and then breathed her warm fairy breath on them, which makes flowers grow right up and blossom straight away. The first to sniff at one of the flowers was the schoolteacher, who had sneezed his way to the fields just beyond the town. He noticed that the little flowers had no scent, but that he stopped sneezing, and remembered he was supposed to be at school. He got the children together, and told them they were all to have a sniff at the . . . 'Whatever was the name of that flower?' he wondered. 'Forget-Me-Not,' the fairy whispered in his ear. Then the children took them to their parents, and everyone stuck their noses into posies of the little flowers, and stopped sneezing and forgetting. And the fairies? They went back to the forest together.

16 May

The Five Pretty Girls

Not so long ago, and not so far away, lived five young girls who were still much too young to be thinking about marrying. Still, they were all terribly concerned as to how they could make themselves prettier. Not that they were ugly, not a bit of it. But they were not at all satisfied with their turned-up little noses. They needn't have worried about them, since everyone else thought they were charming, but they were sure their noses were really ugly. One day the five young girls went to see a conjurer's

show, and it occurred to them that he might be able to do something about their troubles. He could conjure new noses up for all of them, and that would be the end of all their worries. 'Why not?' said the Great Alfonso, though he added that for a conjurer such as him it was much easier to pull rabbits out of hats and coloured handkerchiefs out of people's ears. He told the five girls to hold their noses and pull them forwards, while he said the magic words. He began with an ordinary abracadabra, but then he started to stutter 'Bra, bra, bra ... Goodness me, how does it go on ... Ah! I remember. Eeny, meeny, miny, mo, if it please their noses, let them grow. Tippity, tippity, tippity, top ... er, er, the time has, time has ... oh, yes! the time has come for them to stop!' But by the time the conjurer had remembered how the spell ended, the five little snub noses had grown so long that the young ladies, who had been rather pretty, were now very ugly indeed, and wished most earnestly that they had let their faces be.

17 May

The Tale of the First Long Nose

The five girls burst into a flood of tears. That didn't do much good, since it only made their noses redder and more noticeable than before. 'Hi there, you storks,

come and catch us some frogs!' the children called out to them. The first of the girls, whose name was Sally, decided to run away into the world that very minute. The other four, who were called Polly, Molly, Milly and Lilly, decided to do the same, and they ran off in all directions. But before they went, they promised each other to meet at the same spot in five years' time to tell each other how they had got on. Sally ran off with her head hung low, and the sound of the children's laughter stayed in her ears for a long time. When she was alone, she began to feel lonely. 'Ah, well,' she said to herself in the end. 'After all, laughter is healthy, and children need to laugh more than anyone.' So she went to ask for a job as a children's nurse. She let the boys hang their swing from her nose and use it like a trapeze, and soon she was the children's favourite. Her poppy-red nose attracted butterflies, and so a certain schoolmaster who collected them came to notice Sally. He fell in love with her, and the more he liked her, the smaller her nose became, until in the end it was as small as it had been to start with. And that was when they got married, of course!

18 May

The Tale of the Second Long Nose

When she was little, Polly's father used to say to her, 'Show me your nose, and I'll tell you if you've been good or not.' Now you could tell everything from looking at that long nose of hers. What the weather was going to be like, for instance. If it was covered with dew in the morning, it was sure to be a nice day. If it turned red at night, a wind was bound to get up. A cold nose promised a clear day, and if it was misty in the morning, you could be certain the weather would improve at midday. Polly got herself a job at a meteorological station, because she had become very interested in the weather. Indeed you might

say she had a nose for it. A great many top scientists came to ask Polly's advice, and invited her to conferences. When they couldn't get the long-term forecast right, she would use her long nose to gather together clouds or break them up, so that it was rainy or dry just as the men had said it would be. Polly was so clever and hard-working that it only took her a year to finish a school course that everyone else took four years to do. And the harder she studied, the shorter her nose became until it was back where it started. But she hardly noticed that, she was so engrossed in her books.

19 May

The Tale of the Third Long Nose

It wasn't long before Molly began to say to herself, 'It's no use weeping and wailing. I'm quite different from everyone else, so I might as well find a way of putting that to good use.' So she joined the first circus she came across. They welcomed her with open arms, saying that they had never had a clown like her before. Molly got paid well, and each evening she appeared before a packed audience, which applauded long

and loud. Molly was a great box-office success. They had to put on an afternoon performance, and then they even started playing at lunchtime for school outings. She made sad children happy and poorly ones got better through laughing. Then they brought there prisoners from gaols, and Molly's performance made them decide to reform. It wasn't long before the circus tent was surrounded by reporters and cameramen and fans asking for autographs. One day Molly was so tired that she said to herself, 'I can't go on, I'll have to have a rest.' She slept all day and all night, and when she woke up she found her nose was just as small as it had been before. The manager of the circus was horrified at first, but then he said, 'Never mind! You can wear a false one. No one really believed you had a nose that long, anyway.' And Molly went on being a famous clown.

The Tale of the Fourth Long Nose

For a long time Milly didn't know what to do. She crawled through the cornfields and the undergrowth so that no one should see her. She lived on the fruits of the forest, until at last she had to admit, 'If I go on eating beech-nuts, acorns and raw mushrooms, I shall grow a stag's antlers, and if I chew clover I shall have a hare's long ears.' So she summoned up her courage and went into a town. She chose the biggest town she could find, so that she wouldn't be noticed so much. Quite out of breath, she hurried through the streets until she came to a crossroads. People in the crowd kept grabbing hold of her nose. They mistook it for a railing, or for the baton of the policeman who was directing the traffic. What a mess he was making of it, too! He was new at the job, and he didn't know his right hand from his left. His whistle seemed to stutter, and there was a real old riot going on at the crossroads. It was only when Milly waved her nose about a bit that everything got sorted out. Constable Coppitt was very grateful, and promised to put in a good word if Milly should fancy joining the force. And soon she rose to the rank of chief inspectress in the C. I. D., because that nose of hers could sniff out crime a mile away. Her colleagues grew

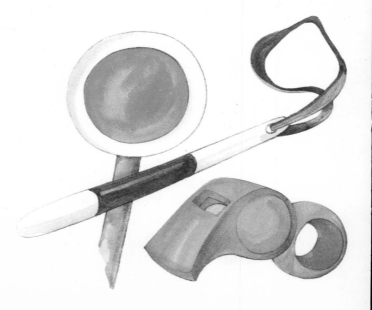

jealous and started to tell nasty tales about her. The more they gossiped, the shorter her nose became, until it was just like it used to be. But it was still sharp, and that was what really mattered.

21 May

The Tale of the Fifth Long Nose

Lilly, the last of the five girls, supposed she wouldn't get on very well in the ordinary world with such an extraordinary nose, so she stepped straight into a fairy tale. There she reached the brow of the first hill and came to a kingdom which had been at war for many years. Lilly didn't know that, of course, and she strode straight up to the castle door and knocked as loud as she could. It was a long time before anyone answered her knocking, and as she stood there up to her ankles in wet grass, she began to sneeze. When she pulled out her large white handkerchief, the generals in command of the besieging army and the besieged both cried out at once. 'They're surrendering — hurrah!' Both armies were most relieved, since they were sick and tired of fighting, and the soldiers climbed out of their trenches and poured out of the gates, and all began to dance. When they finally found out that no one had won and no one had lost, and that it was Lilly who had brought the war to an end, she was given scrolls of honour by both kings. They were written in gold letters, and as Lilly read them, her nose got shorter and shorter, until it was ... well, you know the rest, don't you ... it was small and turned-up again. But Lilly didn't mind any more, and nor did the other four girls. When they meet to tell their tales, they are sure not to complain about their noses at all.

22 May

The Glass Mountain

There were once three brothers, the eldest of whom inherited their father's cottage, the middle one a horse, and the youngest, Jack, just a small piece of garden. He didn't complain about his lot, but got down to work, and was rewarded with beds full of pretty flowers and fruit from the trees. His brothers just lazed about, and in the end they ate and drank away both cottage and horse. They began to wonder how they would make a living without any work, but then they heard that the Princess of the Glass Mountain was looking for a husband, and she would marry the first young man to knock on her palace gates. The two brothers hurried off to try their luck. The first of them tried to climb the slopes of the Glass Mountain, but he hadn't got far when he slipped back down again. His brother didn't get on any better, and nor did the other would-be husbands who had gathered from all around. Jack must have been the only young man who had stayed at home. He was watering his garden, without

sparing a thought for riches, or for the princess, whom no one had ever seen, by the way. When he went down to the lakeside to get water for the third time, a white swan came swimming up to him, and spoke in a human voice. 'I am the Princess of the Glass Mountain, and I should like to marry you, since you are so hard-working and kind-hearted. My wings can easily carry you up the mountain.' And so it was. The moment Jack knocked on the gates of the palace, the swan turned into a beautiful young girl, and before long Jack had become king. And because he was no shirker, he soon taught all his subjects to work hard, and the whole kingdom was like one big garden. Even the slopes of the Glass Mountain became overgrown with beautiful flowers!

23 May

How Jacob Was Dogged by Misfortune

Jacob the merchant closed his shop as usual and set out on his evening stroll. He saw a strange figure sitting beside the chapel, and, being a curious fellow, went to take a look at who it was. 'If you would give me just a farthing,' muttered the woman, who was wrapped in a shawl, and she gazed into his eyes so pathetically that he reached into his pocket and handed her a coin. But instead of taking it, she caught hold of his hand and held it tight. 'What are you doing? Let me go!' the merchant cried. But the woman whined that she would never let him go, that she would accompany him through his whole life. 'Who are you?' Jacob whispered. 'Why Jacob,' she told him, 'I am Misfortune, of course, and you won't get rid of me in a hurry!' Jacob tried to shake her off, to jerk himself free, to run away, but without success. Misfortune had stuck to him like glue. 'I shall serve you well!' she chuckled. And she spoke the truth. When the merchant returned from his walk he found his house and shop ablaze. He lost everything, and was reduced to poverty overnight. The friends who had visited him often when he was a rich merchant now passed him by on the other side of the street. Even the girl he was to have married laughed in his face, saying she wasn't so foolish as to marry such a poor person. What was Jacob to do? He set out into the world with Misfortune at his heels.

24 May

How Jacob Was Dogged by Misfortune

Jacob marched along at a fair old pace, but Misfortune never left his side. 'You must admit,' she boasted, 'that I have made a good job of it. In a single evening I lost

you your home, your livelihood, your friends and your bride.' 'But why?' asked Jacob, bewildered. 'I've never harmed you, and I gave you money when you asked for it.' 'Money, or no money,' snapped Misfortune, 'I have to do my job, and I believe in doing it properly. As long as I am with you, you shall not get back a halfpenny of what you have lost!' 'Is there no way I can get rid of you?' Jacob asked, desperately. 'There is indeed,' replied Misfortune, with a cruel laugh. 'But since you don't know what it is, I shall remain with you for the rest of your days!' At that moment a fair-haired young man was passing by. He must have heard what the two of them were speaking about, for he whispered in Jacob's ear, so that Misfortune should not hear, 'You must get someone to hold out his hand to her.' And the stranger was gone. But Jacob had seen the light. He must find somebody who deserved Misfortune.

25 May

How Jacob Was Dogged by Misfortune

Jacob reached the main square of a large town, with Misfortune at his heels. In the middle of the square a kindly-looking man was standing beside a large pot, pouring soup into chipped bowls to give to poor children. 'Who is it?' Jacob asked one of the crowd. 'Why, the mayor, of course,' came the reply. 'Once a month he performs good deeds.' 'What does he do the rest of the time?' Jacob wanted to know. 'Robs the poor,' snarled the other, and hurried off. 'The very man I'm looking for,' grinned Jacob. He walked straight up to the mayor and asked if he could not spare a farthing for his poor relative. 'It's always a pleasure to be charitable,' replied the mayor, loudly, and he looked around to make sure everyone was watching. As he held out his hand with the money, Misfortune hesitated for a moment. Then she decided. 'Jacob has nothing more to lose, but this rich one will be worth the trouble!' She grabbed him by the hand, and let go of Jacob. He sighed with relief, and said, 'A pity I couldn't have met Fortune instead!' Misfortune bared her teeth and said, 'But you did meet him, though you don't know it. He was the fair-haired youth who told you how to get rid of me . . .' 'But what about me?' cried the mayor. Misfortune bowed to him. 'You are my new master. I shall serve you as faithfully as the last!' And she gave a chuckle of satisfaction.

morning when he got up. But one weekend he disappeared, and for a couple of days no one knew where he was.

27 May

Stodge

In the same town there lived a little girl called Nelly, who was fond of Stodge which was probably because they liked the same sorts of food. One morning, Nelly opened her bedroom door just a crack, and announced that Stodge had come to visit her, and that he was starving, because he had been there since midnight. He rather fancied a couple of bars of hazelnut chocolate, that would do to be going on with. Nelly's mother was horrified. 'Why did it have to happen to us?' she cried. 'Now we'll have two of them in the house, Nelly and the monster. However shall we feed both of them?' When it was time to go to school, Nelly opened the door again, just

26 May

Stodge

A strange monster called Stodge had taken up residence in a certain big town. Just as dragons used to live on a diet of princesses, so Stodge had to be fed on cakes and buns and pastries, and all manner of other goodies. He would always appear on the doorstep whenever someone had just baked a cake, and he went round the families that had a birthday or a wedding to celebrate. In short, wherever there was something for a sweet tooth to be found, there you would find Stodge as well. Everyone was afraid of being visited by Stodge, because he would go quite wild and break things, and only calmed down when he had eaten his fill. On weekdays he would do the rounds of the local schools, begging the children's elevenses off them whenever they took his fancy. Then he would go to the confectioners' shops, which were empty as a rule, since no one much fancied tucking into a cream horn next to a monster. He wasn't a very polite eater, and kept smacking his lips and licking his fingers. His paws were always caked with dried custard and cream, because he never washed them, and his fur was covered in crumbs. It was quite horrible, really, and people would run away from him, even though he smelt of vanilla, because he dusted himself with vanilla sugar from head to foot every

a crack, and declared, 'I can't go anywhere, the monster wants to talk to me. And he would like a box of pralines and an angel cake. If he doesn't get them he'll knock the house down!' The door closed. Mother fainted, and Father went out to buy the things Nelly had asked for. When he wanted to go into her room, Nelly stuck out her hand and told him, 'No one may come in. The monster says so!' Father did as he was told, but he did wonder how he might get the better of Stodge. By evening he had had an idea. He and Mother baked a cake, but instead of sugar they put pepper in it. Nelly took it inside through the half-open door, but before long the door was open wide. There was no monster inside, only a little girl with her mouth full of cake, coughing and sneezing nineteen to the dozen. After that she didn't like either cakes or Stodge. He went off to some other town, anyway.

28 May

The New Gutter

One of the houses had a new gutter. It was all shiny and silvery in the sunshine, and it began to boast. 'I wonder if you know why I am here? Isn't it obvious? I'm here for decoration. They put me right up here so that everyone could see me and admire my beauty.' The lightning conductor felt like saying something rather rude, but it held its tongue. It thought to itself, 'We'll wait and see what you say when it starts to rain. Perhaps then you'll realize that you've got a job to do like everything else, and you'll stop your boasting.' A couple of days later it did rain. The rainwater came pouring off the roof and gushed along the gutter. First of all the gutter began to complain how cold it was. Then it simply turned itself over and let the water run straight off its back. The lightning conductor couldn't believe its eyes. 'I must be seeing things!' it gasped.

29 May

The New Gutter

The owner of the house couldn't believe *his* eyes either, when he came out after the rain had stopped and looked up at the roof. 'They can't have fastened it properly,' he said to himself, and he called the workmen again. This time they made quite sure the gutter couldn't turn over. 'What if it pours with rain again?' the gutter squeaked, desperately, but the owner of the house thought it was just creaking in the wind. This time the lightning conductor couldn't contain itself. 'What do you suppose you are here for?' it asked. 'Precisely to lead the water away! Did you really think a bent piece of metal like you had been put on the house for decoration?' For a little while the gutter didn't say anything, but then it replied. 'Of course. Do you know how beautiful it is when the water gushes through me?' 'Then why did you make such

a fuss about the water last time?' the lightning conductor inquired. 'That wasn't because of the water. I just wanted to show the man that I wasn't properly fixed,' the gutter fibbed. 'Otherwise I should have fallen down and got dented and then I shouldn't have been so beautiful.' The lightning conductor thought it best to gaze across at the opposite roof and pretend it hadn't heard.

30 May

The Doughnut and the Mice

Do you remember the doughnut we last saw in April? His wanderings took him into a field, where he stopped in front of some sort of hole. He hadn't even got round to guessing what might have made it, when a mouse popped its head out. The mouse shivered with delight. 'You must be sent

from heaven, doughnut.' 'You're quite wrong,' the doughnut put it right. 'Nobody sent me. I came of my own accord.' 'Then you heard how hungry we were, and took pity on us?' cried the mouse, gleefully. 'I didn't realize you were so noble!' 'Who's we?' the doughnut wanted to know, but there was no need to ask. One mouse after another emerged from holes all around. He counted exactly ninety-nine of them, and they formed a circle round him. 'We'll have to divide you up,' said the first mouse, 'so that everyone gets his fair share.' The doughnut saw that he was in a real fix. There was no way out of the circle of mice. Putting on a bold face, he began to sing. 'This doughnut's a singer, just the way
                                things should be,
For he's more nutty than doughy, and wants
                                to stay free.'
But it made no impression on the mice. They were grinding their sharp teeth ready to pounce. The doughnut looked beyond them and said out loud, 'Good day, pussy!' The mice were gone in a flash. They didn't wait to check whether the doughnut had invented the cat. Well, he had, of course, just so that he could slip away into June.

31 May

Thief Robs Thief

Pinky was an old burglar who would break into some house or other every evening and make off with anything he could carry that was worth taking. Sometimes he would keep things for himself, but mostly he sold them to a 'fence'. One evening he found himself in the house of some sort of art-lover, and, among other things, he made off with three statues of Apostles, which seemed to be very old. He rather liked the statues, and decided to keep them. As his work was over for the day, he went down to the local pub for a beer. Lightfinger was a rather younger burglar, but he made his

living much the same way as Pinky did.
A little later that evening, he broke into an empty house, whose owner seemed to have slipped out for a drink, and among the interesting things he found there were three old statues of Apostles. Lightfinger was delighted, because he already had three like them, and he looked forward to having the complete set. When he got home, he was surprised to find that he didn't have his three Apostles any more. When he unwrapped his night's takings, he discovered he had stolen his own things back again. He suddenly felt sorry for his crimes, and since Pinky felt the same when he found he had been burgled, there were two more burglars back on the straight-and-narrow the next morning.

June

little parachutes — seeds. One seed flew along for a long, long time. It was looking for the wind elf. When it found him at last, it popped under his hat. At that moment the wind elf remembered the dandelion and what he had promised her. But it was too late. The only thing left was that little grey hair.

2 June

The Cloud Lamb

They say that people meet people on earth, and clouds in the sky, but sometimes it may not be quite like that. One day Betty and her daddy went out for a walk in the country. They were sitting on the grass, gazing at the sky, when Betty asked: 'Did clouds used to be children, too, Daddy?' 'I expect so,' Daddy told her, and he began to go through all the things cloud children probably have to learn at school: drifting and skudding, frowning and puffing up, racing the wind, spotting and drizzling, raining and pouring . . . And as Daddy was saying all this, high above the meadows where they were sitting the cloud children were getting their end-of-term reports. They nearly all had good ones. Only little Fluffy got bad marks in everything. You see, he just didn't like looking threatening and being stormy, and all those things little clouds had to know. He was as gentle as a little lamb. The

1 June

The Dandelion

One evening the wind elf went to sleep in a darkened garden. When he woke up in the morning, he was lying next to a glorious dandelion. Its scent was like the glow of the morning sun, and the wind elf was quite overcome by it. 'I must have fallen in love,' he said out loud, but straight away he thought to himself, 'What am I talking about, a wandering fellow like me doesn't get married!' But the dandelion was so beautiful, gentle and modest, that he had asked her for her hand before he knew what he was doing. He pointed out, though, that he would have to go into the world to make some arrangements, before the wedding could be held. He stretched out his cloak, so that the lovely scent of the dandelion and its warm yellow glow filled all its pockets. But as soon as he flapped the cloak a couple of times and flew along a short way, the scent of the dandelion disappeared, and he forgot all about his love. In the meantime the dandelion was waiting, and it seemed such a long time to her that her head turned quite white with sorrow and anxiety. She looked like an old woman wearing a cotton-wool bun. By and by the wind blew this white fluff off and sent it out into the world in the form of tiny

teacher told him, 'There's no place in *my* school for the likes of *you!*' And he drove Fluffy out into the world. Fluffy was terribly ashamed. He just closed his eyes and floated down, and down, waiting to be blown away into thin air. But instead of that he landed right in Betty's lap and turned into a white lamb, the sort that looks like a little cloud, but eats grass just like any other lamb. 'I've always wanted a cuddly little animal,' Betty exclaimed, and she took her present from the sky back home.

3 June

The Cloud Lamb

Betty bought herself a little red leash, and she took little Fluffy for a walk on it in the park, where the children used to take their dogs. 'Who are you?' barked one of them at Fluffy. 'You look a bit like a poodle, but you keep nibbling the grass. Dogs should eat bones, and have just a taste of grass once a week, to help the digestion!' But the park-keeper was already waving his finger at Betty: 'Get that animal off the grass, or else . . .!' You'd have thought he'd have been

pleased. The lamb was doing a better job than the mowing-machine ever managed. Back home, Mummy complained that she wasn't going to have her nice green carpet spoilt by any sheep. All in all, the people whom Fluffy met seemed to get more and more like his old teacher all the time. He began to feel just as bad as when he had left the sky, so he closed his eyes, changed back into a cloud, and waited to be blown into thin air. That's probably what would have happened, if he hadn't met the wind elf. They bumped into each other with such a bang that the curly cloud's soft locks got all tangled up, and he began to look like a little bush with soft white flowers. He stretched out to tidy himself up, and looked like a bushy tree. Then he looked like a baby elephant, then a rippling pond, then a bearded old man. 'Well, well,' said the wind elf, 'no one else can do that.' Fluffy began to blush, and since the sun was just setting, he looked just like a cloud should look. Not only the wind elf liked it this time, but all the other clouds as well, and they began to take lessons from Fluffy in artistic cloud formation. You can sometimes see him and his school floating about up there.

4 June

The Blackbird's Tale

In the orchard outside the village the cherries were ripe. As long as there were plenty for all, no one bothered about them too much. But as soon as there was only the last cherry swinging to and fro on the last of the trees, the birds nearly fought over it. In the end Blackie the blackbird took it in his beak and chirped that he wasn't going to share it with anyone. He tried to swallow it as quickly as possible, but that was a mistake. It got caught in his gullet, and it wouldn't shift, either up or down. Brownie, his mate, remembered the story of the cock and the hen, and flew off to the spring to beg it for some water. 'Spring,' she began to

say, but at that moment she got a terrible shock, for the spring was dry. But she was not too shocked to fly on. She made straight for the gardener, who was digging one of the flower beds. 'Gardener,' she begged him, 'please move the stones that are blocking the spring. Then Blackie can take a drink. The spring will save his life, and you will have water for your garden.' The gardener replied, 'Very well, but Blackie must sing under my window every morning.' The blackbird was happy to agree. The gardener moved the stones, the water began to flow and the hen blackbird took a beakful to her mate. The moment Blackie took a drink, the cherry went sliding down into his crop with no trouble at all. From then on he shared things with the others, and out of gratitude to the gardener he sang under his window not only every morning, but whenever he had the time.

5 June

A Tinkling Tale

Julie had a terribly inquisitive and terribly choosy chicken, that always wanted the most curious things to eat. One day it swallowed one of those little bells you sew onto things, and after that it walked around

tinkling. Now, that really was something! Maggy, the little girl next door, found out about it, and she caught that awful disease, envy. She wasn't cured of it even when she grew up. In the meantime the chicken had grown into a hen, which laid a single, tinkling egg. Julie rather fancied boiling it and eating it, so that she could tinkle with every step she took, but luckily her mummy persuaded her not to. After all, none of the young men was likely to want to marry a tinkly girl like that, and Julie wanted to get married and have lots of children. Actually, she really did have a lot of them afterwards, and Maggy from next door had even more. But she was still envious of Julie's tinkling hens, because each of their eggs hatched into a chicken with a bell. But there was never more than one tinkling egg at any time waiting to hatch. The last of the tinkling eggs rolled over to the neighbours' fence. Tania, the youngest of Maggy's children, who was just as envious as her mother, picked it up quickly. She said to herself, 'It's mine now, and no one is going to get it!' It wasn't hers at all, of course. But things turned out differently in the end, anyway, because a cock hatched out from the egg, and when he grew wings and a red comb, he flew back over the fence to Julie's. And since cocks don't lay eggs, that was the end of the tinkling tale.

6 June

How Rosemary Found a Marble Hand

There was once a little girl called Rosemary, whose cheeks were as smooth as marble. Though she and her parents lived on hardly any money in their humble little cottage, all three of them were kind-hearted and hard-working, and they got along somehow. Everyone liked them, except their next-door-neighbour, Martin, who was always doing them wrong. One time he bumped into their garden fence with his cart, another time he trampled their rye by riding his horse through their field. He would even shout out, 'We don't want any poor ragamuffins like you in our village!' But the boys and girls liked Rosemary, and didn't mind that she was poor. That year as always, when the Midsummer festivities came round again, the young folk stayed close to her during the dancing, everyone wanting to hold her hand. But Rosemary suddenly pulled herself free from them. She had caught sight of something shining in the grass. She bent over and picked up a small marble hand. Her friends gathered round. 'Show us, show us!' they cried. But then they moved off again like a flock of sparrows

taking flight, and called to her from a safe distance. 'Throw it away! It's sure to be enchanted! It'll bring you bad luck!'

7 June

How Rosemary Found a Marble Hand

Rosemary took no notice of her companions' cries, and she hung the marble hand on a piece of string around her neck. From then on the entertainment lost its sparkle, with everyone looking at Rosemary's strange ornament out of the corner of his eye. One by one they all made their way back home. Only Rosemary didn't want to go home. She wandered along wherever her feet took her, and, without even knowing how, found herself among the ruins of the old castle that crowned a hill overlooking the village. A tiny shiver ran along her spine, when she recalled the old story that was told about the castle, how it was haunted by the ghost of one of its masters, a mean old miser. But the evening was an exciting one, with the feel of early summer about it, and the soft green moss was nice to sit on, and down below the windows of the cottages and farmhouses glowed with the light of paraffin lamps. It seemed to Rosemary that something special was about to happen.

How Rosemary Found a Marble Hand

Suddenly music began to play. At that moment one of the walls of the castle opened up with a loud noise, and Rosemary found herself looking into a vaulted hall. It was filled with noblemen in magnificent clothes, the gentlemen in ruffs and the ladies in brocade. The musicians played on lutes and harps, and servants hurried to and fro carrying rich foods, while others stood around with flaming torches in their hands.

Strange to say, Rosemary's fear melted away, and she stood staring breathlessly at this unaccustomed sight. She was so busy gazing and gaping that she didn't even notice when the lady of the castle suddenly appeared beside her, wearing a golden crown. 'I'm glad it was you who found the hand,' she told Rosemary, kindly. 'None of the others would have dared to come here, and we should have had to wait another year. Are you willing to help my poor husband?' Rosemary nodded her head. And the lady began to explain to her how greedy her husband had been, how he had forced taxes from his subjects without mercy, and as a punishment none of the royal family could rest in peace, but had to feast in this marble hall night after night. But the banquets were sad, even though music played and the wine flowed free, for they were all enchanted. 'You are the only one who can set us free and give us back our peace,' she told Rosemary.

9 June

How Rosemary Found a Marble Hand

'How can I help you?' Rosemary asked. 'Return to this spot where we are standing tomorrow night, and dig a hole,' the lady of the castle told her. 'But you must take no one with you apart from your parents. Whatever you find here is yours. When the riches that were got dishonestly are gone, peace and contentment will reign once more between these walls. But let any greedy fellow who interferes in this business be cursed, for it is between the two of us only.' Then the lady gave Rosemary a bouquet of myrtle, an evergreen shrub, as a token of remembrance, and everything disappeared. She made her way home as if in a dream, and the next morning she thought she had imagined the whole thing. But the bouquet was still lying there beside the bed, and it wasn't of myrtle, but of pure gold. So she told her parents what had

happened, and as evening fell they crept out unnoticed, and made their way to the ruined castle. 'It was just here,' Rosemary told them, and they began to dig. They dug for a long time, taking turns at throwing up the earth and stones, until the pick struck an iron-bound chest. They could not believe their eyes when they opened the lid and saw that it was filled to the brim with gold pieces. They pushed it home on their handcart. After that they were able to buy what they needed, mend the cottage and the fences, and buy another cow and some more land. Then things began to go a good deal better for them.

10 June

How Rosemary Found a Marble Hand

The story of the marble hand might well have ended there. But that was not to be. Farmer Martin smouldered with envy when he saw how his neighbours had suddenly fallen upon good fortune, how well their farm was doing, and that they no longer lived from hand to mouth. He was always hanging around, trying to discover how they had come by such sudden wealth. He didn't believe a word when they spoke of an inheritance from a distant aunt. A year passed by, and Martin, who still had his ears pricked for something that might betray his neighbours' secret, overheard Rosemary say to her father, 'We ought to go up to the castle tonight and say thank you for the treasure the marble hand brought us.' 'A good idea,' he replied. 'And we should return the hand. Perhaps some poor man will find it, and meet with the same good fortune as we have. Who knows if that was the whole of the lord's riches?' That was enough for Martin. 'So that's it!' He laughed scornfully to himself. 'Why should some poor man have the benefit, when I myself wouldn't say no to a pile of gold or a chest full of diamonds?'

11 June

How Rosemary Found a Marble Hand

That evening Martin mounted his fine stallion and followed his neighbours at a safe distance, impatiently awaiting the moment when he might get his hands on the magic piece of marble. His greedy heart beat faster, as he thought of the gold and precious stones that might await him. At last, the moment came. His neighbours went away, leaving the marble hand shining in the grass beneath the moon's pale light. Martin emerged from his hiding-place, grabbed the hand like a half-starved vulture, and leapt onto his stallion. In an authoritative voice he ordered, 'And now you shall show me the treasure of the lord of the castle, the more, the better!' At that instant there was a loud noise, and one of the castle walls opened up. There, in the vaulted hall, stood the lord of the castle, a hollow skeleton. 'I've been waiting for you!' he cried. A violent windstorm came up over the castle, and in seconds it had carried the greedy farmer off into the air, horse and all. No one knows where he was taken. Some days later the exhausted stallion

returned to its stable alone, but there was no sign of its master. And the marble hand? That disappeared with him, and no one has ever found it since — not even you or I.

12 June

Who Wants an Umbrella?

The umbrella's name was Alfonse, and its owner had forgotten it in the woods after the rain stopped. He did look for it, but he couldn't remember where he had put it down, so master lost umbrella and umbrella lost master. 'Don't you want an umbrella?' it asked a passing roe-deer with its fawn. The deer looked up at the blue sky, and replied, 'Whatever for?' 'Don't you want an umbrella?' it asked the squirrels. The squirrels burst out laughing. 'Now, if we could make ten little ones out of you, then we could share you out among us and use you to float from tree to tree. But what use is a great big umbrella like you to us?' 'Wouldn't you like an umbrella?' it asked the woodpecker. 'What on earth for?' the woodpecker tapped out on a tree trunk in Morse code, and the umbrella guessed that he wasn't interested. 'What use am I now?' thought the umbrella, and it gazed up at the cloudless sky. Underneath it a wild strawberry was blossoming. 'Wouldn't you like to stay where you are?' it asked the

13 June

Still the Tale of a Cupboard Goes On

In a mysterious room in a mysterious house, there once stood a mysterious cupboard. It was positively the only thing in the room. There were no chairs and no tables, not even a settee. And no one lived in the house. It was empty, except for that one mysterious cupboard. What do you suppose was in that cupboard? If you want to know more, you'll have to wait until 13 July.

14 June

Two Cocks on One Rubbish Tip

The Wainwrights had a flock of hens with a cock called Hotspur, and the Glovers had a flock with a cock called Proudcomb. In between the two poultry yards was a big rubbish heap. For a long time the two cocks knew nothing about it. But as they led the hens further and further afield, it so happened that one day the two of them met in the middle of the rubbish tip. They both puffed out their feathers and glared at each other threateningly. The hens, meanwhile, waited to see how their masters would settle the affair. 'This rubbish tip,' crowed Hotspur, 'has belonged to the Wainwrights since time immemorial. We are the only ones with the right to go pecking here!' But Proudcomb retorted, 'That is a downright lie! The rubbish tip belongs to the Glovers, and to us!' 'It's ours, fishface!' yelled Hotspur. 'Its ours, fathead!' Proudcomb snapped back. 'If you don't take this gang of yours away at once,' hissed Hotspur viciously, 'I'll scratch your eyes out!' 'And if you don't vamoose with this mangy crew, I'll tear all the feathers off your back, and you can walk round naked!' snarled Proudcomb. So they went on, hurling the biggest insults they knew at each other, and adding the nastiest threats they could think

umbrella. 'I'm terribly scared of the rain. If it comes on heavy, I'm sure I shall be soaked to death.' The umbrella agreed. While the sun was still shining it leaned over a little so that the sunshine fell on the strawberry. But then some clouds came along, and it began to rain again, and the umbrella quickly covered up its little friend. The roe-deer and her fawn came trotting along. The squirrels ran back again, and the woodpecker came flying up, too. 'We've come for you!' they all shouted at once. 'It's pouring down!' 'Too late,' Alfonse replied, 'I belong to the strawberry now.'

of. This went on for one hour, and then two. Exhausted, the two cocks looked around them, and saw that the Wainwrights' hens and the Glovers' were pecking away in the rubbish side by side. Their combs drooped, and they went off home shamefaced, neither of them knowing whether he had won or lost.

15 June

The White Snake

In one strange kingdom, which was ruled over by a king who was the wisest of the wise, there was among the palace servants a young lad called Kit. He was the only one allowed to cook and serve the King's meals, but he was strictly forbidden to taste the food. One day, he received orders to fry a rare white snake and bring it to the king immediately. This time he couldn't resist, and he ate a small piece of the white meat. The moment he entered the dining-chamber, he heard a fly on the window buzzing, 'What a double chin the king is growing these days!' Kit gave a little giggle, but the king noticed it, and knew at once that the young servant had disobeyed him. Though he was anxious that no one else should be able to understand the language of the animals, he did not want to cut off the young man's head, for he had served him faithfully. Instead he had him banished. Kit wandered aimlessly along, and by and by he came to a lake. The water-level had dropped because of the dry weather, leaving a fish stranded in the reeds

beside the bank. Kit tossed it into the lake, and it called out to him, 'I'll never forget this!' A little further on he helped a bee that had fallen into a tub of water. Then for a third thing he released a dove that had got caught up in a net. Then he walked on through the world until he came to a great city, where the king was seeking a husband for his daughter, Princess Cecilia. But the bridegroom first had to perform three difficult tasks. Kit was curious to see whether the princess was worth the effort, and he hurried up to the castle.

16 June

The White Snake

As soon as Kit set eyes on Cecilia, he fell in love with her, and went along at once to put his name down for the contest. But the first of his tasks left him breathless. He was to find a ring that the princess had once dropped in a lake. He stood helplessly beside its banks, not knowing what he should do. Then the fish he had rescued came swimming up to him and placed the ring at his feet, just as if it had been waiting for the chance to do so. Kit was filled with joy, but the moment he was given his second task, his face fell. In the space of a single day he was to collect the pearls from the princess's necklace, which she had dropped all over the meadows. 'Don't

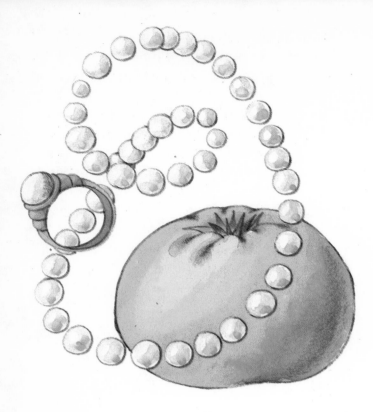

worry,' the grateful bee buzzed in his ear, 'I'll summon all my brothers and sisters, and we will help you!' A great cloud of tiny wings appeared over the meadows, and before long the string was again full of pearls. Kit handed them over to the princess before sunset. Cecilia was not pleased because he was a mere commoner, and she gave him a third task even more difficult than the first two. She sent him to find a golden apple, but she didn't tell him where it was growing. Kit wandered over hills and through valleys, blundered here and there, and had already given up hope of winning the princess's hand, when there was a throbbing of wings above him, and the dove dropped a golden apple in his hands. She, too, had rewarded him for his help. Kit went back to the princess and handed her the apple. The moment her fingers touched it, she fell in love with him, and after that they lived happily ever after, and reigned together for the rest of their lives.

The Ten Lumberjacks

Once upon a time ten lumberjacks were given the job of chopping down a part of the forest where a new hotel was to be built. They chopped away hard all morning, but by then one of them had blunted his axe so much, that after lunch he decided to go and get another one. 'I'll be back in half an hour,' he promised. When he hadn't come back after an hour, another of the lumberjacks said, 'He must have got lost on the way back, I'll go and see.' When neither of them had come back in another half hour, a third lumberjack said crossly, 'I bet the two of them are fast asleep somewhere! I'll soon wake them up!' He added that he would be back in a little while, as did the fourth, fifth, sixth, seventh, eighth and ninth lumberjacks, when they went to see what had happened to the others, and didn't return. 'I'm not so stupid!' cried the tenth, driving his axe into a tree stump and setting off to look for the others. 'I suppose they think they can sit drinking beer while I do all the work for them!' He followed the path down into the valley, but suddenly he saw in front of him a huge open mouth. 'What's this?' the last of the lumberjacks inquired. 'I am the open mouth of the giant Ikonomisize,' boomed the mouth. 'I have consumed your nine companions, and I am about to consume

you, too!' 'Now that would be a stupid thing to do,' replied the lumberjack, who was never short of ideas. 'Why is that?' asked the giant, sitting up. 'Because you would lose a feast for the sake of a snack,' the lumberjack replied.

18 June

The Ten Lumberjacks

The lumberjack explained to the giant that it hadn't been very wise to devour his colleagues. If the lumberjacks didn't cut down the trees, then the builders wouldn't build the hotel, and the hordes of tourists who would have come would never get the chance. And where would the hotel guests go for walks if they did come? Why, down into the valley, of course. Then the giant could just lie there and swallow one after the other. As soon as one lot of tourists had been swallowed, their rooms would be free to let to another lot, and the food supply would be a steady one. It would be good business for both the giant and the owners of the hotel. Ikonomisize was convinced. He spat the other nine lumberjacks out onto the path, told them to get on with their work as fast as they could, and lay down once again with his mouth wide open. Years

passed by. It was one year before the trees were felled. Two years before the plans were drawn up. Three years before the foundations were dug. Four years before the hotel was built. Five years before it was fitted out. When the sixth year had gone by, the first guests moved in. The hotel was quickly full of customers, for where else could they offer a real stone giant, where you could climb down inside his mouth and take a stroll around his stomach? Why had he turned to stone? Well, you try waiting six years for something to eat.

19 June

Kindhearted Christina

There was once a merchant who had three daughters, but only the youngest of them, Christina, truly loved him. She never longed for precious gifts and didn't want new clothes and jewels all the time, like her two sisters. She was satisfied with trifles, such as a ribbon for her hair, or a pretty flower. Her father always remembered her on his way home from business. But one day he lived to regret having plucked a twig off a wild rose bush to bring to Christina. The bush formed the gateway to a certain kingdom ruled over by a fearful king. He was half human,

half animal, a monster so ugly that no one could even look at him without horror. 'This will be the end of me,' the merchant thought. But the creature spoke to him in a gentle voice. 'You shall go free, but in return you must bring me, tomorrow, one of your daughters, who will serve me. If you do not obey my orders, it will be the worse for you.' The two elder daughters declared that it was nothing to do with them, that they hadn't asked for a dog-rose. So Christina had to go through the rose-bush gate, and she went without hesitation. She gave herself up to slavery without any idea of what might happen, all to save her father. She walked across an orchard, through empty chambers whose doors opened in front of her, until she reached a table where the candles lit themselves, and sat down before a blazing fire to await her master.

20 June

Kindhearted Christina

Christina fell asleep by the fireside. She was roused by a pleasant-sounding voice, 'I am here, standing behind you, but do not turn round! You will never see me. You will live like a queen here, and your only duty will be to wait here for me each evening and tell me what sort of a day you have had.' Christina agreed. The king had such a gentle voice that all fear left her at once. After that she would look forward to her evening meeting with the one she was not allowed to set eyes on. She refused to believe that he was as ugly as he was said to be, and began to love him for the beautiful words he spoke to her. For many long weeks she contained her curiosity, and never even tried to sneak a look at him. But one evening she dropped her handkerchief, and as she bent down to pick it up, she looked up at the king by mistake. When she saw his hairy head and huge ears, with fiery eyes blazing down at her, she was seized with horror, and fell into a dead faint. When she came to her senses again, she would have preferred to die rather than meet the monster again. She ran out into the gardens, but the rose bushes that surrounded it were like an impenetrable wall. Suddenly, she saw a mirror lying on the ground. When she picked it up, it spoke to her, saying, 'Wherever you wish to be, I shall take you there.' Without hesitation, Christina cried out. 'I want to be at home with my father!'

And in an instant she was standing beside the table where her father and her sisters were eating their supper.

21 June

Kindhearted Christina

For three days Christina was happy to be back home. Then she suddenly started to feel sad, as though no one needed her. She longed for the monster's gentle voice and the evenings spent talking to him. She began to understand that the creature's kind words were more important than his fearful-looking face. In the end she said to the magic mirror, 'Take me back to the royal palace!' In an instant she was sitting beside the blazing fire again. She waited there till twilight fell, but that evening the king did not come. The next morning she woke up in the chair beside the fireplace. She felt a strange jabbing at her heart, and some unknown force led her out into the gardens, among the rose bushes. They parted in front of her, until at last, in the deepest of the thickets, she spied the beast-king. He was lying among the roses as if dead. Christina lifted his head, and laid it in her lap. Then she bent her ear towards his hideous jaws to see if he was still breathing. 'Thank you,' whispered the familiar voice, and at that moment the creature's face was transformed completely. Looking up into her eyes was a young prince, whom her love had released from an evil spell. The two of them remained together in the rose-hip kingdom for ever, and they would often recall how it had all started with a wild rose.

22 June

The Good Old Days

When King Minimilian IV died, he was succeeded by his son, Billius I. It took the young king a little while to get to know the ropes of ruling, as you might say, but it wasn't long before he discovered that his royal father had appointed a special Minister of Claptrap, whose only duty was to make sure that every last subject knew how well off he was under Minimilian IV. In a fit of youthful enthusiasm, Billius gave the minister the sack, and set about cutting taxes, building schools for the children and hospitals for the sick, and looking after nature. In short, he tried to be all that a good king should be. But because he was a little proud, all the same, he put on a disguise and went among his people to hear what they had to say about him. The people were far from satisfied. 'This new fellow's no use at all,' they told him. 'Always something new. He's got no respect for what his father did. The old boy set things in order round here, you know. Dear me, the good old days of Minimilian are gone for ever!' When he had heard these last words for about the tenth time, Billius stamped his foot and said, 'If that's how you want it, that's how it shall be!' And he recalled the Minister of Claptrap, put the taxes up again, closed down the schools and hospitals, and left nature to fend for itself. And that was that.

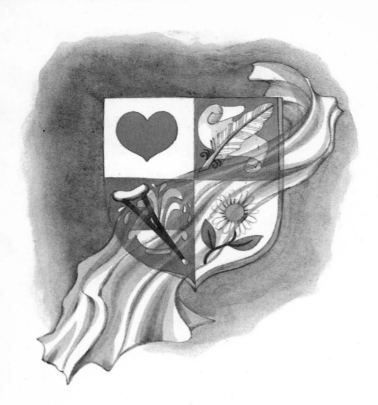

Minister of Claptrap again, and carried on where he had left off. He put the taxes down again, opened the schools and hospitals, and began planting the occasional new forest and cleaning up a river or two. He had this inscription carved in the stone above the entrance to his castle: 'Only a bad ruler thinks of himself, a good one thinks of his subjects.' But he never went among his subjects in disguise again. What if they had started to speak about the good old days?

23 June

The Good Old Days

But that was far from being that. Billius couldn't face up to the idea that he was a bad ruler, that he wasn't doing anything for his people, only filling his royal treasure chests. So he put on his disguise again, and went out among the people to ask how they were satisfied now. This time they would say to him, 'The young king has changed terribly. He's become just like his father, thinking only of himself. Dear me, where are the good old days now, when young Billius first took the throne. We shan't see them again!' 'So that's it,' thought Billius to himself. 'It seems that people always speak well of the past, sometimes rightly, sometimes wrongly. In that case, I shall just rule as I think fit.' And he sacked the

hadn't got that amount anyway, even if they sold everything they owned. And neither of them was willing to admit defeat. There they sat, banging their fists on the table and adding thousands of coins to their offers. And since they couldn't agree, Judy and Thomas couldn't get married after all.

25 June

Friends

There once lived two boys. One of them had a father who was a magician, while the other was from a very ordinary family. They lived near each other, and played hide-and-seek and blind-man's-buff together, quarrelled and made up again, until for no reason at all the magician's son Crispin grew terribly proud, just as if someone had waved a magic wand over him. He began to boast that he could change cats into piglets and make the river run dry in a flash, and make mountains tumble apart into piles of stones whenever he felt like it. 'Whatever is the use of all that sort of nonsense?' thought his friend Hal, but he said nothing. Perhaps he was a little scared that Crispin would get angry with him and turn him into a pumpkin or

24 June

Who'll Give More?

Green and Brown had been friends since childhood. But it was a strange sort of friendship. Each of them always wanted to outdo the other. When they were little boys they would go to the fair, and compete with each other to win the most prizes or have the most roundabout rides. As they were growing up, they would challenge each other to see who could eat the most sausages or drink the most beer. As time went by, Green's daughter and Brown's son grew up, too, and they happened to fall in love with each other. They decided to get married. 'Why not?' said their fathers, and they had a meeting to discuss the couple's future. 'I'll give Judy ten thousand coins for a dowry,' Green began. 'And I'll give Thomas a house worth twenty thousand,' replied Brown, upping the stakes. 'And I'll give Judy furniture and fittings for another twenty thousand,' Green went on. Brown was not to be outdone. 'I'll throw in a piece of land worth another twenty thousand, that makes forty thousand coins altogether.' And so it went on. 'I'll . . .' and 'I'll . . .' and 'I'll'. The two of them continued to offer more and more, even though they both knew they

something. Hal wasn't too brave sometimes, but he had a good head on his shoulders. So he wasn't too upset when Crispin suggested, 'Let's see who can conjure up a better castle by tomorrow morning!' He was a little bit surprised, but he didn't despair, and he certainly didn't lose any sleep over it. He knew Crispin had a big book of spells at home, but he preferred to stick to his own ideas. And Hal wasn't short of those.

26 June

Friends

The next day Hal woke up and saw a five-storey castle standing outside his window. It had lots of towers and domes, and really did look wonderful. 'Wow!' he gasped, and began to doubt whether he could do better. He was just an ordinary boy after all, and Crispin was a magician's son. Still, he hurried outside and began his conjuring. He found a fragment of brick in front of the castle, and began to draw lines on the broad pavement. He added some arches, and before long there was a brick gate, towers and domes, chambers filled with furniture, and tables loaded with fruit and toys. Meanwhile, Crispin was wandering about on his own in his five-storey wonder-castle, waiting for Hal to come and admire his handiwork. Then he leaned out of one of the windows and saw his friend down below, leaping about in his castle hall, popping in and out of its chambers, adding something here and rubbing something out there, as happy as could be. Hal's castle is much better than mine, he thought, and at that moment his wonderful building came tumbling down, and Hal won the bet.

27 June

Friends

The next day Crispin had forgotten how he had lost his bet, and he started to needle his friend again. 'Bet you I can conjure up a better carriage than you can! It shall have velvet seats and a team of fine horses, and we'll go for a ride in it! I *know* you can't come up with anything like that.' But Hal

was silent. He just thought about it. And at that instant there really was a neighing sound from the horses that were harnessed to a golden coach with soft seats, standing in front of the door, ready for them to take their seats. They got in, and off they went. They drove through the town and out into the countryside, but the coach went so fast that they couldn't see anything around them. They only felt the wind in their faces, and held on tight so as not to fall out. But when they got out again, Crispin exclaimed: 'That was great, wasn't it?' Hal didn't speak. He just shifted from one foot to the other and thought about something. Then he brought a battered old basket out of the attic, took it in both hands, neighed like a horse, and ran out into the garden with it. At first Crispin looked at him as though he was crazy, but as usual Hal's game got

tempting for him, and he joined in. Then they really had a fine ride! They stopped where they wanted to, watching the bees sucking nectar from the flowers, looking to see what was swimming about in the lake, and following the ants along the path to find out where they went. They could even climb trees with their light basket. Then they made it into a house, then a cradle, then a boat. 'You win again,' Crispin had to admit, and Hal went to bed the victor again.

28 June

Friends

The next day Crispin went around like a bear with a sore head, trying hard to think of something to surprise his friend Hal with. He was upset at having lost twice. 'Watch carefully,' he told the other lad. 'I shall conjure up a treasure chest. I bet you can't make a better one, no matter how hard you try.' 'If you think so,' Hal replied modestly. In an instant there was a beautiful casket on the table, decorated with gold and precious stones, a sight to take your breath away. Inside was a pile of shiny coins. Crispin carried his casket off home with a smile of satisfaction and a gesture of triumph. But it wasn't long before Hal went into action. He got a shoebox down from the shelf and

went out into the garden with it. There he filled it with all the nicest things he could find, a bird's feather, a pink pebble, a snail's shell, an oak leaf, a beech-nut, a rose petal, a bit of bark, a four-leaved clover, and so on. 'What you got there?' asked Crispin, peering curiously over his shoulder. The boys turned the contents of the box out on the floor, and Crispin had to admit that this **was** a treasure much better than his shining splendour, and that Hal's games were much more interesting than magic. After that he didn't bother making bets with him any more.

29 June

The Doughnut Takes Up Sport

You surely remember our friend the doughnut. One day he wandered into a playground where some small boys were playing football. Since he had never seen a game of football before, he sat down on a bench beside the pitch and watched to see if he could work out what goals and offsides were. All of a sudden big Jimmy, on the losing side, gave the ball such a kick that it flew up in the air and disappeared. His side was 3—1 down. The other players on both sides started calling him all sorts of names. He didn't really mind their insults all that

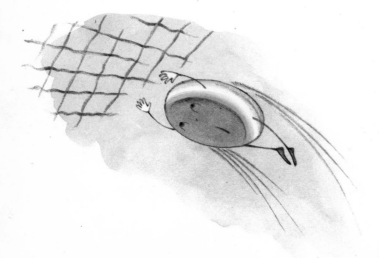

much, but he was sorry they didn't have the chance to draw level, now that there wasn't a ball to play with. Just then he caught sight of the doughnut sitting on the bench. 'Better than nothing,' he said, and threw the doughnut onto the pitch. 'Ow!' cried the doughnut, when Jimmy kicked him for the first time. Then everyone started kicking him. 'Ow! Ow! Ow!' And goal! 3—2 'Ow! Ow!' Goal! 3—3. But the doughnut had had quite enough. He was aching all over. He rolled in front of Jimmy's foot. Jimmy took a hefty kick, and the doughnut went flying. He landed somewhere in the wild thyme in July, and rubbed some into his wounds. While he was still in the air, he managed to mumble, 'Three all! That's enough! That makes it a draw.'

30 June

The Typewriter's Tale

The storyteller who had a fairy to look after him (do you remember?) used to write his stories on a typewriter. One day his typewriter got ideas, and it said to itself, 'Why should I just keep bashing out the things he thinks up? Haven't I been writing his stories long enough to think up some of my own? I shall write my own fairy tale, and sign it Typewriter.' So it began. 'Once upon a time there was a Red Riding Hood who pricked her finger and fell asleep under a briar rose. Along came seven dwarfs. They began to cry because Red Riding Hood, or rather Sleeping Beauty, whose real name was Snow White, had died. But a handsome prince came riding by and ...' But the typewriter couldn't remember exactly what it was that the prince was supposed to do. So it put a row of 'x'es through the bit about the prince, and went on. 'Snow Red, or Sleeping Hood, or Riding Beauty, or whatever her name was, had seven enchanted brothers, or was it six? ...' Just then the storyteller arrived back from the stationer's shop, where he had been to buy a new typewriter ribbon, so that all the words would be nice and clear. 'What's this you've been writing?' he asked. 'Not a fairy tale?' 'Dear me, no,' said the typewriter, hurriedly. 'I was just trying out my letters.' It would have blushed, if it had known how. 'And what did you find out?' the storyteller asked. 'What did I find out?' repeated the typewriter, indignantly. 'I found out that you'd better buy me a new ribbon, that's what!'

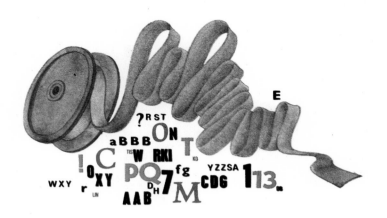

July

1 July

A New Colour for the Wind Elf's Cloak

The start of summer is so green it almost makes your eyes smart. The wind elf covered his cloak with all manner of leaves and grass, and stuffed his pockets with clover and chives. 'There!' he said at last, and leaned over to look at his reflection in the lake. But then he frowned. 'I look more like a water-elf,' he said. 'I went a bit too far with all that greenery.' And off he flew to find another summer colour. But the wind took him over the forest, where there was nothing but pines and spruce, and ferns growing out of the moss, and the sky traveller began to see green rings in front of his eyes. So he flew down to the ground, pulled his hat down over his eyes so that he couldn't see anything, and dozed off for a while. Then, of course, he started to dream green dreams. All he could see was green leaves in a green jungle. Then he was woken up by shouting. When he opened his eyes, he immediately thought, 'I must have been among savages.' A group of children came running past. They had purple patterns smeared all over their faces, as if they were getting ready for some native ceremony. And they were banging on little tin cups. The cups were filled with bilberries. 'So they weren't savages, after all,' thought the wind elf, and off he flew to the glade beside the path. When he returned, his cloak was covered in purple patches, and there was a sweet taste in his mouth.

2 July

The Proud Flower

Underneath her window, little Helen had a garden full of tulips, roses and carnations. For a long time it was great fun, but then she got fed up with watering the flower-beds every day, and said to herself, 'I shall make myself a paper flower — that will be pretty all the time, and it won't need watering!' From breakfast time to lunch time she cut and coloured and glued, until finally she was able to stick her paper flower in the jug beside the window. At that very moment the wind elf landed on the garden fence. It was a hot midday, and the garden was looking very droopy indeed. 'I am a good deal prettier than all you floppy flowers down there,' boasted the paper flower, and this upset the wind elf. When her boasting didn't stop, he flew off to see the wind, and the wind sent rain clouds sailing along. It began to pour, so suddenly that Helen forgot to close the window, and the paper flower was soon soaked from its proud head down to the tip of its stalk. Its colours ran all over, and its petals hung limply. But the garden flowers perked up, and now there was no mistaking who was the more beautiful.

pale. If Drearie failed too, the fate of the school was sealed. Now, we should explain that Drearie was actually not nearly as stupid as he made himself out to be. That was just his way of getting out of doing too much hard work. In fact he was a very ingenious weaver of spells. Now he strode confidently up to the table and drew out the task: 'Conjure up a six-foot-long beard for one of those present in the room.' 'Well, then, whose is the beard to be?' asked the Grand Master, in a nasty voice. 'Yours,' Drearie replied. 'Very well,' smiled the Grand Master, 'but I hope you succeed.' And he quietly mumbled a spell to prevent the tiniest hair from growing on his chin. Drearie walked round and round the Grand Master in smaller and smaller circles, waving his wand and growling fiercely. All at once the Grand Master began to feel uncomfortable. Slowly, he realized that what Drearie was doing had nothing to do with beards. But it was too late. The Grand Master's long, thick hair was suddenly gone. He tried to get it back again, but Drearie had been too clever for him, and had included in his spell a bit that said only he could put the Grand Master's hair back again. The Grand Master first threatened, then persuaded, then begged, but Drearie refused to restore his hair until he signed a report saying that all three pupils had passed with distinction and that there was no question of closing down such an

failed. Gentlemen, let us retire for a moment to change into some clean clothes.' When the board of examiners had returned, wearing dry gowns, it was the turn of Blearie. His question was: 'Take a cloud from the sky and turn it into a ram.' Blearie gazed desperately up at the clear blue sky, while the Grand Master stared at him, obviously enjoying his discomfort. The headmaster tried to help: 'Well, Blearie, if we can't find what we need anywhere, what do we do?' They all expected him to answer, 'Conjure it up,' of course. But Blearie was so nervous he replied, 'Forget it.' 'I think that's just what we shall do,' the Grand Master told him, severely. 'Which means that, like your friend Eerie, you have failed!'

7 July

The School of Magic

The faces of the teachers were anxious and

excellent school. Otherwise he would have had to return to the ministry quite bald, and he would never have lived it down. When the Grand Master was gone, Drearie's headmaster offered him a job as a teacher, but Drearie said, 'No thanks, I'd rather wander about the world. It's much more fun, you know.'

8 July

Farmer Gower's Ghost

The villagers would speak about farmer Gower with admiration. A ghost had begun

to haunt the big farm, but even though it was a lonely place, Gower had no intention of leaving it. 'What does it look like?' the cottagers asked. 'What does it do?' But Gower wasn't very forthcoming. 'A ghost is a ghost,' he would say. 'And, what does it do? Why, it haunts, of course, all night.' Sometimes he would add, 'You ought to come up and see sometime.' And he would grin. No one ever did go to see the ghost for himself, of course. They never went near Gower's farm at night. But Humphrey the blacksmith was a brave fellow, and he began to wonder why the farmer was always talking about his ghost. So he decided to take a look. He took his hammer along with him, just in case there was any truth in the stories, and set off for the lonely farm. It was just before midnight. There was

nothing moving, but a light shone from the farmer's best room. 'Is that where the ghost lives?' thought the blacksmith, and he crept up to one of the windows. He nearly burst out laughing at what he saw. There was Gower, sitting at the table, counting piles of gold pieces. So that was his ghost, money and miserliness. Humphrey didn't keep what he had seen to himself, of course, and before long the whole village was having a good laugh over farmer Gower's ghost.

9 July

The Queen's Clothes

Queen Isabel loved to dress up. Whenever any merchants were passing that way, they always called in at the castle, knowing that the queen always bought the very best they had to offer. Why not, when she had money enough? Money enough, it was true, but her husband King Zaddlezore was very rarely at home. He was for ever roaming around the world. Once, while the king was on his travels yet again, the royal steward tried to have a cuddle with the queen. When she assured him that Zaddlezore was the only man in the world for her, and that she would remain faithful to him till the day she died, the steward was left nursing his wounded pride. Out of spite, when the king returned, he told his master, 'That young merchant from Damascus was here again. I fancy there is something going on between him and the queen.' That was enough for Zaddlezore. He was terribly jealous, and he leaped to his feet as if a hornet had stung him. Without even bothering to hear what she had to say for herself, he ordered her to be thrown off the tallest tower. 'The penalty for faithlessness is death!' he shouted. Isabel knew it was no use arguing, but she asked if she might put on the dress of her choice. 'You can put them all on, if you like!' shrieked the king. So the queen went to get dressed. She put on six underskirts, nine middle skirts, and

a dozen overskirts. When they hurled her from the tower, she floated down as if she was wearing a parachute. 'A miracle!' cried the assembled subjects. 'The queen is innocent!' The king, too, was amazed, and listened to what the queen had to say at last. After that the royal steward was banished from the kingdom.

10 July

Broadshoulder

In the midst of a certain sad landscape stood a lonely cottage where Broadshoulder lived with his mother. Though they loved each other dearly, life was not easy for them, since there was not a patch of fertile soil nor a strip of greenery for miles around. 'This is no place for

a young man,' his mother told Broadshoulder one day. 'You'll have to go out into the world. There's no living for you here.' Broadshoulder was a giant of a man, fit to split mountains open, but he had a soft heart, and he began to cry. 'Boo hoo, very well, I shall go into the world, but you must come with me. I couldn't live without you.' 'How can I go with you?' she asked. 'My legs are too weak, and I love our little cottage too dearly.' But Broadshoulder was not to be put off. 'I'll carry you and the cottage on my back,' he said. 'I am strong enough.' But his mother said, 'Our cottage belongs where it is. It's no use. I must stay here.' And she sent her son off on his own. Broadshoulder strode across the sandy plain and the bare mountainsides. It took him so long to reach a fertile landscape that winter had already come, and tall snowdrifts covered the land.

11 July

Broadshoulder

Broadshoulder grew very sad when he saw that everything in sight was white. The ash-grey sand had given way to cold snow. 'What use is the world to me. There's nothing worth looking for in it,' he sighed, tired from his journey, and homesick for his mother. He lay down on the ground and closed his eyes. In a while he was asleep. He slept all winter, and all spring. He slept through until autumn, and he was still asleep when the next snow fell. Years passed, and the birds and bees stood on Broadshoulder's chest. Rain and snow fell on him, and the spring floods half covered him with earth. The wind blew all sorts of seeds from fields and forests onto him. Soon Broadshoulder was covered with trees and flowers, with grass and grain crops, and birds nested in his hair. He didn't wake up until the middle of a summer storm. Then he stretched his limbs, stood up as if he had awoken from a good night's sleep, and set off back home. As he crossed the barren countryside, he dropped lumps of fertile soil, seeds, clover and ferns, fir trees and appletrees all around him, and the sad and lifeless landscape began to grow green. When he reached his native cottage, he saw his mother sitting on the doorstep, sickly with grief and quite grey-haired. But as she welcomed her son, and heard the birds singing in his hair, she grew stronger at once. From then on they lived together

happily in their little cottage, amid a merry landscape.

12 July

The Butterfly Story

There was once a foolish boy called Daniel, who thought that butterflies grew their wings just so that he could throw his cloth cap over them. Whenever Daniel appeared in the meadow, all the butterflies took off and were gone. This annoyed him. Then, one day, he decided to set a trap for a Red Admiral, a beautifully coloured butterfly, and one of the best fliers in the whole of the butterfly kingdom. He knew the Admiral liked pears, and that it would sit and drink the sweet juice until it was full, without looking either to left or right. So he took the ripest pear he could find, and laid it down on the window-sill. After that it wasn't difficult to catch the Admiral. He locked it up in a little wire cage, and

decided to feed it up. It would eat pears until it grew wings like an aeroplane's. Then he would ride around on it. Only the butterfly didn't seem to be hungry, and just stared sadly out of its cage. At last it said to Daniel, 'You know what? We'll have a bet. If you can stand in the garden for a quarter of an hour without moving, just like a tree, then I'll eat and grow for you. But if you can't, you must set me free.' 'All right,' Daniel agreed. 'That's easy.' And he went out into the garden and stood in the middle of the lawn. He stretched his arms out like the branches of a tree, but he didn't manage to keep still even for five minutes. All the local butterflies came along and landed on his head and shoulders. They tickled his nose, his chin, his neck and his elbows, and so they saved the Red Admiral.

13 July

The Tale of a Cupboard Goes Ever On

In a mysterious room in a mysterious house, there once stood a mysterious cupboard. It was positively the only thing in the room. There were no chairs and no tables, not even a settee. And no one lived in the house. It was empty, except for that one

mysterious cupboard. What do you suppose was in that cupboard? That was just what a certain robber was anxious to find out. But if you want to know more, you'll have to wait until 13 August.

14 July

Enchanted

Half way between the village and the forest stood a little cottage where an old man lived. His wife had died long ago, and one day his son had not returned from the forest. Never a trace of him was found. The old man spent all his time working, which had now became his only comfort, and the days passed quickly enough. One day he sharpened his axe again, and went into the forest to find a piece of wood to make a garden seat. He chose a fine straight birch tree, and as he chopped it down he thought he heard a sigh. The seat was very pretty,

but all who sat down on it grew suddenly very sad. The old man recalled how the tree had sighed, and he went back to the place where he had chopped it down. Beside the stump of the birch stood a small fawn with great, sad eyes. 'You must be an orphan, I suppose,' said the old man, and he took the creature home. He tied it to the garden seat, and in a flash a beautiful fairy was standing before him, with a baby in her arms. 'Thank you for bringing us from the forest,' she said to the old man. 'If we had not been touched by human hand and reunited, we should have remained as we were for ever. We were enchanted by the fairy queen who wished to punish me for falling in love with a human. She destroyed him, but this is his child.' The old man realized that he was looking at his grandchild, and that the woman was his daughter-in-law. He was happy that he would no longer be alone.

15 July

Geoffrey

Near to a city park, where there was a fountain with a huge statue of a lizard, lived a skinny little boy called Geoffrey. He wasn't allowed to chase about with the other lads, or to play with a ball. In fact, there was hardly anything he was allowed to do. That meant he had all the more time to think about himself. He didn't like being thin and weak, and he would dream all day long of how he might beat people in fights. The other boys would laugh at him, and if they met him down by the fountain, they would make fun of him, saying, 'Can you hear what it's saying? It says, "I'm the most powerful lizard in the world, and I'll destroy all skinnyribses!"' Streams of water poured out of the lizard's mouth, and it seemed to Geoffrey that it was terribly evil. It frightened him, and at the same time annoyed him. Perhaps that's why he told the other boys one day that they would see what a hero he was, that he would overcome the lizard all by himself. It was a stupid thing to say really. How was he supposed to destroy a stone monster, when he hadn't even got a hammer to do it with? He began to wish he hadn't been quite so brave, and his knees started to knock. But the boys sat him up on the edge of the fountain and said, 'Go on, then, we can't wait to see this!' Geoffrey hung his head in shame. He saw his own unhappy face reflected in the water, and said to himself,

'Perhaps I shall drown, and I won't have to face the shame!' And he leaned towards the rippling water.

16 July

Geoffrey

Geoffrey's face was nearly touching the water, when the only thing he ever had to play with, a glass marble, fell out of his pocket. It plunged to the bottom of the fountain pool and rolled into the hole where the water came from. As soon as that happened, the lizard stopped spurting water, and the pool began to dry up. It was a hot summer, and the fountain started to dry out altogether. The lizard began to crack, and when it seemed as if it would split apart, it begged Geoffrey, 'Please don't destroy me, you can see that I'm not really the most powerful of all the lizards. You are stronger than I am. Let a little water into

the fountain, so that I may not die.' Just then the mayor came along, and promised Geoffrey the moon and the stars, if only he would save the rare statue. But what was he to do? He only shrugged his shoulders, for he had no idea how the spring had got blocked up. People started to hate him. The boys drove him away, and he was unhappier than ever. When he was already so miserable he didn't know where to turn, a frog came hopping along and said to him, 'I will help you, because I know it is not your fault.' It jumped into the fountain, found the marble, and swallowed it. The spring was released, and the water began to pour from the lizard's mouth again. Goeffrey wanted to thank the frog, but it was gone, leaving his marble lying beside the fountain.

17 July

Alice

Miles the cottager had a pig called Alice. He fed her up until she was round and plump. One evening, he told his wife how he was going to kill the pig the next day and turn it into sausages, ham and bacon. But he spoke a little too loud, and Alice overheard what he was saying. Without giving the matter too much thought, she flung herself against the door of the sty and broke it open. Then she ran as fast as a sow that's

been fattened up for slaughter can manage. 'I'm not just going to wait around to have my throat cut,' she gasped, hardly able to catch her breath. She tried to cross the plank bridge across the stream, but it gave way beneath her, and she fell into the water. It was all she could do to struggle out onto the bank, but the moment her trotters touched dry land again, she went on running for all she was worth. She climbed hills and pushed her way through thickets without rest. She grew quite thin, but never even thought about food. When she finally came to a halt after her wild escape, she found to her horror that she was back where she had started from. In fact she almost bumped into Miles himself. 'We're glad you've come back again, Alice!' the cottager called out. And his wife added, 'While you were away, we realized how much we should miss you. What a good thing we didn't make sausages out of you!' After that they kept Alice like a cat or a dog, and took her out for walks so that she wouldn't get too fat.

18 July

Cheap Is Not Cheap

Everybody spoke with admiration of Mrs. Chary's ways of saving money. She always waited until things were reduced in price, and she always got a bargain. Mrs. Chary herself heard what they said, and the whole

thing went to her head. She started to make economy her life's work. The first thing she did was to buy a pocket calculator in the sales. But it was just as if she had let a mischievous little imp into the house. First of all the calculator informed her that if she bought a hundred boxes of cut-price eggs she would save so much and so much. What a good buy that would be! Only the eggs went bad, because Mrs. Chary couldn't use them up fast enough. Then the calculator told her to buy an ice-cream maker that was on offer. It worked out that it would pay for itself within a year if she were to eat four ice-cream cones a day at home, instead of buying them at the shop. So she bought the machine, quite forgetting that she didn't like ice-cream. Then she bought some cheap shoes that didn't fit, and a cheap dress she couldn't wear. By and by she had collected so many useless items that she had to open her own department store and sell them off even cheaper than she had bought them. She went quite bankrupt. And yet she had been a woman, well known for her money saving ways.

How the Storyteller Found a Mother

It was a hot July day, and the storyteller didn't feel like thinking up a new story. He was sitting in the shade of an apple tree, watching the bumble-bees buzzing around the flowers of the climbing beans. All of a sudden the fairy was sitting beside him on the bench, and she said, 'Mrs. Millett across the way is all on her own.' 'So am I,' replied the storyteller, nodding his head, 'except for the children who sometimes come to ask for a story.' 'No one goes to see her,' the fairy said, as though it was the storyteller's fault. 'Her only son has gone off into the world somewhere, and never so much as sends her a postcard. And she can't walk very well, so *she* can't go visiting.' 'At least she's got peace and quiet to do some reading,' the storyteller suggested, but the fairy didn't agree. 'She can't see too well, either. Someone ought to pop in and have a chat with her from time to time.' When the storyteller didn't say anything, she added pointedly, 'This afternoon, perhaps.' 'All right,' the storyteller said, and off he went to talk to Mrs. Millett. The old lady was pleased to bits, and she said, 'You remind me of my son, you know, before he went

away.' 'And you remind me of my mother,' said the storyteller, trying to remember how many years it was since she had died. 'Shall I come again?' 'Come every day if you want,' she smiled, and little wrinkles fanned out around her eyes. So the storyteller found a new mother.

20 July

The Princess and the Gardener

Princess Constance was for ever getting magnificent presents from her royal father, but she didn't really get any pleasure out of them. What she liked best was to visit her nurse in her simple chamber. One day the two of them were looking out of the window when Constance saw the young gardener weaving a daisy chain. 'Give me the garland, please,' she called out. 'I have never seen one so pretty!' 'You may have it in return for a kiss!' called the young man, without any real hope of getting one. But the princess ran downstairs and kissed him. She took the daisy chain, and wore it until it withered. The next day she heard curious sounds coming from the garden. She leaned out of the window and asked the gardener what it was. 'A willow whistle, and it's yours for two kisses!' came the reply. In an instant she was in the garden. She grabbed the

whistle, and the gardener got what he had asked for. On the third day Constance ran out into the garden as soon as it was light. Without a word the gardener gave her a ring woven from grass and decorated with dew. He got three kisses for it. But this time the king saw them. As a punishment he made Constance marry the gardener and live in a humble cottage. It was the nicest present he had ever given her.

21 July

Too Much of a Good Thing

In the house of a certain merchant there were ten cooks for every type of dish. So

there were ten meat cooks, ten fish cooks, ten pastrycooks, ten makers of sauces and so on. In short, there was no other house in the land where one could eat better, and people began to refer to it as The House of Good Food. If anyone stayed there for more than a day or two, he ended up with a huge pot-belly, and his cheeks puffed out so much one could hardly see his eyes any more. The master of the house was so fat he could scarcely walk, but he still enjoyed his food. Then, one day, it happened. The merchant fell ill from all that overeating. He had aches here and pains there and cramps nearly everywhere, and he started to think he might die. After that he quite lost his appetite. He sent for ten doctors from each branch of medicine, but though they all had enormous brass plates beside their doors, they didn't know how to cure him. Instead they moved into the merchant's house, where they ate and drank with such enthusiasm that they soon had huge stomachs of their own, and their eyes had practically vanished into their cheeks. But in time they too began to have aches and pains and cramps, and they couldn't eat any more either. They felt so ill they thought they would die. And people started to call the merchant's house The House of Indigestion.

22 July

Too Much of a Good Thing

The merchant's cooks might have taken a holiday, but he ordered them to go on cooking. What if he or one of his guests was to get better all of a sudden and start to feel hungry? The piles of food grew higher and higher, but he wouldn't let them give any food to the poor, saying that it didn't do to spoil them. 'I'll show you!' said Annie, one of the kitchen-maids, to herself. She sent the master a message to say that she had a cure for his illness. 'Is it a herb, or a powder?' asked the merchant, when Annie came to see him. 'Nothing like that,' Annie told him. 'But if you like I can cure you and all your guests. All I ask for in return is that every day of the year you give me a pint-pot full of food.' The merchant agreed and signed a contract with Annie. The next day he and the doctors all lined up for their treatment. Annie's method was very simple. She drove them all out into the fresh air and gave them forks and spades. Instead of medicine they got hard work in the garden and an apple each for elevenses. They ate them core and all, and their digestion improved remarkably. When they were all cured, the kitchen maid collected her reward. There was rather a lot of it, for she had written the words 'Pint-Pot' in the contract with capital letters. The merchant didn't know it, but that was the name of the local fishpond. The poor had a grand time of it that year, though, with so much to eat.

23 July

The Mushstool

The mushroom and the toadstool were growing side by side between a larch and a pine. 'See what a lady I am,' declared the toadstool. 'Tall, slim and pale, and dressed in the latest fashion. Everyone must like me!' When the mushroom said nothing, she added an insult. 'But *you* are horrible and a *very* shabbily-dressed sort of fungus!' Only when the mushroomers came along, they took the mushroom with a yelp of delight, and almost kicked the toadstool. It was long time before she got over the shock of their insults. 'Horrible old toadstool!' 'Am I to grieve over not being sliced up and dropped in a pan of soup?' she comforted herself. But all the same she, too, wanted to be picked, rocked in a basket, and eaten. So she called a passing slug and got him to alter her dress a little. He took a bite here and a nibble there, and in a while the toadstool looked quite edible. She was in luck. Who should come strolling along, but the great mushroomer Gadby. 'Hurrah!' he shouted. 'I've discovered a new fungus — the mushstool, henceforth to be known as Gadby's mushstool.' So the toadstool got what she wanted. She was taken home to the mushroomer's cottage, fried, and eaten. I know you're thinking that Gadby must have poisoned himself. But actually he had in his time eaten so many half-edible and quarter-edible fungi that not even a toadstool in disguise could hurt him. He was packed full of antidote. And a coloured picture of Gadby's mushstool appeared in all the encyclopaedias of fungi. But no one ever found another specimen.

24 July

The Soap Bubble

Frances sat down in front of the house with a straw and a jar of soapy water. You don't have to be a detective to guess what she wanted to do. But the first time she dipped the straw in the jar, she sucked it a bit too hard and got a mouthful of soapy water. Ugh! How horrible it tasted! But then she managed to blow a marvellous bubble. It was big, gleaming with all the colours of the rainbow, and it flew into the air like

a fairground balloon. To her amazement, Frances could understand what it was saying. It must have been because she had taken a drink of soapy water. She could hear it quite clearly saying, 'Look, everyone, see how beautiful I am! And how elegantly I can fly! I'm lovelier than the sun, more colourful than a bed of flowers. Even the aeroplanes can't compare with me. Actually, I'm perfect. You can look at me for hours on end, for days, for weeks. You might delight in my beauty for mon . . .' POP! And that was the end of that marvellous sight. Frances reached for her straw, but then she changed her mind, and went to fetch her ball instead.

25 July

Where Have All the Faces Gone?

In the town of M. in the county of N., the strangest of things occurred. Mr. P. went for a walk in the nearby woods, and came back without a face. Since he didn't have a mouth any more, he couldn't tell anyone how it had happened. Soon after that, Mrs. Q., who used to take her handcart into the same part of the woods to gather firewood, came running back to town without her cart. But that wasn't the important thing. She, too, was quite faceless. Without any eyes, she couldn't even write down what had happened. The third victim was R. the blacksmith. He too had gone to the woods and come back with just a pale oval where his forehead, eyebrows, eyes, nose, cheeks, mouth and chin had been. He couldn't smile and he couldn't frown. He didn't have any expression at all. In fact, no one really understood how the three of them could go on living, when they could neither eat nor breathe. But live on they did. The son of R. the blacksmith, Rudolph R., tried to get something out of his father, but all he could do was wave his hand in the direction of the woods and make a gesture as if someone had lifted his face off his head. 'There's nothing for it,' said Rudolph R., 'but to go and see for myself.'

26 July

Where Have All the Faces Gone?

When Rudolph R. reached a woodland clearing, he saw a beautiful golden-haired girl sitting on a tree-stump. He had never seen her before, either in the town of M., or anywhere else in the county of N., and there weren't many pretty girls he didn't know by sight, since he had always gone round shoeing horses with his father. 'Who are you?' he asked. 'And where do you come from?' 'I am Goldenhair,' the girl replied in a sweet voice, 'and I am waiting for you.' 'For me?' He couldn't believe his ears. 'What do you want with me?' 'The door of my cottage has come off its hinges,' said the golden-haired girl, 'and I need you to lift it back again for me. I am not strong enough.' 'That's no problem,' said Rudolph, with a wave of his hand. 'Only I don't know where your cottage is.' The girl led him along a forest path, telling him that she hadn't lived there long, that she was an orphan, and shy of people, so she liked to live in solitude. The cottage door was

indeed lying in the grass in front of the doorway. Rudolph took hold of it and . . . And found that his hands had become stuck fast to it. Try as he might, he couldn't let go of the door. He turned to look at Goldenhair, and saw that she was no longer a beautiful young girl, but an ugly hag, with a nest of snakes where her golden locks had been. 'Give me your face, and I shall set you free!' she croaked. 'Give me your face . . .'

27 July

Where Have All the Faces Gone?

Now young Rudolph R. saw how his father, and Mrs. Q., and Mr. P. had lost their faces. But what use was that, when he had a great heavy door stuck to his hands? He decided to play for time. 'What do you need my face for? You've got three already.' The hag cackled with laughter until she nearly choked. 'Three?' she said. 'I've got three thousand, three hundred and thirty-two of them, that's how many I've collected in the counties of S., T., U., V. and Z. I only need one more to make a full set.' 'What use will

that be?' Rudolph wanted to know. 'Whoever has three thousand, three hundred and thirty-three faces is ruler of the whole world!' the hag replied. 'Now, let me take yours!' The blacksmith's son realized that unless he agreed the hag would take away neither his face nor the door. Only cunning could help him now. But how? 'I'd like to learn something from you, before you take my face,' he said. 'And what might that be?' croaked the hag. 'I'd like to know how to take people's faces, too,' Rudolph explained. 'Tell me how to do it, and I will take off my own face and give it to you. Only you'll have to hold the door for me.' For a long time the hag pondered whether this young man was not by any chance trying to trick her. In the end she decided he was much too simple a soul for that sort of thing, and agreed, 'Very well, I shall tell you.'

28 July

Where Have All the Faces Gone?

The hag took the door from Rudolph and told him: 'All you have to do is take hold of the person's chin with one hand and his brow with the other. Then you must say, "false fairies filch fools' faces." It's very simple.' But Rudolph looked at her as if he didn't quite understand. 'You say it's easy, but I never get anything right,' he told her. 'What if you were to repeat the spell, while I try out the grip on you?' 'I saw you were stupid at once,' hissed the hag, but she signalled the snakes on her head to lie still for a minute, while Rudolph took hold of her chin and forehead. Then she repeated, 'False fairies filch fools' faces.' At that instant her face came off in Rudolph's hands like a mask. You can imagine his surprise when he saw the face of the beautiful Goldenhair underneath. 'Thank you! You have set me free,' she told him. 'I was under a spell, and if I had obtained your face today, I should have been a witch for ever.' Rudolph was about to ask what they were to do with her collection of faces, but at that moment he saw crowds of people with ovals instead of faces approaching the cottage from all sides. Each of them found his own face without any trouble and put it back on. And Goldenhair? Rudolph took her back to the blacksmith's shop with him.

29 July

The Goat-Kid and the Wolf

Nell the goat lived with Nellie the goat-kid in a cottage on the edge of the village. Every day, Nell would go down to the shop for a cabbage, and when she set off she would say to Nellie, 'Don't open the door to anyone except me!' And Nellie would shoot the bolt and wait for her mother to return. But one day the wolf came along and called out, 'Open up, my dear little goat-kid, it is I, Nell, your mother.' Nellie thought the voice sounded a little strange, so she didn't open the door. The next day the wolf came back again, and this time he spoke in a much squeakier voice, more like that of a goat: 'Open up child! It is I, and I have brought a cabbage home!' Nellie shot back the bolt and opened the door a crack, and in a flash a black wolf's paw pushed its way in.

'You're not my mummy!' cried Nellie, with a start, and she slammed the door shut again. It all turned out all right. When Nell came home, the little kid told her what had happened. 'Just you wait, you wicked old wolf!' said she. The next day she stayed at home, and waited beside the door. Soon a silky soft voice was asking to be let in. When the goat opened the door a little, the wolf stuck in two flour-covered paws, to try to fool the kid. But before he managed to get right inside the door, the goat had grabbed a stout stick and given him such a hiding that he quite lost his appetite for goat-kids after that.

30 July

The Doughnut and the Ants

Do you remember the doughnut? We left him lying in a patch of wild thyme in June. Well, he's long since climbed out of it. He went rolling on through the world, until late one afternoon he wandered into a deep forest, where he lay down next to some sort of hill and fell asleep. The next morning, when he woke up, he found that someone or something was slowly moving him up the slope. He looked all around him and underneath him, and saw that there were ants everywhere. They were shouting and whooping. 'Long live the doughnut! Hurrah for the doughnut!' they were calling. The hill they were carrying him up was a large

anthill. 'Why are you cheering me?' the doughnut asked. 'Because you are brave!' the nearest ant told him. At first the doughnut felt proud. It was very pleasant to be praised for one's courage. 'How right they are,' he thought. But then he began to wonder. 'How do they know how brave I am?' So he asked them. 'How do we know? Why, it's obvious. There aren't many would let themselves be carried off to our larder without batting an eyelid!' the nearest ant explained. Then he went on shouting with the rest, 'Hurrah for the brave doughnut!' 'Well, I never,' thought the doughnut, 'they call out "long live the doughnut", but then they're going to eat me.' He watched the ants for a while, and noticed that all the orders were being given by a particular ant general. The doughnut imitated the general's piping little voice, but he yelled so loud that he shouted him down. 'Drop the doughnut! About turn! Quick march!' And before the confused ants could recover, he whispered to himself, 'Doughnut, at the double — into August!'

31 July

Veronika and the Musician

There was once a certain musician called Cornelius Tralto, who plonked away at his piano until late into the night, composing all sorts of sonatas and symphonies. When Veronika, his landlord's daughter, came up to the attic to visit him, he would play his compositions over to her. But Veronika would only shake her head, as if she didn't like the music at all. Maybe she didn't understand music, maybe she just wanted Cornelius to whisper sweet nothings in her ear. But Tralto took it very seriously. He was quite upset, and worked even later into the night, trying to put together a composition that would make Veronika leap up with delight and clap her hands. He didn't eat any more, and he didn't sleep. All he did was compose, until finally he himself turned into a piece of music, that just floated around the garret. Veronika came and called out to him, 'Where are you hiding, Mr. Tralto?' And she looked under the piano, behind the door and behind the curtains. Then the landlord came, and the landlady, and all the other tenants, and they searched high and low for him, and couldn't work out where the music was coming from. Veronika didn't realize it was her dear Cornelius she could hear, though the melody did seem a little familiar. She grew to like it more and more, and started to go to the empty flat to listen to it. One day she forgot that it wasn't a concert, and started clapping. At that moment Tralto appeared before her, happy at last, no less happy, that is, than Veronika.

August

1 August

Rock-a-bye Baby

Summer can sometimes be so hot that it wears people out. Children are more trouble than usual, too. One mother put her baby's pram under the shade of an old apple tree, because it was nice and cool there. But by midday the heat had got in everywhere, and the baby began to cry again. It was Sunday, and her mother said, 'What a pity the shops aren't open! If I were to buy little Lizzie a new toy, she'd play with it, and that would be that.' The wind elf was passing by, and he thought, 'If only I could make time go quickly.' But not even wind elves can do that! He looked around anxiously for something that might help, and saw a garden beyond the apple tree, and on the other side of that a mown cornfield. 'Dear me, there are enough toys here for a dozen babies!' he exclaimed. He gathered up a few ears of grain and picked a flower in the garden. Then he called the wind, and they played above the pram. The baby began to smile, then fell asleep to the gentle swishing sound. She dreamed that a new ear grew from each little grain, there, beneath the apple tree.

2 August

An Ordinary Hat

Eleanor's daddy gave her a linen hat for her birthday. 'How ordinary it is!' she cried. 'I won't wear it.' And she shoved her present in a cupboard. The wind elf, sky traveller, saw and heard all this, and he knocked on the cupboard door and reassured the hat, 'You won't be there long, you'll see.' And he was right. On Sunday Eleanor and her mother set off on an outing, and in their bag there was not only lemonade and some buttered rolls, but the linen hat as well. When Eleanor found it there, she said she didn't like it and she wouldn't wear it, and threw it on the ground. The wind elf, who had gone along on purpose, stroked the battered hat and said to Eleanor, 'Watch this!' A lizard came along, and tried to make itself a cradle out of the hat. Then a jay flew up, thinking it would be a good place to build a nest. A squirrel wanted it to put nuts in it, a cabbage wanted it to keep the butterflies off, and a mole wanted it to use as a boat to cross the lake in. A hedgehog would have liked to make his bed in it, and

a mouse wanted to store grain there. They began to argue over the hat, and who knows what might have happened to it if Eleanor hadn't come to her senses. She quickly put it on her head, and just in time. Everyone knows how useful a linen hat is when the midday sun is beating down!

3 August

Redcap and Bluey

In the garden was a house, and in the house lived a mummy and daddy. The mummy and daddy had a little girl called Vicky, and she was their only child. She was a good little girl, really, but there was one thing wrong — she could never get to sleep at night. 'Someone must have cast a spell on her,' thought Mummy, and she wasn't far wrong. Underneath Vicky's window stood a couple of garden gnomes. One of them was good and kind, while the other was a rascal who was always causing people trouble. Keeping Vicky awake at night was his idea of fun. It was terrible, because she would walk about half asleep all day long, yawning her head off, but when evening came her eyes opened wide and she couldn't get to sleep for the life of her. Mummy and Daddy had

to read her stories all night, and in the end they were so tired and sleepy themselves that they couldn't work properly, and things began to go badly for them. 'I can't let things go on like this,' said the good gnome to himself one day. His name was Redcap, and you can guess why that was. 'I like Vicky, and I must try to help her,' he added. But he couldn't think how to do it. And all the while his brother Bluey was standing there beside him, sniggering quietly to himself and thinking how he would enjoy upsetting Redcap's plans.

4 August

Redcap and Bluey

'You don't know any magic anyway,' Bluey the gnome teased his younger brother, from morning till night. 'You won't think of anything.' But he was wrong there. One afternoon, when Vicky appeared in the garden, Redcap called out to her and handed her a silvery sprig of herb. 'If you

put it under your pillow,' he told her, 'its scent will make your head whirl, and you'll drop off to sleep without any trouble.' Vicky's mother heard what he said, and she grabbed handfuls of the herb and sewed them inside a silk pillow. Actually, that was Bluey's idea. 'Why wait till evening?' he asked. 'Why not try it out at once?' So Vicky's mother put her in the rocking-chair, pushed the sweet-smelling pillow under her head, and waited to see what would happen. Vicky took a deep breath, and before you could count to five, she was fast asleep. But she slept so soundly that they couldn't wake her up. She lay in the rocking-chair, eyes shut tight, for days, and weeks, and years. She grew bigger and more beautiful in her sleep. Mummy and Daddy didn't have to read stories all night now. They had a good rest, and began to work properly again, but they weren't too happy, of course.

5 August

Redcap and Bluey

'See what you've done now!' Bluey scolded his brother, though he knew very well he was the one to blame. Poor, innocent Redcap couldn't answer him, because Vicky's parents had taken him away and locked him up in the toolshed. They went to see him from time to time, but that was just to give him a piece of their minds. 'Whatever will become of poor Vicky? She just goes on sleeping like a log! She can't even choose herself a husband!' Redcap thought about it for a long time, then he decided what to do. 'If that's how it is, then I shall ask for Vicky's hand in marriage myself.' So he did. Vicky's parents weren't too pleased, but they didn't have much choice. As their future son-in-law, Redcap moved into the house. When the day of the wedding came round, the gnome took the silk pillow, which Vicky still had her head on, and threw it into the fire. At that instant Vicky woke up, and instead of a garden gnome, a handsome young man was kneeling before her. Out of sheer envy, Bluey's blue cap fell from his plaster head. That was a good thing, because it was under that cap that all his nasty ideas were hidden. From then on Bluey the gnome wasn't nasty any more.

6 August

Who Shall Be King?

King Peniwise of Nohopia called his two sons and said to them, 'I am older than the two of you put together, and the time has come to think about retiring. Reigning takes up too much of my time, and I don't get the chance to go fishing.' 'From now on you can do all the fishing you want to, Father,' the

elder son, Albert, told him. 'I shall be happy to take over the kingdom for you, and I'll buy you a new fishing rod as a retirement present.' 'I used to enjoy collecting stamps when I was younger,' Peniwise went on, 'but now my albums are locked away in the treasury, gathering dust.' 'You just go and sort out your stamps to your heart's content, Father,' said Adam, the younger son. 'When I am king I shall have a special stamp issued with your picture on it.' 'That's just the trouble,' said Peniwise, with a shrug of his shoulders. 'I don't know which of you to hand the crown over to. I think about it day and night, but still I can't decide.' 'It's easy, Father, I'm the best!' cried both princes at once. 'Better,' said the king, rather sternly. 'You mean, "I'm the better." I'm sure you're both better. What I want to know is which of you is the betterest. I mean bester . . . no, that's not right either. What I mean is, which of you should I choose?'

7 August

Who Shall Be King?

King Peniwise asked his ministers, and he asked the wise men, but no one could give him any sensible advice on how to tell which of his sons would make the better king. Then, one day, a ragged old poor man asked to see His Majesty. When he saw him, Peniwise said at once, 'I never give charity, as a matter of principle.' 'I haven't come

begging,' replied the old man, smiling a little. 'I have come to advise you.' Since that was free, the king told him to speak. 'Send for your two sons,' the old man requested. 'I shall pose them three questions, and you will see for yourself which of them has answered better.' So Peniwise had the two of them summoned, and listened as the old man asked: 'Do you know what is troubling the blacksmith who shoes the royal horses?' And Albert replied gruffly: 'I don't know, and I don't care.' But Adam said: 'I didn't know he was troubled. I shall have to ask him.' The second question was, 'Why did Annie, the pawnbroker's daughter, refuse to marry the Minister of Justice?' 'What's that?' snapped the elder brother. 'The minister wanted to marry a pawnbroker's daughter? I shall put a stop to that sort of thing when I am king!' But the younger brother had a guess: 'I expect she didn't like him.' Then the old man asked, 'What would you do if your wife tried to advise you on affairs of state?' Albert gave a coarse laugh: 'I'd pack her off into the kitchen!' But Adam said, 'It all depends on what her advice was.'

the man behind the counter was the same who had advised his father. 'Why did you come to the castle poorly dressed and ask us such strange questions?' the young man wanted to know. 'It wasn't my idea,' was the reply. 'My daughter Annie sent me, and told me what to do.' The prince was more curious than ever to meet young Annie. But the pawnbroker said, 'Do not be angry, Your Highness, but Annie says you won't see her until you come as king.' Adam felt like shouting that such impudence deserved a severe punishment, but he stopped himself in time. Instead he took his leave and went to see the blacksmith, wondering as he walked what this Annie was really like.

9 August

Who Shall Be King?

The blacksmith was pleased to see Adam. He invited him inside, and laid all the food and drink he had in the house before his guest. 'I haven't come to be feasted, blacksmith,' smiled the prince. 'I want to know what is troubling you.' But the smith replied: 'It troubles me no more Adam, for I wanted only to sit down at the same table with you.' Then he revealed to the young man that he was his real father. How had that come about? Well, the queen and the blacksmith's wife had both given birth at the same time. The royal child had died at once. The midwife who attended the queen was in

8 August

Who Shall Be King?

King Peniwise looked at the old man, the old man looked at the king, and it was quite clear to both of them that Albert was rash and conceited, while Adam tried to judge things on their merits. 'My successor is to be Adam,' the king decided at last. Albert only grated his teeth and sneaked away. He was thinking of how he might get his revenge, for he was determined to do so. 'I am honoured by your choice, royal Father,' said the younger son with a bow. 'But first allow me to visit the blacksmith and the pawnbroker's daughter to find out what I do not know.' The king agreed. How astonished Adam was the next day when he entered the pawnbroker's shop and saw that

the smithy when she heard the news, and she persuaded the blacksmith's wife to swap the two children. Thus it was that Adam was brought up in the royal family. 'In that case, I have no right to be king,' Adam declared. 'I must hand the throne over to Albert.' 'What, that conceited good-for-nothing?' roared the blacksmith. 'You mustn't do that. Why shouldn't a blacksmith's son be a better ruler than a true-born prince?' Adam fell into thought. Perhaps his father was right. 'Why have you told me all this now?' he asked. 'The midwife, the only one who knew about it, told her daughter the secret before she died,' the smith replied. 'And she persuaded me to tell you. She said it was important for both you and her that you should know the truth.' Adam didn't bother asking who that daughter was. He was quite sure he knew.

10 August

Who Shall Be King?

Adam became king, and the first thing he did in his new lifestyle was to visit the pawnbroker's shop again. He was enchanted by the shopkeeper's daughter the moment he saw her. 'Why did you send your father to the castle?' he asked. 'For selfish reasons,' Annie told him. 'I have loved you for a long time, and since I was a child

I have wanted to be queen. That is why I thought up the sort of questions you must answer sensibly and your adopted brother stupidly. At the same time, I had to make you notice me.' 'But why didn't you speak to me the first time I came here?' Adam wanted to know. 'Isn't it obvious?' replied the pawnbroker's daughter. 'Since you had never seen me, you were sure to think of me. That, too, was a selfish reason.' 'Very well,' Adam went on, 'but I still don't understand why you persuaded the blacksmith to tell me the secret of my birth.' 'Oh, but I'm sure you do,' Annie smiled. 'How could I be sure you would marry me, if you didn't know that you are not of royal blood? That was selfishness also.' 'Then I have never known a selfish person who was so charming,' Adam admitted. 'But how can you be so sure that I shall marry you?' 'Because I know you are no fool, and you recognize what a treasure you have found in me,' Annie told him, modestly. I suppose Adam *was* no fool, for he did marry Annie. After that the gossips would say that Nohopia was really ruled by a woman, but the important thing was that it was a woman who knew what she was doing, and made a very good ruler indeed.

11 August

Who Shall Be King?

There was still Albert, of course. He couldn't forgive his brother for having succeeded to the throne, for having married a girl of low birth. Not only that, but he took her advice, and was much too friendly with that blacksmith fellow. Albert went down to the lakeside to complain to his father, but the old man had other worries. 'Shhh!' he whispered. 'Can't you see I've got a bite? Looks like a big one, maybe a pike!' So the prince tried again that evening, but this time his father began to shout at him.

'Shut the door! You're causing a draught! My stamps are flying all over the place!' So Albert got together a company of the young nobility who were most hostile to the new king, and plotted to overthrow Adam by force. The king knew nothing about it, but it wasn't long before Annie had discovered the conspiracy, and she was quick to advise her husband. 'For a long time now Black Dan and his band of robbers have been hiding in the mountains of Nohopia. The only one who can bring him to justice is ...' 'Is I,' interrupted Adam. 'Oh, no,' she corrected him with a smile. 'Albert, of course. You must send him there this very day, along with this company of noblemen.' And she handed the king a list of conspirators. Do you suppose they went? You may be sure they did, and they were only too glad to escape the gallows. And did they manage to capture Black Dan? They haven't yet. There is one battle after another up there in the mountains. Sometimes Albert wins, sometimes Black Dan, and there seems to be no end to it. But otherwise there is peace and quiet in Nohopia.

12 August

The Traveller

At first sight it looked just like an ordinary bush. Except that it was chock-a-block full of spiders' webs. In fact it was a spiders' school. If you put your ear up against it, you would have heard 'You must try to spin your webs in a place where the fly can't help bumping into them. As soon as the fly gets caught, you must run straight to it ...' And so on. That was the spider teacher telling his pupils what to do. Among them was little Lanky, who had nearly finished his course. When at last he had got his weaving certificate, Lanky picked a nice spot between a currant bush and a gooseberry bush, wove the strongest web he could manage, and sat down to wait. The first fly gave the web a wide berth. The second one buzzed scornfully and flew straight under it. When the third fly noticed the trap in good time as well, Lanky called out, 'Wind, help me!' He cut the strands that were holding his web down. The wind caught it up, and Lanky set off to catch flies in mid air. The spider pupils saw him, and began to shout, 'Hurrah! Three cheers for Lanky, the first

airborne spider!' And ever since then you can see spiders' webs flying about from time to time. Do you suppose Lanky caught his fly? Not a bit of it, but there's a whole chapter woven into the spiders' schoolbooks about him.

13 August

The Tale of a Cupboard Reaches a Climax

In a mysterious room in a mysterious house, there once stood a mysterious cupboard. It was positively the only thing in the room. There were no chairs and no tables, not even a settee. And no one lived in the house. It was empty, except for that one mysterious cupboard. What do you suppose was in that cupboard? That was just what a certain robber was anxious to find out. He put on his mask so that no one would recognize him, took with him his skeleton keys and his torch, and made for the mysterious house. He went at night, and if you want to know any more, you'll have to wait until 13 September.

14 August

Every Dog Has His Day

Mr. Barker had a beautiful house, a large garden, and a lot of valuables. So he got himself a dog to look after the house, the garden and the valuables, and hung a big notice on the gate saying 'BEWARE OF THE DOG!' The dog's name was Sheik, and he was about the size of a calf and looked fearfully dangerous. He continually wrinkled his brow, rolled his eyes and bared his teeth, so that everyone kept their distance from Barker's property, and his master was extremely satisfied. But as time went by, Sheik began to yawn, and got bored running about the garden all by himself and sniffing away at the fence to make sure no one had climbed over it. 'If only a thief *would* come now and again,' he thought, 'then at least there'd be some action.' And when Pongo, one of the neighbouring dogs, passed by one day, trotting along at a respectful distance from the Barkers' fence as usual, Sheik stopped him to have a chat. Then he found out that the other dogs didn't spend all their time guarding property. He was surprised to hear about the dog parties that were held down in the valley by the dogs' club, and he began to long for the company of other dogs.

15 August

Every Dog Has His Day

Mr. Barker was just, as it happens, going on holiday. He gave Sheik a long speech, telling him to guard the house well and not to let anyone into the garden. Sheik listened patiently, but he had his own ideas. As soon as Pongo passed by, Sheik told him to invite all the other dogs to a party in the Barkers' garden that very evening. Then he set to work making ready for his visitors. He dug a secret entrance underneath the fence. Then he buried tasty-smelling bones in the flower beds among the dahlias and the roses, and prepared some refreshments beside the swimming-pool. By six o'clock in the evening there were fifteen dogs of various breeds dashing around the garden. They broke down the flowers as they all tried to be first to dig up a bone. They stuffed themselves with doggie goodies, fought, raced, barked, and all in all had the time of their lives. The most excited of all was Sheik. This went on day after day, for the whole fortnight Mr. Barker was away, worrying his head off over his property. Sheik never even bothered to walk round the house, so that it was burgled in turn by three different gangs. When Mr. Barker came home and saw that scene of desolation, he felt quite faint, but he came to

his senses enough to see to it that his faithless guard-dog went out on the street, to start with. Sheik glanced back at the house and garden, and barked, 'It was worth it, though!' And he hurried down to the valley by the dogs' club because it was nearly evening, and time for another dog party.

16 August

The Heavenly Pastures

Winifred loved Ambrose the shepherd-boy, and Ambrose felt the same way about the girl from the mountain village. Though it was a good hour's walk from the village up to the mountainside pastures, the two of them would meet each evening after Winifred had fed the cattle and Ambrose

had settled his flocks down for the night. Ambrose would set off down the hill and Winifred up the hill, until they reached the old oak tree, which people had called the wise oak since time immemorial. Then, one day, the villagers heard a terrible din from up in the mountains, as if the giant Pennfillion, who was said to dwell there, was grinding the rocks between his fists. Winifred was worried stiff, and she finished the milking, gave each of the cows an armful of grass to chew on, and hurried up into the hills. The old oak was rustling soothingly, but Winifred did not stop there. She hurried on up to the pastures, to see if anything had happened to her loved one. When she reached them, she was horrified to see that, instead of a hillside meadow with a sheep pen and a shepherd's hut, a huge ravine now stretched before her. Had Ambrose and his flocks disappeared beneath the ground? Something made Winifred look up to the sky. High up there she spotted something that wasn't a cloud. In a little while she could make it out more clearly. It was the meadow, floating like a balloon, and at its edge she could see Ambrose waving to her. 'The main thing is that he's all right,' she said to herself, but she had no idea how she might get him down again.

17 August

The Heavenly Pastures

Winifred was a pretty girl, but loveliest of all was her long hair. When she let it down, it reached to the ground, but she usually

wore it in a plait, twisted into a bun. Deep in thought, she unwound her bun as she walked back down the hill, and nervously wrapped it around her hand. 'Whatever am I to do?' she kept repeating mournfully. 'You're doing the right thing now,' said a deep voice somewhere above her. 'Keep plaiting your hair, until it is long enough for you to touch the heavenly pastures with the end of your plait. Only then can you save Ambrose.' Winifred looked around her, but she could not see a giant, or any other living creature. Then she realized that it was the wise oak that had spoken to her. 'I shall be old and grey before my hair is so long,' she said, sadly. But the tree told her, 'If you think of your loved one all the time, neither you nor he shall grow old...' Day by day, year by year, Winifred's plait grew longer. She had no idea how long she would have to wait before it was long enough, but at last she was able to stand beneath the heavenly pasture and throw the end of her plait up to it for Ambrose to catch. Then Winifred hauled him and the whole of the meadow back down to earth as if it were a feather bed. The pastures fitted exactly in the hole in the ground, and everything was just as it was before. The two lovers embraced, and looked into each other's eyes. It seemed as though they were really no older than before. But in the meantime there were ten times as many sheep, and they all belonged to Ambrose, for his master had long since died.

18 August

Tina and the Water Imp

Tina was not terribly fond of washing, even though her mother was quite hoarse from telling her off all the time and lecturing her about how important it was to keep clean. Whenever she was being talked to like that, Tina would stand there looking as if she had cotton wool in her ears. Then, one day (it was by accident, of course) she happened to

pick up a bar of soap. She liked the way it made foam under the running water, just like whipped cream. Then, suddenly, she heard the voice of the water imp, calling out to her from the tap over the bath: 'Soap's not for playing with! You can't keep going around like a chimney-sweep, Tina. If you don't buck up, then . . .' 'Then what?' Tina asked, and she went over to the tap to try and find out what a water imp looked like, and maybe fish him out with her little finger. But he was gone. Tina was just a little bit scared by this warning, but her dislike of water won the day. 'If only it wasn't so *wet*,' she would say to herself. But she started to pretend to get washed, at least. She would lock herself up in the bathroom and fill the bath with water, then she swished it around with her little finger, so as not to get *too* wet. Outside the door, her mummy heard a splashing, and brightened up at once. She hurried off to tell the neighbours that Tina was improving. It was all a mistake, of course.

19 August

Tina and the Water Imp

Then one Saturday, Tina spent longer in the bathroom than usual, because she heard the

water imp again. He spoke just like one of the men on the television adverts, and told Tina exactly what she must do. For instance, she might drop some green and scented bath salts in the water and pretend she was in the sea. 'The sea's got too much water and I don't like it,' she answered, stubbornly, and just to be awkward she sat down in the empty bath with all her clothes on. She picked up the shower head and pretended to be talking to the imp on the telephone. But he had stopped talking to her. 'It's no fun at all playing with you,' the little girl said, grumpily. She hung up the shower and pretended to dial a new number on the tap. Only the tap came off in her hand before she knew what was happening. In a flash

the bath was full to the brim with water. Then the water poured over the side, and went on rising until it covered the stool, the cupboard and the clothes-basket. In the end it lifted up the bath, crashed it through the bathroom door, and sent it spinning round Tina's startled mother out in the kitchen. The next thing she knew, Tina's strange boat had floated all the way down the staircase and out of the front door.

20 August

Tina and the Water Imp

The little girl in the bath caused quite a sensation as she floated down the main

Tina and the Water Imp

It's one thing for a fidgetty little girl like Tina to decide she's not going to move, and quite another thing actually not to. Tina managed to stay sitting on her chair for half a day, but in the end she had to stretch her legs. She took another little walk around the whale's stomach, and pondered how she might get out of there. She remembered the water imp, and the moment the thought of him crossed her mind, she came across a metal box. When she opened it, she found a bar of soap inside. Since she had nothing better to do, she went round washing everything she could find, making lots of soapy bubbles, which weren't at all to the whale's taste. 'Stop that washing at once!' it called out. 'I can't stand bub-bub-bubbles. I'll get hic-ic-iccups!' 'So that's it!' said Tina, opening up some more boxes of soap, so as to make as much lather as possible. There was soon so much foam about that she slid across the whale's stomach as if it had been a polished floor, and went on slipping down the wonderful slide until she passed out of the animal's jaws and into the open sea. The whale tried to slap her with its tail, but she was hidden in the soapsuds, and a large octopus got slapped instead.

street, but before the passers-by could get round to wondering what she was doing there, Tina had shot down to the riverside and slipped into the water. The bath seemed to be making for the sea. Then Tina remembered the water imp, and she was quite sure it was all his doing. The bath overtook one river steamer after another, and before she knew it, Tina found herself floating on the sea. A wave broke over her, and she felt herself and her bath-boat sinking towards the bottom. Soon the bath was full of lobsters and mussels, and it decided to stay where it was. Before Tina had a chance to take a proper look around, a whale swam up and swallowed her. There were so many things lying in the creature's great stomach that it looked like a sort of store-room. As Tina was wandering about helplessly among all these things, a deep voice said, 'I like the way it tickles when you walk up and down, I think I shall keep you for ever!' Tina was startled. For one thing she was surprised to hear the whale speak, but most of all she was upset to think she might have to stay in its stomach for the rest of her life. She quickly sat down in a chair she had just stumbled across, and decided not to budge. 'If this whale thinks I'm going to do what *he* wants,' she thought, 'then he's mistaken!'

22 August

Tina and the Water Imp

'How strange,' sighed Tina, as soon as she was out of reach of the angry whale. 'I should be glad to be free again, but I feel more like a drop of water lost in the sea.' And she thought of the imp again. No sooner had she done so, than along swam a huge turtle, bigger than she was, who said soothingly, 'There are a lot of ways out of the sea, and you don't know which one leads to the shore, do you? You look as though you want to give the sea a salting — you were about to cry, weren't you?' Tina swallowed a salty tear, flung her arms around the friendly turtle's neck, and all of a sudden woke up. She really was holding a turtle, but it was the sort you blow up. Her mother was whispering to her, 'It's a present for you. Had you forgotten it's your birthday today?' Tina hurried off to the bathroom. The bath was standing in the corner as usual, and the tap was right as rain. 'Well, then?' asked a familiar voice. 'Can I go and live somewhere else now?' 'Yes, you can,' Tina replied, and she took off her pyjamas and had a good wash without having to be told, for the very first time.

23 August

The Travels of a Vase

Larkin, the mayor of Gotham, once brought a beautiful cut-glass vase home from his travels. He stood it on the table, put three asters in it, and surveyed it with pride. Suddenly, it started to rain, and a wet patch appeared on the ceiling. Larkin hurried up to the attic, and found the roof had sprung a leak. He sent for the roofer, but the roofer told him: 'You know what, Larkin, I must be getting lazy. I don't feel a bit like mending your roof. The ceiling can soak through and fall down for all I care. Mind you, if you were to offer me that nice vase of yours on top of the price ... Yes, it's a nice vase, that is.' With a heavy heart, Larkin agreed, and before long his roof was mended and the roofer was the proud owner of a cut-glass vase. But not for long. Soon *he* had a burst pipe in his house. The bathroom and kitchen were flooded, and the plumber didn't feel a bit like mending the pipe until he was offered the vase. But the plumber got the 'flu as well as the vase, and the doctor didn't

want to cure him until *he* got the vase. Now, the doctor had one great ambition, and that was to get on to the Gotham town council. Of course, the very person to help him there was Larkin the mayor. So the doctor got on the council and Larkin got his vase back. How long for, I wonder?

24 August

Death Goes to Gaol

There was once a man named Mr. Muggins, who knew a gipsy fortune-teller. Mr. Muggins believed every word the old gipsy-woman spoke. Whatever she read in his palm, it was sure to happen. When he was a boy, she foretold that he would have an accident on the old motorcycle he drove up and down hills all day, but that he would soon get over his injuries. Well, he did have an accident, and it really was nothing serious. When he grew into a young man, she told him he would get married and be the father of twins. He was going out with Polly Proctor at the time, and before long

he got married and they had two children. One after the other, it's true, but then you mustn't expect fortune-tellers to get it exactly right all of the time, must you? After all, it's not written very clearly on your hands, is it? And you can't really hope that they'll manage to read it from all those lines and squiggles without slipping up a little bit now and then. Then the gipsy told him he would be ill, get a better job and have a rise in salary. That's just how it turned out. His friends all said the gipsy was a fraud, and that she always predicted the sort of things that happen to everyone, but Muggins went on believing her, just the same. So he was very upset when she foretold that he would die in exactly a month's time. But he ordered himself a coffin, put on his best suit, and spent the whole of that fateful day lying in the coffin waiting for it to happen. But it didn't happen that day, or the next, or the next. Or even that week. His friends laughed like anything, but Muggins was determined to get to the bottom of the matter.

25 August

Death Goes to Gaol

Muggins made some enquiries, and discovered that no one had died that week for miles around. Not even in the whole country. Soon the newspapers, radio and television were full of it. People weren't dying any more, not even those who were seriously ill. Muggins took a couple of weeks off work and set out to find out what was going on. One thing he found out was that the gipsy-woman had predicted that the town gaoler was to die on the same day he, Muggins, was supposed to have. The gaoler, too, was a picture of health, but he refused to talk to Muggins about the gipsy or her prophecy. Nor would he let anyone into the part of the gaol that was reserved

had come to get him on the appointed day, but he had tricked her into entering the cell and slammed the door on her. In the end he had to give the chief justice the key, though he first tried to persuade him to wait a couple of weeks more. Death had a busy time that day. She began with the gaoler, then went on to the judge's father, and finally got round to Muggins. 'Well, it was you who set me free, so I'll leave you alone,' she whined, and before he found his tongue she was gone. 'Botheration!' Muggins cursed. '*Now* how am I going to prove to everyone that the gipsy was right?'

for especially dangerous prisoners, though he claimed that it was empty. Muggins was not too anxious to die, but he was determined to prove to his friends that the gipsy-woman had been right, and that only some accident or other had prevented her prophecy form coming true. So he went to the chief justice and told him of his suspicions. The judge heard what he had to say, and then said, 'Any other time I would throw you out and call you a madman. But my father is gravely ill. The doctor can't do anything for him, and only death can set him free. Let us go to the gaol!'

26 August

Death Goes to Gaol

The chief justice went with Muggins and a couple of constables to visit the town gaoler. The gaoler kept making excuses, saying he had lost the key to the special section, but in the end he admitted that, in a cell with no windows and a heavy iron door, he had Death under lock and key. She

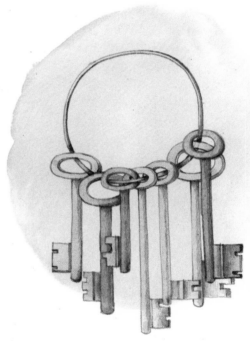

27 August

The Three Gossips

They looked rather like a trio of witches, but actually they were just three gossipy old women. When the storyteller woke up in the morning, they were already standing by the fence and having a go at the whole village. When he went to do his shopping,

and it was quite plain who the neighbours were going to blame. At first the passers-by thought the whole thing was very funny, but after a day or two they began to get upset. 'I don't know why we put up with that strange fellow. Who knows who he'll put a spell on next. It's no joke being a statue you know, and if anyone decides to take a hammer to you, there's nothing you can do about it, is there?' People began to forget how much they had disliked the three gossips. Now they just looked on them as neighbours who had got a raw deal. And they made no

they were still there. They went home for lunch, but in the afternoon they were back again, only this time they were leaning on the fence. Their legs must have been aching, poor things! The storyteller caught the words: 'At it all day he is, crouched over his typewriter...' But then the gossip changed the subject, as she saw the very person she was talking about coming out of his cottage: 'Then you just add three eggs, ladies, and mix them in well.' All three of them burst into laughter, which sounded just like the rattling of tins full of nails. As soon as the storyteller got round the corner, he heard: '... and writes, and writes, well, is that work for a normal sort of fellow, I ask you? He'd do better to go out in the garden and cut the grass!' But one day the storyteller came back from town and noticed that everything was strangely quiet in front of his cottage. The three old women were standing in front of the fence, stock still and silent. When he got nearer, he jumped in surprise. They had been turned to stone.

28 August

The Three Gossips

There was every reason for the storyteller to be startled. The statues of the three old ladies were right beside his garden fence,

secret of the fact that as far as they were concerned the storyteller could take himself off where he had come from, or appeared from, or whatever. It was no use trying to tell them that he couldn't cast spells on people even if he had wanted to. 'Fairy,' he called, late one evening, when the villagers were tucked up in bed. 'Fairy,' he repeated, 'I know you're here somewhere. Show yourself to me.' 'What can I do for you, storyteller?' she asked, appearing only a couple of feet away from him. 'You'll have to take the spell off those three old gossips, or the neighbours will beat me up,' the storyteller said, quietly. 'True, I much prefer them as stone statues, but it won't do, you know...' 'The trouble is,' replied the fairy, even more quietly, 'that I can't take the spell off them, because it wasn't me that put it on them.'

29 August

The Three Gossips

That was another shock for the storyteller. 'Who was it, then?' he asked, mournfully. 'A distant cousin of mine,' the fairy answered, sounding even more crestfallen than he did. 'They call him Old Stony, and he lives in the ruined castle on Pixie Hill, up in the middle of the forest. It's the only bit of magic he knows. Try taking him my regards. I daresay he won't turn *you* into a statue.' With a heavy heart, the storyteller left his typewriter behind, and set off into the forest. He scrambled up Pixie Hill and stopped in front of the ruins, which were surrounded by stone figures of antelopes, deer and foxes. There was even a petrified mushroomer, but he might have been grateful that he didn't get home, since his basket was full of poisonous toadstools which had turned to stone as well. A hairy figure emerged from the ruins and gave a wave of his hand. 'I know everything,' he said. 'You bring me greetings from my cousin, and you'd like me to take the spell off those three old women. More's the pity for you,' he added. 'But then you humans always were a funny lot. You can rely on me, but don't go writing any nasty things about me in your stories!' As the storyteller drew near his cottage, he heard the three women gossiping away nineteen to the

dozen, as if they were trying to make up for lost time. 'There you are,' he thought, 'as bad as ever.' And they say fairy tales should have a happy ending. But then I didn't write this one, it just happened to me.

30 August

The Doughnut Takes a Plane

Do you still remember the doughnut from July? Well, one day he crawled into some luggage out of curiosity, and started reading some cookery books. He got so interested he didn't even notice he was being put into a taxi, or getting unloaded at an airport, or being put on a plane. Since he was in a piece of hand baggage, he ended up in the cabin, and when he finally crawled out again he was surprised to see how many people were sitting there. He glanced out of a window, and began to feel quite dizzy. How high up they were! However had he got there? And what were all the others doing there? Then the voice of the stewardess came over the loudspeaker, announcing how high they were and what they were flying over. As soon as the doughnut noticed that there were children sitting there, and that they weren't crying, he stopped being frightened. He saw one pretty little girl with ribbons in her curly hair, and decided he would make her smile.

He climbed up onto the seat beside her and said 'Boo'. The little girl burst into tears, and they couldn't get her to stop. She just kept pointing at the doughnut as if he was some sort of monster. So the people asked the stewardess to throw him away. She did it so well that the doughnut found himself falling through the air, faster and faster. And where did he land? You'll find out in September.

31 August

How Mr. Gascoyne Invented School

The Gascoynes had five children. 'Children, indeed!' Mrs. Gascoyne used to say. 'More like five baby dragons!' She was right. The five of them would squabble from morning till night, shouting their heads off, and one after the other they would run home in tears with a bump or a bruise to show. 'We can't go on like this!' cried Mrs. Gascoyne, wringing her hands. 'I don't get a moment's peace, and I'll soon have lost what's left of my poor nerves.' Gascoyne just agreed with everything she said, and that made her crosser than ever. 'Don't just sit there nodding, do something!' she shouted at him. But what was he to do? He'd have to think of something, that was for sure, because a house full of yelling kids and a nagging wife to boot were more than he could take. That day he happened to meet a friend of his who didn't have any children, and who was looking for a job. Suddenly, Gascoyne had an idea. What if they were to build a special house in the town, where people's children could be shut up for half the day at least, and his friend could look after them? To stop them getting too bored, Gascoyne's friend could teach them something now and again, like reading, writing and arithmetic. It might be quite useful for them. So it was that the very first school was started, and the children of that town had the very first teacher. He soon turned grey, because among all the other children he had to put up with were the Gascoynes' five little monsters.

September

1 September

The School for Cats and Dogs

The wind elf always liked to sleep late in the morning, for it was usually long after midnight before he spread out his cloak to go to sleep. On the day before the start of the new school year he had made his bed on the roof of a country school. But he was woken up early in the morning by the sound of shouting and laughing, and the tramp of dozens of pairs of new shoes, in which the children were hurrying towards the school gate. The sleepy sky traveller saw that the children's faithful holiday friends, cats and dogs, were running along behind them. The moment the school doors closed, the animals showed their disapproval. They began barking, and howling, and miaowing enough to awaken the dead. No one could get them to move away from the school, and so the wind elf decided to do a good deed. He flew down from the roof. He was going to spread out his cloak like a blackboard, and teach those four-legged creatures to read and write, so that they wouldn't be jealous of the children. But he didn't get the chance. The moment Frosty the kitten caught sight of him, she got him mixed up with the moths she liked to catch sometimes, and pounced on him. The wind elf only just managed to escape, with Frosty chasing underneath. And Sultan, the Alsatian dog, chased after Frosty, and then the rest of the the cats and dogs pursued Sultan. So that was the end of their moaning and groaning. It was the end of the school for cats and dogs, as well. They're not as lucky as children, are they?

164

2 September

Jelly-Knees

There was once an unfortunate mother whose little boy answered almost everything you said to him by saying, 'I'm scared.' Do you suppose she could send him down into the cellar in the evening for some apples to finish off their supper? Not a bit of it. And as for telling him spooky bedtime tales, well, that was out of the question. From morning till night he would just keep on repeating that cowardly little sentence. Even if she only asked Jelly-Knees, as they started to call him, to pop round to the neighbours and borrow a little salt, he would reply, 'I'm not going out there, someone might jump out on me!' Jelly-Knees didn't want to play with the other children, in case someone tripped him up, and he wouldn't go out for a walk in case he should stumble over a stone and fall down. 'I don't know what we shall do with that boy,' sighed his mother, late one night, and this time the wind elf heard her. He was just getting ready to go to sleep in the window-box, and as soon as he heard this, he tried to remember all the magicians, good and bad, that he had ever come across, so that he might think of something to cure the boy of his fear.

3 September

Jelly-Knees

Jelly-Knees's mother had a vivid dream that night. She dreamed she saw a little tiny man with wings land on the end of her bed. Actually, it was none other than the wind elf, with his cloak lined with good ideas. He handed her a little box containing a white powder, and whispered to her, 'Get Jelly-Knees to take a little every morning, but just a speck on the tip of his tongue. In a few days he won't be afraid of anything.' The little man was gone as quickly as he had arrived. But the next morning Mother was still holding the little box in her hand, so she told Jelly-Knees what had happened in the night, and after breakfast she gave him a speck of the wonderful powder. They were both looking forward to getting rid of his fear. And it worked. That same day Jelly-Knees went out to play hide-and-seek with the other boys and girls. Then he went all on his own to get the letters out of the mail-box. After he had had his third lick of the courage powder, he went all the way to the greengrocer's for a cabbage. By the end of the week he was picking over the apples all by himself in the dark cellar. He grew bolder day by day, until one evening he declared, 'I shouldn't be afraid to go into the deep forest at midnight, even if there were devils on the loose!' As soon as he had said this, the wind elf landed on the end of his bed, and smiled. 'There you are, you see,' he said. 'There's no magic in being brave. Your courage was just hidden away inside, and all you had to do was find it. You see, that box had ordinary sugar in it!'

4 September

How Wise Our King Is!

The king of Lotzovrania was called Petiwit III. If you had seen him sitting there on his throne with his crown on his head and his sceptre in his hand, you would have said he looked very dignified indeed, every inch a king. But it didn't do for him to open his mouth. The moment he started to move his

lips, out would come some piece of foolishness that few village idiots would have been able to match. Of course, only those nearest to him, the ministers and courtiers, knew that the king wasn't right in the head, because they didn't let anyone else near him. To keep up appearances, they even spread the word that the king was especially clever and judicious, in short, the wisest of the wise. And the people believed it. One day, a young nobleman arrived at court. Aldred was Lord of the Northern Marches, and he was looking forward to serving the world's wisest monarch. Well, the Northern Marches were a little out of the way, and Aldred had never actually met his sovereign before. So you can imagine how surprised he was at the first audience he attended, when the king started to utter his pearls of wisdom, and each of them was more stupid than the one before, so that you wouldn't have believed that a single fool could manage them all on his own. 'Why, the king is an idiot!' said Aldred out loud, before he could stop himself. Everyone flinched, but luckily the king was the only one who didn't notice the nobleman's remark.

5 September

How Wise Our King Is!

The nearest of the ministers hurriedly bumped Aldred out into the corridor with his huge stomach. 'Of course the king is an idiot!' he hissed in the young man's ear. 'We all know that. But at least he doesn't interfere in the affairs of state, because he doesn't even know he's got a state. That's just how we like it, so that we run the country, and not the king. So you'll either have to learn to praise his wisdom, double quick, or you can crawl back into those marches of yours and stay there!' Now that was the last thing Aldred wanted. Having been summoned to the royal court at last, he was anxious to stay there, and he agreed at once to do what was required. He stepped back into the hall and cried out resolutely, 'How wise our king is!' Unfortunately, Petiwit had just made one of the dottiest pronouncements he had ever come up with, so that now the whole company burst out laughing. Now the king was a fool, but he was also easily upset. He thought the young nobleman must be making fun of him, and had him locked up for insulting the royal person. So Aldred stayed at the castle after all, but a couple of floors lower down than he would have wished. And if he hásn't died, he's sitting in the dungeons of Lotzovrania to this day.

6 September

Jack and His Cat

One foggy day old Briggs passed away, leaving his son Jack just one solitary thing in the whole wide world, a fine-looking tomcat. Jack had a good cry, and after the funeral he said to the cat, 'Why should

I have to struggle to keep the two of us? Better for each to look after himself.' But to Jack's surprise the cat answered him in a human voice. 'Don't be in such a hurry, master. Better to get me a pair of tall boots made and find me a strong sack. You won't regret it, you'll see.' Jack was so confused to hear a cat speaking that he went and did as he was told at once. He didn't even bother to ask what the cat needed such things for. The cat set the sack up in the middle of a field like a trap, and shoved a cabbage into it. Then he lay down beside it and pretended to sleep. A hare came hopping

along, popped into the sack, and started to gnaw at the cabbage. Without more ado the cat snatched up the sack, threw it across his shoulder, and set out for the royal palace.

7 September

Jack and His Cat

The king was a gullible sort of fellow, with a kind enough heart. The things he loved most in this world were his daughter Rosalind and receiving presents. He always

wore such a funny little crown that his courtiers would sometimes say in jest that it was really a saucepan from the royal kitchens. It was to his royal court that the booted tomcat came and knelt before the throne. 'O most mighty of kings,' he said, 'my master, Baron Briggs of Catford and the Feline Hundreds, begs you to accept this humble token of his esteem.' Luckily, the king's geography wasn't very good. 'A hare?' he said. 'How nice. We shall look forward to having it for supper. Please convey our gracious thanks to your master.' A week later the cat was kneeling before the king again — this time with a pair of partridges he had lured into his sack with a handful of corn. He took the king's even warmer thanks away with him. A couple of weeks later he arrived with a pheasant. The king ate his gift with relish, and kept saying the baron should come in person some day, so that he might see his generous benefactor in the flesh. And Princess Rosalind, who happened to be passing, nodded and said that the Baron of Catford really should come to the royal palace to pay them a visit.

Jack and His Cat

How could poor Jack go before the king
and his charming daughter in a pair of
patched trousers and a rough linen shirt
that was out at the elbows? There wasn't
much future in that. But the cat knew what
he was doing. He learned from the royal
steward that each day on the stroke of four
the king and the lovely Rosalind used to set
out in a carriage accompanied by the
coachman and a few servants. Their ride
always took them along the banks of the
River Gryme. The cat led Jack to a bend in
the river which the royal carriage must pass,
and told him to undress and jump into the
water. He then concealed his master's poor
clothes among the willows, and when the
king's party approached he began to shout
at the top of his voice, 'Help! Somebody
help! Catch them! Robbers! There they go!'
The king ordered his coachman to drive
straight to the river. There they spied
a young man up to his neck in water and
a familiar tomcat standing on the bank. The
king asked at once what had happened.
'Alas, mighty sovereign,' lamented the cat,
'my master was attacked by a band of
robbers. They stole his fine clothes, his
sword and his purse, and threw him into the
river.' The king immediately ordered his
servants to return to his palace and bring
a suit of clothes worthy of the Baron of
Catford, and invited Jack to take a seat in
his carriage.

9 September

Jack and His Cat

When Jack put on the fine suit of clothes
they brought him, the princess was unable
to take her eyes off him. She whispered at
once to her royal father that they should
invite the baron to the royal castle. But the
cat had other plans. He bowed to the king
and said, 'Allow my master to entertain you

Thurgon, where he banged on the gate. 'What do you want, you flea-ridden moggy?' the magician greeted him roughly. Thurgon was not only a fearsome sight, but also a cruel and treacherous wizard, and all trembled before him. 'O greatest of the great wizards,' the cat began, for he had heard that the magician was fond of flattery, 'I have heard that you can change into anything you want. I could not resist making the long journey to this magnificent castle of yours, to see for myself such a rare

at his castle in Catford.' The king agreed, and the princess agreed, and the coachman had no choice in the matter. But Jack looked very dismayed indeed, seeing nothing but a shameful end to the affair. The cat was already running along in front of the carriage, and since his tall boots were very fast, he had soon put a good distance between himself and the team of royal horses. He came to a large meadow, where herdsmen were grazing a great many cows. 'Listen to me,' the cat addressed them. 'If you don't tell everyone who passes by that the meadow and the cows belong to Baron Briggs of Catford, then the keepers will come and give each of you twenty-five lashes.' When the king passed by and asked whose the meadow and the cows were, the herdsmen naturally told him that everything was the property of the Baron of Catford. It was the same story when the royal coach reached a huge field of rye with mowers at work, and the edge of a vast forest, where the gamekeepers were setting out hunting. The king just nodded his head and muttered, 'That's what I like to see, that's what I like to see!' But Jack hadn't the faintest idea what was going on.

and wonderful sight.' The wizard replied, 'I should put you to death for your impudence, but since you come to me so humbly, then I shall do as you ask. Transformation is a minor task for such as me,' he added, and with a couple of magic words he had turned into a lion. The cat gave a shriek and shot up one of the curtains, without even stopping to take his boots off. What if the lion were to take a fancy to catmeat? 'Very impressive, very impressive,' he admitted, from his place of safety below the ceiling.

10 September

Jack and His Cat

Meanwhile, the booted tomcat had reached the castle of the powerful magician

11 September

Jack and His Cat

'Now I see that the stories were not exaggerated,' said puss in boots, slyly, the

moment Thurgon had returned to his usual shape. 'But I still cannot imagine how you could change into something small, like a mouse for instance.' 'Huh!' The wizard gave a scornful laugh. He enjoyed showing off, and never suspected he might be falling into a trap. Again, he muttered a couple of magic words, and in an instant a mouse was scurrying about on the floor. The cat pounced, and that was the end of the mouse, and Thurgon. Just in time! The king's carriage was arriving at the gates at that very moment. The cat went out to meet the guests, welcoming them to the castle of Baron Briggs of Catford. And then what? There was a grand wedding, of course. Only the cat didn't enjoy the wedding-feast a great deal, for the wizard had given him indigestion. And then? Then the king retired, and Jack was ruler of the whole country. I must add that he ruled wisely and with justice. Which was only natural, when his chief advisor was a booted tomcat!

12 September

The Cottager and the Landowner

A poor widow and a miserly landowner were neighbours. And because the landowner was so greedy, he even picked his neighbour's apples, as if he hadn't enough of his own. He claimed that because the tree was touching his fence it belonged to him. 'I daresay things will go better for me one day,' the woman said to herself, 'and maybe that old miser will get what's coming to him.' One day she set off into the forest to gather firewood, taking a piece of bread with her in her bundle. On the way she met an old beggar. She could see he hadn't eaten all day, so she gave him all except the crust from her bread. She didn't expect anything in return, but the old man pointed to a nearby field. Where there had been nothing a moment ago, she saw a couple of potatoes. 'Take them, in return for sharing the last of your bread with me,' he told her. The next morning the old woman was woken up by an unusual glare. It seemed as though the sun was wrapped up in her bundle over by the stove. She peeped inside it, and saw that each of the potatoes had become a little pile of gold. The miserly

landowner was passing by, and when he saw the strange glow, he went inside without knocking, to see what it was. The woman told him truthfully what had happened. The landowner hurried to fetch his wheelbarrow and five loaves of bread, and scurried off to the forest with them. He met the old man there, and you know what happened then. He took a whole barrowful of potatoes home with him and locked them up in his barn. But when he woke up the next day, he was in for a nasty shock. Each of the potatoes had turned into a dozen mice, and they had eaten up all his corn.

170

13 September

The Beginning of the End of the Tale of a Cupboard

In a mysterious room in a mysterious house, there once stood a mysterious cupboard. It was positively the only thing in the room. There were no chairs and no tables, not even a settee. And no one lived in the house. It was empty, except for that one mysterious cupboard. What do you suppose was in that cupboard? That was just what a certain robber was anxious to find out. He put on his mask so that no one would recognize him, took with him his skeleton keys and his torch, and made for the mysterious house at night. How surprised he was to find that the house wasn't even locked, nor was the room, and nor was the cupboard. And anyone who wants to know more will have to wait until 13 October.

14 September

The Clever Prince

There was once a certain forest that everyone used to get lost in. In the middle of the thickest part of that most confusing of forests, wicked King Balthasar had a special castle built for his only daughter, Vashti. Then he pronounced that whoever desired his daughter's hand in marriage must find his way back home from the gates of that castle. When the king's heralds had announced this royal decree, only three princes came to try their luck, Lotto, Totto and Otto. The first of these was clever, but not clever enough. As they led him through the forest to the castle, he secretly dropped peas along the way to mark the route. Although the king's servants didn't notice, a hungry pigeon did, and it followed behind, gobbling up the peas. Lotto got lost on the way home, and didn't win the princess's hand. Totto was just as anxious to gain the princess, but he didn't get on any better than his rival. He snapped little branches on the trees along the way, but he shouldn't have chosen living trees. The wind got angry with him, and blew all the broken branches away. Totto is wandering the woods to this day, simply because he should have been cleverer. Otto dressed up sensibly for the journey, none of your silver shoes and tight-fitting tunics, but walking boots and a loose leather jerkin. And right from the

start he made friends with the forest and its inhabitants. He shared his bread with the birds, gave the ants a piece of cake, and praised the spiders' webs. They all helped him to find his way out again, and the next day he drove to the forest castle to collect his bride.

15 September

A Tale of an Armchair

Mr. Newcombe was moving into a new house and, as you can imagine, he wanted everything there to be new. Some of his old furniture he sold, some of it he chopped up for firewood, but he got left with a tattered old armchair that stood on four bear's paws. 'Look here, old son,' he said to it. 'Your back's not what it used to be, and you let out a sigh every time I sit on you. I don't want you any more. I'll take you out in the country, and you can live in retirement there.' And before the sun had slipped behind the horizon, the armchair really was standing on the edge of the forest, sticking out like a sore thumb. 'Brrrh, it's cold here,' the chair complained, and it started to get gooseflesh. Or was it the evening dew

settling on it? Whatever the case, the armchair had cold feet standing there in the grass, and it was starting to feel terribly sad. Now, when someone is sad, he should try to think of something pleasant. So the armchair recalled the time when it was brand new, smelling of fresh varnish, and without a single little mark on its light green upholstery. Mr. Newcombe had mostly bought it because of its bear's paws. He liked them a lot, and he was very proud of the armchair, until it went out of fashion.

16 September

A Tale of an Armchair

'Is it an animal, or isn't it?' rustled the spruce tree, bending to take a closer look. 'It's got feet like a bear, but it isn't a bear,' added the pine. 'It stands there like a tree-stump, but it's certainly no tree-stump,' chipped in the oak, adding, 'It's got no business here, anyway.' The armchair tried to move, thinking it might find a better place, but voices from all sides cried out, 'Don't come this way! Go somewhere else! You're in the way here!' 'I know I don't belong here,' sighed the chair, and it slipped down into a hollow and hid amongst the

bracken and thistles, so as to get away from them all. But the forest is always curious about intruders, and every so often a hare would come running along to hide there. A squirrel threw nuts at the chair's arms, the birds took a few threads from its upholstery to line their nests, and a fox came to ask it where it had come from. But the armchair stayed silent. Up above it the forest swished like a distant sea, and was full of scents and the signals the birds sent from one end to the other. They would often call out, 'Watch out! Mushroomers!' That was the message the birds gave the forest when Mr. Oldfield appeared with his basket. He wanted to make his grandchildren a nice bowl of mushroom soup, but instead of mushrooms he brought home an old armchair.

17 September

A Tale of an Armchair

'I don't think I'll ever get used to a carpet beneath my feet and a roof over my head again,' said the armchair, looking around the cosy room. 'Oh yes you will,' Mr. Oldfield soothed it. 'You'd have come to a sticky end in the forest, you know. In winter you'd be covered in snow, and in spring you'd be soaked through. It's warm and dry here. And it's fun, too, because the children come.' So the armchair stretched itself out comfortably until its joints creaked, and thought how nice it was to have someone want it again. When Mr. Oldfield's five grandchildren came visiting, they all squeezed into the roomy chair, and sat there wide-eyed. You see, they heard one story after another of hares and squirrels, beetles and birds' nests, ants, a tall spruce, a stunted pine and all about the mysterious life of the forest. The armchair told such interesting stories that Mr. Oldfield's grandchildren forgot all about the television, and would secretly creep into Granddad's room instead. The story of the armchair with the bear's feet found its way back to Mr. Newcombe. He pricked up his ears at once, and decided he must have that chair at all costs. It was getting fashionable to collect antiques, and the chair's old master was hard at work collecting them. But he never got his rare old piece of furniture back again, either for money or for free. He should have thought of it sooner.

18 September

The Storyteller's Hazel Nuts

In the storyteller's garden there was a tall hazel bush. When the nuts began to ripen it had twice as many as the other hazels in the neighbourhood. A speckled nutcracker, which is not a very well-known bird, came flying along and began to pick the nuts and crack them open against the trunk of an apple tree. It flew back and forth from hazel to apple tree and back again, picking nuts and gobbling them up at a fair old speed. The storyteller tried to persuade the bird to leave the nuts alone, but the next day two nutcrackers appeared, then three, then four, and they spent the whole day bashing away at the nutshells and stuffing

themselves like mad. So the storyteller bought himself a gun and started to shoot at the birds. It was only a child's toy, that wouldn't have hurt a chicken, but the birds were scared of it, and as long as the storyteller was in the garden with his gun, they kept their distance. But the moment he went inside the cottage, they were back in the branches of the hazel. The storyteller was most upset, and he did his best to pick as many nuts as he could himself. Why didn't he want the birds to have them? Well, those were no ordinary hazel nuts, but fairytale ones. Each one had a fairy story inside it, and all you had to do was crack it open. Only those nasty birds with their long beaks were pecking to pieces at least four dozen stories a day!

19 September

The Storyteller's Hazel Nuts

The storyteller called the fairy, who had often helped him in the past, but she was nowhere to be found. She must have wandered off somewhere. Even fairies do that sometimes. To make matters worse, one day he left his gun on the table outside, and that evening the four nutcrackers picked it up by its strap and carried it off into the forest. Not even a snowman could have stood by and watched that sort of thing! The storyteller took his stick and his

torch, and set off along the woodland path after the birds. It suddenly got dark, for autumn was on its way in, and in the light of the rising moon the forest looked rather mysterious, not at all as the storyteller knew it from his daytime strolls. The path between the spruce trees wound like a snake, and the storyteller suddenly realized that he was lost. 'I'll have to end up somewhere!' he said to himself out loud, so as not to be scared, and he carried on walking. In a while he saw a light among the trees. 'Well, well,' he reassured himself. 'Someone seems to live here. So nothing can happen to me at all, not even the wolf from Red Riding Hood can eat me up!' Then he spied a cottage, but what a cottage! Now the storyteller really got a shock. It was standing on a stalk, turning round and round, and at each of the four corners of the roof there was a cage with a nutcracker asleep inside.

174

20 September

The Storyteller's Hazel Nuts

Suddenly, the cottage on a stalk stopped turning, and a searchlight shone out of a window in the roof, quite blinding the storyteller with its light. He tried walking to the right, stepping backwards, hiding behind the trunk of a pine tree, but it was all in vain. The light followed him wherever he went. Then a staircase let itself down from the cottage, a door opened, and out stepped an ugly old hag. Well, ugly is really too nice a word, for this hag was absolutely hideous. 'I am Yagga the Hag,' she croaked, 'and you can't imagine how pleased I am that I managed to lure you here.' 'I'm a storyteller,' the man with the stick and the torch introduced himself, and he was going to add something about chasing nutcrackers, when the hag screeched at him, 'Don't say a word! I know all about it! You sit there cracking nuts and telling poor little children all those terrible stories! Now I'm going to shut you up, and I shan't let you go until the nutcrackers have eaten the rest of

those cursed nuts!' 'But why?' asked the storyteller, with a gulp. 'I don't like fairy tales, I can't stand them!' the hag snarled. 'I'm always cruel and evil in them, and I won't have it! I shall wipe all fairy stories off the face of the earth, do you hear me?'

21 September

The Storyteller's Hazel Nuts

Just then a familiar fairy stepped into the illuminated clearing. She was out of breath, and had obviously been hurrying. As soon as the hag saw her, her face fell. 'Yagga,' the fairy addressed her, in an angry tone, 'is this how you keep our agreement? Have you forgotten your promise?' The hag hung her head in shame. 'Well, he keeps on writing, and writing, and I . . .' she began to make excuses. 'But I thought we had agreed that your nutcrackers could pick their nuts anywhere else but in the storyteller's garden,' the fairy interrupted. 'Otherwise . . .' 'I know,' said Yagga the Hag apologetically. 'Otherwise m-my c-cottage will b-be overg-grown so thickly with hazels, that I'll n-never g-g-get out ag-g-gain!' She handed the storyteller his gun. 'Here's your weapon,' she told him. 'I promise you won't need it again. A pity!' As they walked back out of the forest, the storyteller said to the fairy, half gratefully, half as though he was telling her off, 'I thought you were never going to turn up.' The fairy smiled. 'We fairies

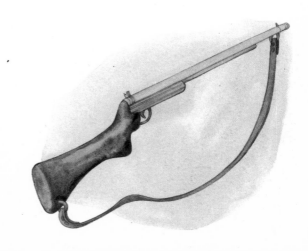

mustn't be around *all* the time, you know, or people will take us for granted. The important thing is that we turn up in time. Don't you think you ought to write a story about this?'

22 September

The Chestnuts

Just outside the town of Pilchester was an abandoned and neglected garden with a huge chestnut tree growing in it. Every autumn the grass beneath the tree was full of fine big chestnuts. Two merchants from the town found out about this, and each of them said to himself, 'If I put a charcoal stove in my shop and sell roast chestnuts, I shall make a fortune!' The two of them met in the garden, and realized they had both come with the same idea. But neither of them was willing to share the chestnuts. So in the end they agreed that whoever found the first ripe chestnut would keep the whole crop. They shook hands on it and, looking up at the tree, they both said that they thought it would be a week before any of the chestnuts were ripe. But really they both knew that the chestnuts were ready. So each of them set off secretly that very same evening to the garden where the chestnuts grew. The first of them sat down beneath

the tree with a piece of sacking spread out to catch the first chestnut as it fell. But the second merchant saw him sitting there, and thought he could get the better of him. So he silently climbed up to the top of the tree, so that he might hear the skin of the first ripe chestnut crack, and grab it before it fell. But both of them fell fast asleep. When the chestnuts began to fall, early the next morning, the one in the tree gave a start and fell straight into the other's sack. While they were arguing over who had won, some boys crept up behind their backs and carried the whole crop of chestnuts away.

23 September

Scouse the Mouse

Barbara actually went into the pet shop to buy a parrot, but she forgot all about parrots the moment she set eyes on Scouse the mouse. 'I'll take this one please,' she said, pointing at Scouse. But the shopkeeper said, 'Dear me, the mice are not for sale, they're to feed the snakes with! Can't you see that it's the python's lunchtime, and he just

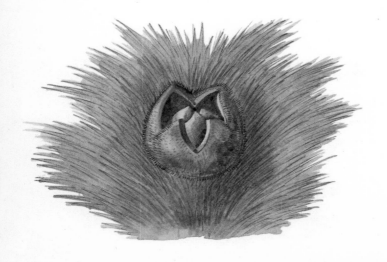

fancies this particular mouse?' But Barbara shouted out, 'If you don't give me Scouse the mouse, I shall never buy anything here any more, and I shall tell all the other girls to get their goldfish and budgerigars somewhere else!' Now that was enough to put the wind up any shopkeeper, so he quickly wrapped Scouse up in tissue paper, tied a piece of string round him, and gave him to Barbara for free, because he didn't have a pricelist for mice. As soon as she got round the corner, Barbara threw the paper in a bin and put the mouse in her pocket. A little voice from her pocket said, 'Thank you for saving my life. I'll pay you back, you'll see.' Barbara just gave a little wave of her hand, as if to say, 'I don't want paying back. I'm glad to have you, that's all.'

24 September

Scouse the Mouse

When Barbara got to school, she found out they were going to have Physical Education for first lesson instead of maths. She wasn't very pleased, because she didn't like P. E. very much. Just to make matters worse, they were going to have races, which she always lost. 'You'll win today!' the mouse told her, and he was right. The moment Scouse appeared on the track, the other girls ran off in all directions, and Barbara was the first past the post. Scouse tried to help Barbara with everything. When she forgot her ruler, she was able to draw lines in her exercise-books using his long tail. Or when she had an art lesson, the mouse dipped his tail in the paints and drew such lovely pictures that they could have put them on show right away. One day, Barbara went to visit Bertie, who was known to be the quietest and most obedient boy in the street. His mother had decided she would set all the other children an example, and she invited the rowdiest of them to tea and biscuits, where she was going to lecture

them about good manners and proper behaviour. Bertie sat at the head of the table, behaving terribly well, but only till Scouse gnawed away one of the legs of his chair. Then the best-behaved boy in the neighbourhood crashed down under the table, slice of bread and all. He quite liked it, and from then on he was just like the rest of the children.

25 September

Scouse the Mouse

One day, Barbara's class were going on a trip, and their teacher said to the children, 'You can run about and enjoy yourselves, but each of you should try to be useful in some way. All right?' 'Yes!' cried the children, and they all started to clap; all that is except Barbara, since she had Scouse in her hand and her hand in her pocket. But the teacher frowned. She thought Barbara didn't want to be useful, and as a punishment she told her to write out thirty times, 'I am to clap if it is useful.' 'Don't

worry, I'll do it for you!' squeaked the mouse. The children set off in a procession behind their teacher, making for the countryside. As soon as they got out of town, they came to an orchard, where a strange old man was picking pears in a lazy sort of way, and putting them in sacks. 'There you are, children!' said the teacher, and she sent them to help the old man. That was the end of the trip, but the girls didn't even get a pear for their efforts, as you might expect. The old man was mean. When Scouse found out, he gnawed a corner off each of the sacks, so that all the pears fell out on the way to market. They say you should repay evil with good, but Scouse the mouse didn't know much about proverbs. And what happened to him after that? If he hasn't run away, Barbara has still got him.

The Enchanted Pipes

Nothing very much had happened all summer in the village of Tingleford. Then suddenly one day things changed. The day began just like any other, but as soon as midday came along, the parents lost their children. Just as they were leaving school, they heard the distant sound of pipes playing. The music was so strange and wonderful that all the children ran towards it as though they were under a spell. The last of them was Simona. She watched as the houses got fewer and the trees more frequent, until she and the others found themselves in an unknown landscape. They came to a mysterious gate, and on the other side was a paved path. When they reached the path, they all stopped, because the sound of the pipes had ceased. In a hollow in front of the path Simona found some coloured chalks. There were exactly as many as there were children. Simona drew a cat on one of the flagstones, and you can imagine how surprised she was when it first miaowed, then stretched its paws, and then hopped up onto her lap. When Peter drew a bread roll, he was able to eat it. Eddie's red toy car hooted and drove away. In

a little while the path was covered in toys, animals, cakes and ice-creams. Everyone got what he drew. 'I do hope this goes on for ever,' wished Simona, but in the evening the pipes led the children back home.

27 September

The Enchanted Pipes

The next day the worried parents came to school to meet their children, so as not to lose them again. But the moment there was a whirring sound in the church tower, and the clock began to strike midday, the sound of the pipes could be heard again, and the children ran off towards it at such a speed that their mothers and fathers soon lost sight of them. And once again they came to the strange countryside, the mysterious gate, and the paved path with its coloured chalks. The children had spent all morning thinking about the nice things they would draw themselves, and all the wonderful toys they would be able to play with, so that they

hadn't paid any attention to their lessons. They didn't have time to do any homework that day because it was after sunset when they returned, and they were so tired that they fell asleep at the supper table. They weren't hungry anyway, since they had eaten their fill of cakes and ice-cream on the other side of the magic gate, and didn't fancy beans on toast or scrambled eggs any more. But not one of them said a word about their adventure with the coloured chalks and the pavement. This went on all week, and on Friday the headmaster called a parents' meeting to try to decide what to do. But no one came up with any ideas, so in the end they went home, having decided to wait and see.

28 September

The Enchanted Pipes

On Saturday the children were in a state of high excitement, but they didn't miss the sound of the pipes when it came. They ran towards it like wild things, and when they got to the pavement they were still as wild as ever. When Paul drew himself a plump sausage and wanted to eat it, Harry drew some bars across it, and the sausage was in prison. To get his own back, Paul gave Harry's tortoise hare's legs. Then Harriet's dachshund flew away. Someone had given it wings like an elephant's ears. 'Wait

a minute,' said Simona, 'don't be silly!' But it was too late, and from then on lemonade ran out of holes in glasses, and cakes slid away from children's mouths on little rails. The girls were doing their shoes up with worms instead of laces, and the boys grew donkeys' ears or horns. They all tried to outdo each other in mischief. Before Simona could sit on her tricycle, its wheels were gone, and the ice-cream in her cornet turned into a cabbage. She tried in vain to tell the children that you mustn't mess about with magic, or it will disappear forever. She'd read that in a book of fairy tales. But they wouldn't listen. The children started to pull each other's hair, nudge each other, and fight. After that the enchanted pipes disappeared forever. They led the children home, and were never heard again. Only Simona was a bit better at painting than the others, and she won a prize in a painting contest. It was a whistle, but a quite ordinary one.

29 September

The Doughnut and the Albatross

Do you still remember the doughnut from August? Well, after they threw him out of the aeroplane, he went on falling and falling, singing to keep up his courage,

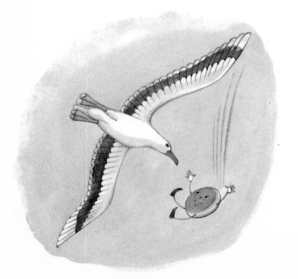

'This doughnut's a singer, a singer is he,
He's rather more nutty than fresh and
                              doughy,
He doesn't know where he is falling and
                              tumbling,
But thinks it's no use to be rumbling and
                              grumbling...'
'This is it,' he whispered to himself, and closed his eyes. Then he suddenly felt more as though he were moving sideways than downwards. When he opened his eyes, he saw that he was sitting on the wings of a big white bird. 'Who are you?' he asked. 'I'm an albatross,' replied the bird. 'Allow me to express my gratitude,' said the doughnut, with feeling. 'You have saved my life!' 'It's an ill wind that blows nobody any good,' replied the albatross mysteriously. The doughnut thought about this for a moment, and then he said to himself, 'The opposite's true too.' 'It's a good wind that blows nobody any ill,' he said out loud. 'Quite so,' replied the albatross. 'I see we understand each other well. You have clearly perceived that the albatross is a greedy sort of bird. So we can be friends, until I reach some rock or other, that is ...' But the doughnut didn't seem too interested in a brief friendship with a greedy bird. He preferred to jump off the albatross's back and go sailing over the sea towards October.

30 September

A Hard Living

Little Ernie loved to read detective stories, but do you suppose he wanted to be a detective? Not a chance! He had decided to become a robber. There was nothing else in the world that attracted him. As soon as he grew up, he pulled a stocking down over his face, shoved a pistol (a cap-pistol) in his pocket, and went out to rob a bank. 'H-H-Hands up!' he stuttered to the bank clerk pointing his pistol at him, but at that moment the alarm began to ring. Before

Ernie knew what was going on the police had arrested him, and he went to gaol for attempted armed robbery. 'Fair enough,' he thought, 'bank robbery is a bit too much to try for starters. I'll have to begin more modestly.' So when they let him out, he broke the window of a delicatessen and shoved everything he could lay his hands on in a big sack. But they caught him as he was crawling out of the window again, and he soon found himself behind bars for a second time. The day they let him out, he found an empty house and broke in. But on the way out he met a gang of burglars, who took everything off him and gave him a good thrashing for muscling in on their territory. All the same, the detectives found his fingerprints in the house, and he was off to prison again. And so it went on, except that the sentences were getting bigger and bigger. In the end, Ernie realized that there were better careers around than a life of crime, and he got a job feeding the polar bears in the local zoo. Sometimes he tells them about the things that happened to him while he was still a criminal.

October

1 October

Mousey-Mousey

The wind elf had never lent anyone his cloak before. But on the day of his October birthday he did, and I'll tell you why at once. He flew back to the old attic where he had been born, under the eaves. Everything was the same as ever under the old beams, except that the butterfly which used to flutter there was gone, and there were more mice around. Granny Mouse, who had lived there for many years, was tying on her apron to stir a pot of gruel. She was looking after ten little grandchildren, who were each as small and pink as a baby's little finger, but wouldn't stay still for a minute. 'Whatever am I going to do with you all till Mummy and Daddy get back from work?' she was saying. 'My back hurts, I can't get the stove to draw properly, and you lot keep squeaking away fit to set my ears singing!' The wind elf saw and heard everything and immediately offered to keep the children busy. 'Where are your toys?' squeaked the little mice, and the wind elf didn't know what to say. But then he shook all sorts of berries he had collected out of his pockets, and they rolled about the attic floor like little coloured balls. After that he spread his wind cloak out so that the baby mice could slide down a rafter on it like on a slide. Granny Mouse could have a rest at last. So you can celebrate your birthday by making others happy, as well as the other way round!

2 October

How the Wind Elf Almost Lost His Cloak

The children were flying their kites down in the ploughed field, and little Lucy only had a kite made of leaves, the sort that flies just above the ground, and that you have to run around with to make it fly at all. The boys kept laughing at her, and they didn't like the way she was interfering in their kite contest, a little girl like that. But all of a sudden the wind elf appeared, and caught hold of one of the crisp leaves. Then he carried the humble kite high up above the others. But the sky traveller got dizzy. He had never been so high up before, and suddenly he tumbled down, right into the middle of a thorn bush. His frail cloak got torn, and the wind elf, though he hadn't hurt himself, suddenly felt like crying. However was he going to fly again? He could no more float on the breeze in a leaky wind cloak than a ship can cross the seas with a torn sail. Little Lucy took the unhappy elf in her hand and said, 'It was my fault. I wish I hadn't won the silly contest now. How am I going to help you? I don't even know how to sew patches.' And *she* started to cry. But as her tears fell into the carpet of needles beneath a spruce tree, she had an idea. She could use the needles to fasten a couple of the leaves from her kite onto the wind elf's cloak, and cover up the holes that way. As soon as she had done it, the sky traveller was on his way again.

3 October

Notnow and Waitawhile

Lydia was a little girl who always had all the time in the world. Whenever her mother asked her to help with something, or her father wanted her to do her homework, she always said the same thing: 'Not now, wait a while!' And then she would forget all about whatever it was she was going to do. Lydia's mummy and daddy couldn't put up with any more of this always putting things off, and so they asked around everywhere trying to find out how to cure it, but no one could tell them what to do. One day her mother was so upset that she shouted: 'Your "not now" and "wait a while" go flying round and round the house like a couple of ugly moths!' As soon as she had finished saying this, two little pairs of wings began flapping over her head. The grey ones belonged to Notnow and the brown ones to Waitawhile. Lydia laughed because she thought it was going to be great fun with this pair of moths, but she soon changed her mind. When she wanted to sit in the rocking-chair, Notnow got there first. Waitawhile stopped her from opening the refrigerator, and from taking a bite of chocolate. Then he wouldn't let her turn the television on. In the end she couldn't even read a book of fairy tales, take her toys out of the cupboard, or eat dessert. Notnow and Waitawhile spread their wings everywhere. The only thing they avoided was Lydia's school satchel, so all she could do was learn her lessons from morning till night.

Notnow and Waitawhile

Daddy just shrugged his shoulders, and was glad that Lydia was going to learn something at last. He secretly fed the two moths, to try and persuade them to stay around as long as possible. But Mummy was worried. 'You can do too much of anything,' she sighed, 'even homework. Lydia's getting pale and sickly. Before you know it she'll start getting poorly, and then what?' Lydia was just reading aloud the chapter of her natural history book that described how butterflies go through part of their lives in a cocoon. Mummy suddenly began to pay attention. 'What if we were to persuade the moths to make themselves some sleeping bags, and take a rest?' she asked. 'But Mummy,' Lydia corrected her in a learned sort of way, 'it's butterfly *larvae* that spin cocoons, not butterflies. That's like saying that a mummy had a granddad instead of

a baby, and that he got younger and younger until he was a child.' Notnow and Waitawhile heard this, and it sounded like a good idea. 'Why not get younger?' they said. They agreed to be wrapped up in cocoons, which Mummy quickly knitted from the finest thread she could find. And since Lydia had got used to having them flying around the house, she got herself a butterfly. It was called Straightaway.

5 October

The Innkeeper and the Magic Money

Fandangle the magician had lived in the solitude of his mountain home all his life, just conjuring up whatever he fancied, or whatever he happened to need. But one day he decided he would go out into the world. He had probably had enough of living on his own. Fandangle arrived in town, and since he was hungry after his long journey, he went into an inn to have something to eat. The magician had a liking for peas and beans, so he ordered bean soup and lentils with egg. After lunch the innkeeper brought him his bill. 'What's that?' asked Fandangle, who, though he knew practically all there was to know about charms and spells, had no experience of everyday life. 'That,' said the innkeeper, just a little sourly, 'is your bill.' 'What do I do with it?' asked the wizard, mildly. The innkeeper felt like suggesting something you wouldn't usually do with a bill at all, but, remembering that the customer is always right, he explained, 'The number at the bottom tells you how much you have to pay.' 'Ah!' said the magician. Then he muttered a couple of words and a crisp new banknote appeared

between his fingers. The innkeeper rubbed his thumbs over the note, and then held it up to the light. His face darkened. 'You don't think you can catch an old hand like me out with a forgery like that, do you?' he scowled. Fandangle was so taken aback that he couldn't think of a clever way to get him out of the mess he was in. He just looked nervously up at the innkeeper's huge bulk, and thought, 'He looks ready to throttle me!'

6 October

The Innkeeper and the Magic Money

Just then the magician noticed a pack of cards lying on the bar. 'What if we were to play for the cost of my lunch?' he suggested. 'Why not?' grinned the innkeeper, who was a very good poker player, and had never been known to lose to a customer. A couple of other cardsters

drew up their chairs. One of them shuffled and the other one dealt. 'But mind you,' warned the innkeeper, 'if you haven't got enough money, you'll have to work it off in the kitchens!' 'I trust that won't be necessary,' the old wizard said with a smile. He already had both his sleeves full of aces. Well, to cut a long story short, Fandangle won all the money the innkeeper and his other companions had within a couple of hours. He could have ordered the finest foods on golden dishes, if he'd felt like it. But for supper he asked for lentil soup and beans in white sauce. Then he played cards again. He sat there in that inn for a whole week, and took the last halfpenny off anyone who cared to play with him. He was finding it difficult to get anyone to sit down with him by then, and even the innkeeper had given up when he lost his inn. Fandangle would probably be sitting there to this day, if the innkeeper hadn't lost his temper. He picked the magician up out of his chair and gave him a good shaking. Fandangle's spare aces fell out of his sleeves, and he had to make a quick exit. The wizard returned to his lonely home, and because he didn't have anyone to play with there, he had to take up Patience.

7 October

Angie and Her Shoes

Angie could never walk past a shoe shop without stepping inside. And once inside she would always buy a pair of shoes, or a pair

of boots, or sometimes two pairs, and even occasionally five pairs. At home, she had cupboards full of high heels, low heels, ankle boots, calf boots, moccasins and flip-flops. She couldn't have worn them all out even if she hadn't bought another shoe for the rest of her life. There were shoe boxes everywhere, under the settee, in the larder, in the hall, in the bath, and even in the washing machine. But Angie would always find another pair that she just had to have. One day, her shoes organized a revolt. 'We want to walk. We want to be worn. We don't want to lie around doing nothing any more!' But Angie didn't hear them. She wouldn't have understood what they were saying, even if she had. The shoes whispered to each other all evening. The next morning they crawled out of their boxes, jumped down from their shelves, and set off ten abreast after their owner. When the lights were green they crossed the street behind her. Then they all squeezed into the bus she was taking, and when she got off they continued to follow her in tight ranks. ''Ere, 'ere, my girl,' said a policeman, stopping her, ''ave you got a permit for a shoe parade?' 'They're not mine,' lied Angie. But the moment the shoes heard this they ran off in all directions and found themselves new owners right there in the street. Angie was left with the pair she was standing in.

8 October

The Clever Minister

King Pewniwitt sank down onto his throne and frowned like thunder. Then he confirmed three death sentences, sacked the royal treasurer, and gave the Minister for Special Affairs a good telling-off. The minister was the only one who knew why the king was on the rampage. That morning Her Majesty his wife had told him he was weak and indecisive. The king had to put up with a lot from the queen, and he used to take it out on his subjects. The next morning

the minister overheard the royal missus yelling at the king that idiots such as him were hard enough to come by, and why had she been unlucky enough to get stuck with one. That did it. The minister decided it was his patriotic duty, and the best way to keep body and head together, to get the queen out of the way for a time. 'Your Majesty,' he said to her, 'I hear it is all the rage for monarchs' wives to travel the world.' The queen, who hated any suggestion that she was behind the times, snapped back at him, 'Of course I know that you fool! Don't you know my bags are packed?' He didn't believe her of course, but he was quietly confident that they soon would be. 'I shall

write to Pewniwitt every day,' the queen declared, 'just so's he doesn't forget who the real boss is.' So the minister opened all her letters, which were full of threats and angry attacks, and rewrote them full of loving phrases before handing them over to Pewniwitt. The king was amazed at the change that travelling had brought about in his wife. He was fair and kind, and the whole kingdom flourished. The minister rubbed his hands with glee.

9 October

The Clever Minister

All good things must come to an end, and one day the queen returned from her travels. Pewniwitt was amazed at how quickly she changed again, and he passed his annoyance on to the rest of the nation. 'We shall have to think of something,' thought the Minister for Special Affairs. And fortune sent the chance his way. A new lady-in-waiting, the beautiful Hortensia, arrived at court. When she was presented to the king, he only mumbled something irritably, but a plan was taking shape in the minister's head. 'Did you notice the new lady-in-waiting?' he asked the queen, in a meaningful sort of way. 'What of her?' The queen could tell that the minister wasn't just making conversation. 'Nothing,' said the minister, carelessly. 'Just that the king seemed to take a lot of notice of her. Well it's not really so surprising. It's a good thing you're not the jealous type, eh?' 'Too right, I'm not!' thought the queen, but when she had thought it for about the tenth time, she was about as jealous as it's possible to be. 'It's my fault!' she said to herself. 'I never have a kind word to say to him. No wonder he looks elsewhere for kindness.' 'Pewniwitt!' she called. 'Where are you, my pearl? Come and give me a big kiss.' From then on the king was in clover, for his wife was sweetness itself, but he never could understand why she had insisted that a certain lady-in-waiting be dismissed.

10 October

The Mist Maiden

Eliza was as pretty as a picture, and kind and hard-working as well. No wonder Bernard, a rich landlord's coachman, fell in love with her. Whenever he drove past the cottage where Eliza lived, his fine team of horses would neigh out a greeting as Bernard had taught them to do. And Eliza? Her heart belonged to Bernard. They both looked forward to the day they would be married. But the ways of the world are cruel, and one day two kings decided to have a war. Bernard was forced to join the army and march off to battle. 'Come back to me!' cried Eliza, in tears. 'Of course I will!' Bernard promised. But he never did, for he fell dead in the very first charge. A friend of his who had lost a leg in the war came home to tell Eliza the sorrowful news. 'I don't believe it!' said Eliza, stubbornly. 'He promised me he'd come back!' So she decided to go and look for him. Her parents and friends tried to dissuade her. 'How can a frail young girl go wandering about the battlefields, which are savage enough places for men?' they asked. 'I'll manage somehow,' said Eliza, firmly, and she began to get ready for her journey. Her friends tried to stop her, but that was a waste of time. She grew paler and paler, until she finally turned into a milky-white cloud that floated off towards the battlefields and then disappeared from view. Since then the Mist Maiden has wandered the world, and if you listen very, very carefully, you can hear her calling, 'Bernie, where are you?'

11 October

The Stork and the Crow

Late one evening a stork flew in the Larkins' open window, carrying a bundle in its beak. It laid the bundle carefully in the cradle that was waiting there, and when it was unwrapped there was a baby inside,

a fine, healthy young lad. But at that moment a crow came flying in through the window, and made straight for the cradle. It was carrying a bundle as well, this time with a chubby-cheeked baby girl inside. 'I have a feeling you've got the wrong house, my dear colleague,' said the stork. 'I never make a mistake!' snapped the crow. 'Mrs. Larkin sent me a telegram asking for a raven-haired little Mabel.' 'That's very interesting,' replied the stork, 'since I got an express letter from Mr. Larkin ordering a blond-haired little Godfrey. It looks like they couldn't agree, and now they're sure to argue about it. What are we going to do?' 'It's no business of ours,' said the crow, pointing its beak in the air. 'I don't know about you, but I don't intend to get mixed up in any family quarrels!' 'I've got lots of better things to do myself,' said the stork, and the pair of them flew off out of the window. As if they had been waiting for this, the two infants began to howl. The Larkins were both beside the cradle in a couple of seconds. 'What a lovely little Mabel!' cried Mr. Larkin, and Mrs. Larkin looked at the baby boy with pride. 'And isn't Godfrey lovely?' she said.

12 October

The Cat and the Mouse

One morning the tomcat caught a mouse in front of the larder door. As he held her in his huge paws, the mouse said, 'Can't you even let me eat my breakfast before you devour me?' 'The important thing,' said the tomcat, showing his teeth, 'is that *I* get *my* breakfast.' 'Can't you see how pretty I am?' tried the mouse. 'Isn't it a pity to destroy such a fine specimen?' The cat looked his prey up and down, and it *did* seem to him that the creature was exceptionally good-looking. The mouse pretended she liked the tomcat, too. 'What a pity we are not both the same size,' she said with cunning. 'How well we should get on together.' She went on to tell the cat how it might be arranged. From then on the mouse lounged on a cushion in the back room, and the tomcat went back and forth with all manner of good things for his little friend to eat. The cat, though, got thinner all the time. He was on a diet, so that he would grow smaller. When the tomcat finally fell ill from lack of food, the mouse had to go hunting herself. But she had grown so fat that she got stuck in the crack below the larder door. The housewife found her there, and put her in a cage. When the cat was a little better, he came to have a look at the prisoner. 'Pussy, you *will* let me out, won't you?' begged the mouse. 'Think yourself lucky you're locked in a cage,' grumped the cat. 'You're so fat and I'm so thin. I would be sure to gobble you up if you were free!'

13 October

Nearly the End of the Tale of a Cupboard

In a mysterious room in a mysterious house, there once stood a mysterious cupboard. It was positively the only thing in the room. There were no chairs and no tables, not even a settee. And no one lived in the house. It was empty, except for that one mysterious cupboard. What do you suppose was in that cupboard? That was just what a certain robber was anxious to find out. He put on his mask so that no one would recognize him, took with him his skeleton keys and his torch, and made for the mysterious house one night. How surprised he was to find that the house wasn't even locked and nor was the room, nor the cupboard. He opened all the doors and pulled out all the drawers, but couldn't find anything at all. But anyone who wants to know any more will have to wait until 13 November.

14 October

The Lord of the Clocks

Father Time was rushed off his feet. Ever since people had invented pocket watches and wristwatches and tower clocks and corner clocks and calendar clocks, he had had to make sure that they all knew just what the time was in hours, minutes and seconds. And that is no easy job, I can tell you. Father Time only has to leave them alone for a moment, and they get mixed up between summer time and winter time. If he stops paying attention for just an instant, some clock or other somewhere is sure to forget to move one of its hands. In the old days, when they had hourglasses, things were a good deal easier. Father Time just turned them over once in a while, and the sand trickled happily down through its little

hole. And before there were any clocks at all, Father Time could laze about for days on end, and no one minded. But the older he got, the more people were in a hurry, and that made them irritable, and they'd always be looking at their wrists. Father Time could hardly keep up with it all. One day he was comparing the times in some school races, when a girl in a coloured vest and running shoes came up to him. 'What a nice old man you are,' she said to him. 'Is it true that you are the lord of all the clocks?' He nodded, and asked her not to interrupt him, but he was pleased that she thought him a nice old man. 'I was first, wasn't I?' the girl said, giving the time lord a broad smile, and she added, 'I like you ever so much. You look terribly young for your age.'

15 October

The Lord of the Clocks

Father Time puffed out his chest, trying to look even younger, but he shook his head. 'I make you fourth, Miss . . .' he started to say. 'Denise,' said the girl. 'My name is Denise.' And she stroked his beard. 'But you must have made a mistake somewhere, 'cos I *know* for certain I was first. And if you were to put that mistake of yours right, I should give you a big kiss.' 'What is it you want me to do?' asked Father Time. 'Just tell the timekeepers that I won, and that they timed it all wrong.' Father Time would have liked to get a kiss from Denise, but he was an honest sort of fellow, and he didn't want to deceive the timekeepers. So he began explaining at great length that it wasn't fair for Denise to jump the queue like that. 'But you don't understand, Grandad,' protested Denise, 'I don't want to win the queue jump, only the four hundred metres. And I *might* make it two kisses.' Father Time forgot all about time and kept talking away with Denise, and Denise kept talking away with him, and upping the number of kisses she was

offering. And when Time forgets about time, everything stands still, not just the clocks.

16 October

The Lord of the Clocks

To say that everything stopped while Father Time and Denise talked wouldn't be quite true. What actually happened was that everyone went on endlessly doing whatever it was he happened to be doing at the time. The referee in the football match, who had just been blowing his whistle for a goal, kept on blowing it again and again, until in a while the score was 99—0, and went on rising. The competitors who were running a hurdles race kept going round and round, and became the first sportsmen in history to run the marathon over hurdles. A customer in a restaurant who had been eating goose got one fresh portion after another until he burst. The radio broadcast a programme on fossils for hours on end, until the listeners almost fossilized themselves. But Denise had only got up to ten kisses for winning the four hundred metres by that time. Father Time was beginning to waver a little, but then he took a look around, and saw the marathon hurdlers with their tongues hanging out, the whistling referee, the burst goose-eater, and all the other things he had caused to happen. He quickly confirmed with the timekeepers that Denise had really been fourth, and dashed off to catch up with

But the worst thing of all is when a name gets too popular, so that there are five Dianas or half a dozen Jimmies all in the same class. How can one tell them apart? So then they change their names to Curly, Rusty, Carrots or Titch. But there was once a certain town where things had got so out of hand that not even the town itself had a name it could really call its own. Some folk called it Ashford and some called it Ashworth, but there were those who called it Appleby, and a few who called it Appleton . . . But I'd better explain how it all came about. Many years ago, Yagga the

everything else. The lecture on the radio finished half way through a sentence, the soccer match finished at 666—0, the burst eater was taken to hospital and sewn up, and all in all everything got back to normal. But Father Time didn't get his kiss from Denise. Luckily, he didn't hear her calling after him what a nasty old man she thought he was. If he had, he might have stopped his pendulum in mid-swing again.

17 October

What's in a Name?

Names can be troublesome things at times. Everyone knows that poor Mr. Savage is probably the meekest, mildest fellow in town, that Charlie Little is six-foot-two, and that there is always some poor fishmonger around called Pike or Roach. Not even christian names always suit their owners, so they try to change them any way they can. If one didn't know, would one ever guess that Jack was really John, or Peggy was really Margaret, or that Polly was Mary?

Hag moved into the town and opened a shop selling names. All the inhabitants bought themselves new names, not one each, but two, three and four at a time. So, for instance, the cleverest girl in the first form was called Eleanor Elizabeth Margaret Mary Perkins-Dorkins-Fanshawe. You can imagine the time it took the teacher to write all the names in the register!

18 October

What's in a Name?

By and by there was so much work to do at the town hall with all those new names around that they had to employ extra people. Then they started to run out of paper. All the postmen handed in their notice. They couldn't find people's addresses any more, because rich people kept buying new names for their streets. Everyone competed to see who could change the name of his or her street the most times. The schoolteachers nearly went mad because they couldn't remember what any of their pupils were called that week. Whenever one of the children was in trouble he would say that he wasn't called that any more, and that his father had bought him a new name the day before. Everyone would probably have ended up in the mental hospital if the whole thing hadn't come to an end when Yagga the Hag suddenly moved out of town again, and her shop closed down. She swallowed all the names that were still in stock when she went, so that no one else could sell them. Slowly the townspeople got back to normal again. There was just one special custom that they kept, which was that they always give names to the things they own. So

maybe a washing-machine gets called Mabel, a car Albert, or a carpet William. Shoes get called things like Peter and Paul. But no one minds that, do they?

19 October

The Lowly Bridegroom

There was once a certain kingdom where the bakers were so famous that even the capital was called Rolltown. In it lived a certain baker's apprentice called Philip. He was born on the very same day as a princess at the royal palace, and an old woman who was passing by at the time foretold that the two of them would be married as soon as they were twenty years old. 'Never!' the king had shouted when he heard of the prophecy, and when the fateful day arrived, and both the youngsters were

twenty, he yelled angrily, 'My daughter marry a dusty baker's lad? I should rather marry her to Beelzebub, king of the devils!' The whole castle began to shake at the foundations, and in at one of the windows flew a real live devil, a servant of the Prince of Darkness himself. He announced that he had come to collect his master's bride, since the king had proclaimed before witnesses that it was to be so. There seemed to be no way out of it. As soon as the princess found out what was going on she whispered to one of her chambermaids to run and fetch Philip at once. She was in love with him, and they had been meeting in secret for ages. She believed in the prophecy, and didn't mind a bit that Philip was only a baker's apprentice.

20 October

The Lowly Bridegroom

Before the king could think of some excuse to make to the devil's messenger, Philip had arrived at the palace. The king was quite helpless, but not the young baker. 'Tell Beelzebub,' he said, 'that the wedding will be held, but on one condition. It is the custom in this kingdom that before the wedding the bridegroom must eat a dry bread roll because our capital city is called Rolltown, and otherwise the wedding cannot be held.' The devil gave a cackling laugh and disappeared. Back in hell the rest of the devils thought the terms of the agreement were a great joke. True, devils

are not terribly keen on foods made with flour, but to eat a single roll was no problem at all. Meanwhile in his castle the king was moaning and groaning about how the young baker had interfered in the royal family's affairs, but he never thought of locking Philip up, which was a good thing. Otherwise the young man wouldn't have been able to bake the devil's wedding roll. He mixed a mountain of dough that took three whole days to rise, and when it was kneaded into a roll it reached from the castle gates to the frontier with Bombastia. On the day of the wedding Beelzebub arrived dressed in the finest of clothes and full of good humour, but the moment he spotted his breakfast, he put his tail between his legs and set off back home without a bride. To be on the safe side the king married his daughter to Philip, and ever since then they have baked bigger rolls in that country than anywhere else in the world.

21 October

The Envious Hare

In a certain field there were two cabbages growing side by side. They had been planted there by the hares Bigear and Littletail, and they were looking forward to having a great feast with all their friends when autumn came. So the pair of them competed with each other at watering the cabbages and turning over the soil. They even drove away the butterflies, to make quite sure their caterpillars didn't eat the cabbages before they were fully grown. At last the day arrived when they were to pull the cabbages up, divide them into portions, and eat them. But Bigear said, 'We should wait another week, because my cabbage is smaller than yours. But in a day or two mine will not only catch yours up, but will be bigger!' The other hares all teased Bigear

about it, saying that both the cabbages were already the size of houses, and what was he waiting for. 'He wants to hold a party inside it!' they laughed. Bigear should have been well satisfied with his crop, but he was a stubborn fellow. He sat in front of his cabbage and refused to budge. Meanwhile Littletail prepared his feast and the other hares had a fine old time. Only Bigear didn't join them, because he was too busy watching his own cabbage. He sat there day after day, and didn't even notice that the cabbage had grown overripe before becoming wrinkled and brown. In the end it was quite dry and totally unfit to eat. And unless that envious hare has come to his senses, he's sitting in that field to this day.

22 October

The Story of an Orchestra

Once upon a time there was an orchestra. The musicians played their instruments beautifully, and kept time with the conductor's baton, so that the audience always clapped like anything to show how much they had enjoyed it. 'They were really applauding me, of course,' said the piano proudly after one performance. 'I was the one with the main part, while the rest of you were just accompanying me.' 'Rubbish!'

piped the flute. 'If it weren't for me that sonata wouldn't make sense at all.' 'You are both wrong,' said the violin, screeching a string. 'It is clear that the applause was ...' 'Mine!' blurted out the trumpet, the trombone, the clarinet, the cello, the bassoon, the drum, the bass and all the other instruments. They argued about it all night, and when the morning rehearsals came along they were all quite out of tune. It certainly sounded like that as well. 'Pull yourselves together a little!' the conductor told the musicians, thinking they were tired. 'Now take a rest and make sure you get it together this evening, so that we don't make complete fools of ourselves!' The musicians hung their heads in shame, even though they were not to blame. 'We'll put it right this evening!' they promised.

23 October

The Story of an Orchestra

The auditorium was filled with people in their Sunday best. They were all looking forward to the concert, and the musicians climbed onto the stage determined to play as they had never played before. And that was just how it turned out, although not quite in the way they had planned it. The instruments decided they would show each other once and for all which of them deserved the most applause. So from the very first beat they paid no attention at all to the composition and to keeping together, but each of them went solo. The trumpet blared to try and drown the bass and the violin did its best to shout the flute down. Each instrument played the way it wanted, and the result was the most awful noise. It sounded like dogs howling, cats wailing and an earthquake taking place, all at the same time. Try as they might, the musicians couldn't keep their instruments under control. The conductor was so upset by the

pandemonium that he snapped his baton in half. The audience began to whistle in derision. To make matters worse, the notes jumped down from in between their lines and trooped off to the cloakroom in shame. Then the instruments began to calm down when they finally realized what they were doing. For a moment there was silence. The musicians gazed at the audience, while the audience stared at the stage. Then the violin came to its senses, and asked the bow to play the theme. The other instruments followed its lead. When they were given their final applause (louder than they had ever had before), they completely forgot to worry about who it was for.

24 October

How Jimmie Went Looking for the End of the World

The neighbours always said that Jimmie wasted his time on silly things. His house was in poor repair, his garden full of weeds, but he had a telescope sticking out of an attic window with which he observed the stars. There was more corncockle, the purple flower, in his field than there was corn, but Jimmie spent his time wondering if there was an end to the world somewhere. He worried about the whole thing so much that in the end he decided to go and find it. He wandered the world for a long time. He asked people, and they shook their heads sadly and winked at each other. He looked from hilltops down into valleys, and from valley floors up at hilltops, but he could find the end of the world nowhere. 'Perhaps there really isn't one,' he began to think. 'Of course there is,' said the journeyman who was travelling with him. 'If you don't believe it, then I will take you there.' Jimmie became really excited, imagining that he was going to see the end of the world with his own eyes, and he promised the journeyman thirty silver pieces if what he said turned out to be true. So they walked, and walked,

walked along with his eyes and ears wide open. In the forest he spotted a couple of learned fellows with green jackets and jay's feathers in their hats. One said to the other in a learned sort of way, 'There haven't been as many cones seeded in years!' On the road near a town there were two wise men leaning over the engine of a car, and one said to the other, 'I reckon your battery's flat.' Then he passed a pair of sages who were walking along a ploughed field in their wellingtons, and one of them nodded his head in a knowing fashion and said, 'If we use more manure from the cowsheds we're sure to get a better crop.' Jimmie wrote all this down, and learned these three pieces of wisdom off by heart. Then he hurried on home to show Jenny what an educated fellow he had become.

past forest and lake, through meadow and ploughed field, along highway and byway, until they reached a ravine, on the opposite side of which stood a neat-looking building. It was a tavern, and the sign on the roof said: 'The End of the World'. The journeyman got his silver pieces, and Jimmie was proud at having indeed found the end of the world at last.

25 October

How Jimmie Went Looking for the End of the World

When he had seen the end of the world, Jimmie decided to return home. So as not to idle away his time on the return journey, he decided to educate himself. Whenever he came across any wise or learned man, he would write down what the fellow said and then put it to good use at the first opportunity. When Jenny, back in the village, heard him speak she surely wouldn't think he was still foolish, and she might even consent to marry him. So Jimmie

26 October

How Jimmie Went Looking for the End of the World

Jimmie didn't waste any time in going to ask Jenny to marry him. 'I thought of you even at the end of the world,' he told her. Jenny liked that of course, even if she didn't really believe there was an end of the world. 'Maybe Jimmie has changed on his travels,' she thought. So she said to him, 'I cried as

27 October

The Gorilla from the Zoo

In a certain zoo, apart from an elephant, a crocodile, a rhinoceros and a lot of other animals, they had a gorilla. He looked terrifying, and everyone was afraid of him. The gorilla didn't make friends with anyone and he didn't tell anyone his name was Pete. One day little Josephine stopped in front of his cage with her mummy, and she didn't want to leave. 'Come on dear,' Mummy told her, 'we've still got to see the baboons, and the kangeroos, *and* the giraffes.' But Josephine shook her head. 'The gorilla's the nicest,' she said. 'I'd like to play with him!' Pete the gorilla heard this, and his heart went out to the little girl. The next morning

well when you went away without saying goodbye.' 'Now's my chance to show my bride-to-be how clever I have become,' thought Jimmie. 'There haven't been as many cones seeded in years!' he said. Jenny didn't know what he was talking about, but just so he wouldn't get the idea that she was crazy about him she added, 'But then I got used to your being away.' And Jimmie replied, 'I reckon your battery's flat.' 'He must have gone off his rocker, out there in the world,' thought Jenny. For safety's sake she asked him, 'Do you think we shall get on well together?' To which Jimmie proudly replied, 'If we use more manure from the cowsheds we're sure to get a better crop.' That was a little bit too much for his loved one. She grabbed a broom and gave him a sound beating with it, shouting, 'I'll give you cones, I'll give you batteries, I'll give you manure!' This made Jimmie forget all his newly-acquired wisdom, and he began to speak as he always had. After that Jenny married him. During the day he works, so as not to have weeds in the garden and corncockle in the field, but at night they both go up to the attic to watch the stars through his telescope. Well, why not, if Jenny likes it?

the keeper discovered the gorilla was gone. It had simply forced open the door of his cage, climbed over the zoo wall, and gone off to town. The alarm went up at once. The firemen turned out with their ladders, the policemen with their truncheons, troops of soldiers with tanks, and a small army of doctors and vets, all looking for the gorilla.

Loudspeaker-vans toured the streets playing loud music and announcing that everyone was to stay well out of the way of the fierce gorilla, and to report to the nearest police station the moment he was seen. Faint-hearted girls swooned on the spot, and amateur big-game hunters climbed into attics and onto roofs with loaded air-rifles. But there was no sign of the gorilla. It was as if he had vanished into thin air.

28 October

The Gorilla from the Zoo

For five, six, then seven hours they searched for the gorilla, but he was nowhere to be found. Then one general had the bright idea of sending for Al the Alsatian, who had always sniffed out anything they were looking for. Al took one sniff at the gorilla's cage, barked for a while, and then raced off. After him ran a regiment of soldiers, a platoon of policemen, and a unit of firemen, who lost their ladders on the way. Al followed the scent until he arrived at a block of flats. When his handler opened the door the dog leapt up the stairs to the fourth floor, and the rest of the pursuers, including the doctors and vets, all chased up

the stairs after him. The dog handler nervously rang the bell of the door that Al had stopped at. The policemen gripped their truncheons tight. But the door was opened by Josephine, her finger on her lips. 'Do be quiet,' she whispered, 'I've just sent him to sleep with a story.' 'Who?' breathed the four hundred and seventy-five policemen, soldiers and firemen who were squeezed together on the staircase. 'Why, Pete, silly!' Josephine explained. They woke the gorilla up of course. And he went quietly back to the zoo with them, once Josephine had promised to go and see him every day.

29 October

How Hatty Swapped and Swapped

Hatty's auntie knitted her a scarf and sent it to her, saying she should come and see her in it. 'Why not?' said Hatty, and she put the scarf around her head and set off for the next village to visit her aunt. On the way she met a stray cat that was shivering with cold. 'Give me your scarf to keep me warm,' he begged her, 'and I will give you my ribbon.' Hatty agreed, but she had scarcely tied up the ribbon when she met a mongrel dog. He had a hemp cord around his neck instead of a collar. 'If I were to have such a fine ribbon,' he whimpered, 'I should not look quite so ugly.' Hatty gave the dog the ribbon without any fuss, and got the hemp cord in exchange. She hadn't even decided what she was going to do with that before a little bird fluttered over her head and told her the cord was just what she needed to mend her nest with. All she had to do was pull it to pieces. 'Take it, then,' Hatty told the bird, and in return she got a soft feather. She stuck it in her pigtail, but soon a spider asked her for it. She wanted it for a bed. Hatty was happy to give her the feather, but then she thought, 'Whatever is Auntie going to say when I turn up without my present

Afghan gave him a sympathetic smile. 'I never eat anything made of flour, because I want to stay slim. Only meat and vegetables! Does that satisfy you?' It did, and so the doughnut was happy to agree, and he hid in the cabin of the dog's mistress for the rest of the voyage. In the evenings he would tell his new friend all about his adventures. The Afghan hound was glad that he could live through some of the excitement in the doughnut's stories at least, since he led such a quiet life. As soon as the ship docked, the hound took the doughnut ashore and showed him the way to the station. There he took an express train to November and a bit nearer home.

from her?' 'Don't worry,' said the spider, 'since you've been so kind, I will weave you a spider's web scarf that's just as nice. Your auntie won't even notice. And even if she does, I'm sure she'll understand why you made so many swaps.'

30 October

The Doughnut Aboard Ship

Do you still remember the doughnut from September? Well, he was lucky yet again. When he jumped off the back of the albatross he didn't smash himself to pieces on a rock, or drown in the sea. Instead he found himself smack on top of a whale's spout, bobbing around like a ping-pong ball. 'Whatever are you up to?' snorted the whale, and before the doughnut could answer he sent him flying up in the air in a powerful spurt of water, straight onto the deck of a passing ship. The doughnut made quite a soft landing, right next to an Afghan hound that was guarding a lady in a deck-chair. 'Well I never,' said the dog. 'If it isn't a stowaway! I'd better hide you quick, before one of the crew finds out you haven't got a ticket.' 'Are you sure you won't eat me?' asked the doughnut, nervously. The

31 October

Hilda

Hilda was the name of one young lady who wasn't altogether bright. To make matters worse she was rather greedy as well. One day her auntie invited Hilda into her

cottage and said, 'I've got a wedding dress for you, and I'm going to give you one extra thing as well. I've put something in two chests and you must choose which one to have. The first chest contains a gift made of feathers, the second one made of metal. One is valuable, and the other is not. Both of them weigh the same. Think over carefully which of them you want.' It didn't take Hilda long to decide. She reasoned that metal was more precious than feathers, and heavier as well. Without hesitation she tapped the second chest. Her aunt lifted both the lids. In one chest there was a soft eiderdown which would made any bride happy, and in the other an old, leaky saucepan. Hilda realized how hasty she had been and from then on she was a little more sensible. When she got married her auntie gave her the eiderdown anyway.

November

and blobs, and squiggles, was finally laid on the table in the decorated dining-hall, the king, who had woken up by now, ordered all the lights to be lit. Up on the chandelier the sky traveller tossed and turned in his sleep. He dreamed that all the celebrations were in honour of him. Then he woke up blinded by the glare of the lights, yawned, stretched himself and, plonk! He fell straight into the cream-covered cake. 'What was that?' asked the king, with a start. It occurred to him that the royal family was threatened by some danger, so he ordered the cake to be sliced up, crumbled to pieces, and examined. Luckily the wind elf managed to crawl out of the sea of cream in time. He washed his cloak in orangeade, and out of the window he flew. It was almost evening again when he noticed his head was all white, like cream. And from then on it stayed that way.

2 November

How Stephen Got to Know the World

On the very top floor of a tower block, sitting on the balcony in an armchair, carefully wrapped in blankets, was a pale young lad called Stephen. He would dearly have liked something exciting to happen, because all he could do was look down at the street below through the gap in the parapet, or stare at the four walls of his room. True, he had read a lot of books, and he was always turning the radio on to play some merry music, but sometimes a terrible sadness came over him. He was so poorly he couldn't even go out for a walk. So he was as pleased as Punch when a strange little figure with white hair and a black cloak came flying along. He smelt of orange juice. The sky traveller wanted to bid Stephen good day, but instead he sneezed. He must have caught a chill in the fairytale kingdom he had visited the night before.

1 November

How the Wind Elf Went Grey

It was the wind elf's November birthday, and he flew in through the dining-hall window of a certain royal castle. There he settled on the crystal chandelier that hung over the table and, since he had been travelling all night, soon fell fast asleep. The king and queen and the young prince were also asleep up in their bed-chambers, but the servants had been up and about since before dawn. The busiest place of all was the kitchen where they were making a cake the size of a cartwheel to celebrate the prince's birthday. It took several tubs of cream to decorate it, and when this sweet marvel covered with snow-white towers,

'Shhh!' said Stephen, offering him a handkerchief. 'My mother's scared of colds like the Snow Queen's scared of fire. She'd send you away at once.' Just to make sure, he shoved the wind elf in his pocket. Just in time, for in a minute or two his mother came to take him inside. 'It's lovely here!' gasped the wind elf, when he had crawled out and taken a look around him. 'Oh no it isn't!' came the boy's voice from above him. 'You wouldn't think so if you were shut up here all the time!'

3 November

How Stephen Got to Know the World

The wind elf felt quite down-in-the-dumps, because he wanted to think up a lovely

game for Stephen to play and he just couldn't come up with an idea. So he flew off to see what the other children were doing, but he couldn't find any of them at home. But on the stairs he found a postage stamp, which must have fallen off a letter. Without any hesitation he picked it up and took it to Stephen. They laid the little picture with its zig-zag frame in front of them. It showed a beautiful island with strange animals on it. Some mountains rose up in the background. 'Do you know what?' asked the wind elf and then continued, 'We'll set off on our travels, and maybe we'll have some great adventures.' And they did. Their expedition was exciting, especially when they drew a map of the island. As soon as they had travelled across one continent, they wanted to go to another one. So Stephen started to collect stamps. He visited many countries, picture galleries, sports grounds, saw exotic plants and looked into history and space. Then he began to write letters and swap stamps with children from all over the world. Though he never went further than the balcony, he travelled the world, and saw more of it than . . . yes, than even the wind elf, who has a heart of gold, but only tiny wings.

4 November

The Lost Song

As she always did every morning, Libby wanted to sing a song. She opened her mouth but not a sound came out of it. So she went to see her loved one, and said to him, 'Lionel, sing me my morning song, I seem to be out of voice today.' 'Why not?' smiled Lionel. He opened *his* mouth but again nothing happened. Not a single note came out of it. So they asked the neighbours and they soon found that no one in the village or for miles around could sing

a single song. 'I'll tell you what,' Lionel told Libby, 'I'll go and look for your song.' And off he went. He walked through a strangely silent landscape, where not even the twittering of the birds could be heard. By and by he came to a crossroads, where a man with a spinning-wheel stood. 'Old man, play me something,' Lionel begged him. 'I haven't heard a song since I set out on my journey, nor for a day or two before.' 'Nor will you now,' sighed the old man, 'for my spinning-wheel is silent, too.' 'But why?' the young man asked. 'Have we offended the songs somehow?' 'Maybe we have, maybe we haven't,' the old man replied with a shrug of his shoulders. 'Perhaps they were shocked by something, or we took them too much for granted. How should I know? Anyway, they're gone.'

5 November

The Lost Song

'Then I shall find the songs again,' Lionel announced. 'Not just Libby's, but all of them.' And he looked around him to see which of the roads he should take. 'But that is why I am waiting here,' the old man told him. 'And how did you know I should pass this way looking for the songs?' asked the

young man, in surprise. 'I didn't know that you would be the one to come along,' the old man told him, 'but someone had to come. Whenever men lose something,' the man with the spinning-wheel went on, 'there is always at least one of them who tries to find it and restore it to the rest. If it were not so, then it would be a poor life here in this world. And since it happens to be you, I shall give you my spinning-wheel. It is the only thing you may use to catch a song, for neither sack nor net will hold one.' 'Not even a tape-recorder?' asked Lionel. 'I don't know what a tape-recorder is,' the old man told him. 'I am one of the old ones. But when I say that only a spinning-wheel will help you, you must believe me.' Lionel took the spinning-wheel, thanked the old man, and was about to ask which way he should go in search of the songs. But the old man had vanished. In the spot where he had stood was a signpost with three arms that read: 'To the Major Key', 'To the Minor Key' and 'To the Keymaster'.

6 November

The Lost Song

Lionel chose the road to the keymaster. He supposed that when he found him he would have the keys to all the songs. He walked for a long, long time, but finally he found himself in front of a low building, whose roof was lifting like the lid of a boiling kettle. That was because there were thousands of songs being sung inside all at the same time. 'How unfair it is!' cried Lionel to the man who came out of the house. 'You have so many songs here it's a wonder you don't go deaf, and yet everyone else is almost turning grey with sadness for lack of them!' The man beckoned to Lionel to follow him. They sat down in a garden bower, around which the birds were singing their heads off. Don't worry,' the keymaster said, soothingly. 'Fill the spinning-wheel with as many songs as you want, and then you may give them back to the people.' 'Now wait a minute,' said

Lionel. 'There's something wrong here. I have to perform some impossible task first, escape some danger, defeat someone in combat. Isn't that right?' 'Whatever for?' asked the keymaster. 'It is enough for me that you overcame laziness and indifference and made the journey here. I shall give you the songs because you were willing to enter into danger for them.' And so he did. The very next morning Libby sang her usual morning song, and again at ten o'clock, and again before lunch, and again after lunch. Then Libby and Lionel sang it together at their wedding, with the sound of the spinning-wheel to accompany them.

7 November

The Magic Glove

One day the wind came whistling down the street and sucked up everything it could carry. It blew away little Clare's mitten, and just for a joke it hid it round the corner of the house. Judy found it there. She picked it up and looked at it with pleasure. It really was pretty, with many different colours and a little heart sewn onto the thumb. Anyone would have liked it. Judy knew very well whose it was, but she didn't want to give it back. She thought to herself, 'Why shouldn't I keep such a lovely thing? I can wear it first on one hand, then on the other. Clare can make do with one just as well. She can warm her other hand in her pocket!' But the moment Judy slipped the mitten on her hand, it felt as though the wool was clinging to her fingers, as if it was glued to them. And try as she might, she couldn't get the glove off again. 'Heavens,' she whispered to the wind, 'I can't even tell anyone what has

happened to me. They'd know at once that I had taken something that wasn't mine.'

8 November

The Magic Glove

But Judy didn't have to tell anyone. Before long the whole town knew about her mitten anyway. As she ran up some steps on the way home she touched the railing at the side, and it got stuck to the mitten too. Startled, she ran on with the piece of railing in her hand, and a dog that grabbed at the railing couldn't let go again, just as if it had grown onto the piece of metal. So now Judy was running along with a mitten, a piece of railing and a dog. Then a boy tried to catch hold of the dog by the tail. You can imagine what happened. The boy got stuck to the dog as if they were sewn together. He tried to save himself by catching hold of a tree, but the tree came up by the roots and was soon trailing along behind them. So there was poor Judy, running and dragging along a piece of railing, a dog, a boy and a tree. The wind came flying past, touched the crown of the tree, and couldn't get away again. Round and round it blew, driving the strange procession before it. As she ran

Judy sobbed to herself, 'If only the two gloves were together again. I don't want one any more.' As soon as she had said these words, Clare appeared, and the magic drained out of the glove. The wind flew away, the tree sank back into the ground, the railing went back to the steps, the boy and the dog ran away, and Clare got her glove back. As for Judy, she learned a lesson she'll never forget.

9 November

The Animals Build a House

As winter was coming on the bear thought about where he should make his bed so as to sleep comfortably. He found an overturned spruce in the forest and started to make his den in its roots. He brought along branches and brushwood, and pushed up the soil where it was necessary. A fox came along to have a look. He praised the bear's house to high heaven and asked, 'May I build a lair on the first floor?' 'If you like,' the bear agreed, and he even helped the fox to make some clay bricks to build his home with. 'How beautiful!' cried a passing badger. 'How I should like to live here with you! It would be enough just to build a balcony onto the fox's flat.' So they mixed mud and stones and set to work. They hadn't even completed it before a squirrel came along. 'The only thing missing is a tower,' she said, 'and that would be just right for me.' Without even waiting for them to agree, she began building. Then a bird flew along and asked, 'May I make a perch on your tower?' And he pushed a twig into the dome. But the moment a little gnat landed on the twig to ask if it could live there too, believe it or not, the

whole house fell down. How the bear, the fox, the badger, the squirrel, the bird and the gnat got through the winter without it, we never found out.

10 November

The Thirteenth Room

Peace and quiet reigned in the kingdom of Ruddiface II until Princess Nosita, the

youngest of the king's many children, went and did something very stupid indeed. What was it? Well, she couldn't control her curiosity. Her father always warned her saying, 'You should have an inquiring mind, my dear, but never an inquisitive one. And above all you must not be inquisitive about the thirteenth room.' For there was a certain door in the castle which bore the number thirteen, and no one was allowed to open it. This included the whole of the royal family and all the servants, and everyone obeyed this rule, even though they could no longer remember which of the king's ancestors had made it, or why. But then one day Nosita turned the key in the lock and went into the thirteenth room. The only thing she found there was an old chest, and when she drew near it she heard a muffled voice moaning, 'Let me out! I won't hurt you! It's so cramped in here, ow, ow!' 'How terrible!' gasped the princess. 'I should never have believed my father could torment some poor creature in a trunk.' So without another thought she threw open the lid.

11 November

The Thirteenth Room

Out of the chest, which had been placed in the thirteenth room in ancient times, leapt a fiery hound. It rolled its huge eyes, grabbed Princess Nosita in its teeth, and ran off with her. A little path of fire trailed behind it, which showed the king that trouble had returned to the kingdom. He knew at once what had happened. The fiery dog carried the princess across hills and forests, and the last of the mountains, which it leapt over in a single bound, caught fire behind it like a bale of straw. After that it

burned continuously from peak to foot, and prevented anyone from getting past it to reach the fire dog's castle. There the dog imprisoned the princess in an iron-clad chest in the thirteenth room. Many years passed. King Ruddiface shed many a tear in his kingdom, while the fire dog started to raise a family in his castle. His mate was an equally horrible bitch with eyes like a pair of dinner plates and jaws that constantly belched flames. By and by they had puppies that looked exactly like their parents and obeyed them in all things. Only the youngest of them, Longsnout, was always sniffing about in places where he shouldn't, and was terribly, terribly curious. He knew he was never to go into the thirteenth room, but one day he could no longer resist the temptation.

12 November

The Thirteenth Room

In the middle of the thirteenth room the youngest fire dog saw an iron-bound chest. When he drew closer he heard a muffled groaning coming from inside, 'Let me out! It's so cramped in here! Whoever sets me

free will receive a sack of gold from my father!' Longsnout pricked up his ears. 'Why should someone else get the gold?' he asked himself. He loved shiny things. 'I'll open the chest and see,' he said. 'After all, I am a fire dog, and what can happen to me?' So he let his curiosity get the better of him and threw back the lid. The moment he did so the fire in the mountain that divided the grim castle from the rest of the world, went out, and the fire dogs turned into wolves. They ran off howling terribly, except for Longsnout, that is. He turned into a dear little Alsatian that never left his new mistress's side. The castle disappeared and the countryside around it turned green. The princess was able to set off home. She hurried over the hill and

never returned to that place again. No one else ever went there either, for it was said that there were as many snakes there now as there once were flames. From then on the hill was known as Snake Hill.

13 November

Very Nearly the End
of the Tale of a Cupboard

In a mysterious room in a mysterious house, there once stood a mysterious cupboard. It was positively the only thing in the room. There were no chairs and no tables, not even a settee. And no one lived in the house. It was empty, except for that one mysterious cupboard. What do you suppose was in that cupboard? That was just what a certain robber was anxious to find out. He put on his mask so that no one would recognize him, took with him his skeleton keys and his torch, and made for the mysterious house at night. How surprised he was to find that the house wasn't even locked and nor was the room, nor the cupboard. He opened all the doors and pulled out all the drawers, but he couldn't find anything at all. Then, in the very bottom drawer, he came across a little mouse. 'Mouse, can you tell me how you came to be in this mysterious cupboard?' asked the curious robber. But if you want to know the rest, you'll have to wait until 13 December.

14 November

How King Valentine
Learned to Rule

King Valentine was looking forward to his funeral no end. Not that he was terribly keen to leave this world, but he was anxious to know how his subjects would mourn and grieve. But then he realized, 'When I really die I won't be able to see anything. If I am to enjoy the people's mourning for me, I'll have to hold my funeral while I'm still alive.' So he had it announced that he had died, ordered the city to be hung with black and a thousand black flags to be flown, and lay down in his coffin. From there he could see the sad ceremonials without anyone noticing him. The chief minister, who was the only one the king had let in on the secret, gave the signal and the funeral procession moved off. But what was this? Valentine couldn't see a single tear, not even a hint of sadness. The people were talking about everyday matters whether they were following behind the coffin or watching from the pavements. Several times the king actually heard someone say, 'Well we've got rid of him at last. Let's just hope the next one isn't worse than ever!' 'Couldn't be worse than this one!' others would join in. Lying there in his coffin, Valentine broke into a cold sweat. So he

was not going to leave this world surrounded by grief. Quite the reverse, his subjects would be glad to get rid of him. When he realized this Valentine really felt like dying.

15 November

How King Valentine Learned to Rule

King Valentine didn't die in his coffin, even though he felt far from well. First of all he was angry. 'All who spoke ill of me shall be executed!' he said. But then he thought, 'Who would do all the work then?' The more he thought about it, the more it became clear to him that he was the one at fault and that he should change. He told the chief minister he wanted to learn to rule properly, starting from the beginning. But how? 'That's easy,' smiled the chief minister. 'All you have to do is go among the people in disguise, work with them and listen to them, and you will soon see what they like

and what they don't like. You'll find out for yourself what the king is doing wrong. If you don't forget what you have learned, you will rule wisely when you return to the throne.' 'But what if they recognize me?' asked the king. 'Don't worry! They always looked at your crown and your fur cloak. They won't remember your face at all,' the chief minister assured him. 'But who is going to rule in the meantime?' asked Valentine. 'The country can't be without a king!' 'Oh yes it can,' smirked the chief minister. 'I'll announce public mourning until you return. If anything has to be decided, I can always pop along and ask you.' So Valentine agreed, and went off to learn how to rule.

16 November

An Autumn Love

A certain young man left town for good because he wanted some peace and quiet. He found himself a pleasant place and built a cottage there, at the foot of a high mountain. All around grew trees with huge leaves, and in the autumn they glowed with reds and yellows. The leaves of the oaks, beeches and elms crackled above all day long like little fires. The mountain grew more beautiful day by day. As he gazed out of his window, the young man grew to like it there more and more, until he fell in love with that mountain. He praised it and admired it, and who wouldn't have liked that? The mountain perked up no end. It had never heard a kind word said about it before, since no one lived for miles around. So it protected the cottage and the young man from wind and storm, and repaid one kindness with another. The autumn seemed longer than usual that year. The leaves

stayed on the trees until the first frost came, but then they fell as always. The mountain lost its green grass and moss, and it was no longer decorated with coloured flames. The young man closed his window, and hardly even looked out of it any more. And when he did look out, it was to say, 'How sad and ugly you are now, mountain. I don't love you any more.' The mountain began to cry. Little springs of water ran down from its peak to its foot. They joined together and gushed down the slopes, flooding the land all around. The water carried the cottage and the young man away with it, and no one ever saw them again.

17 November

The Foolish Farmer's Bet

Joshua was a clever young fellow and he roamed the world making a living out of bets which he always won. Here he would win a loaf of bread, there a piece of cheese or an egg, a handful of dried fruit or a cup of buttermilk. But as time went by he got tired of travelling and of living from hand to mouth, and he decided to settle down somewhere. He arrived in the village of Candleford, where he asked a conceited farmer called Hedges if he could answer ten questions with the words 'why, of course', without getting mixed up. The farmer burst out laughing and said, 'There's nothing easier. Let us have a bet! If I lose I shall give you my farm, but if I win you will work for me without wages till the day you die.' Joshua was happy to agree to these terms and at once began asking his cunning questions: 'Do you go poaching?' 'Are you as poor as a church mouse?' 'Do you steal the mayor's barley?' 'Do you tell tales about the vicar's wife?' The farmer answered 'why, of course' over and over again, laughing as he did so. After all, it was only a bet, and both he and the crowd of neighbours had a merry time. But when Joshua suddenly asked, 'Is it true that you are the biggest fool in the village?' Hedges got mixed up and called out, 'Oh no, there are some who are a good deal more foolish!' But he had to admit at once that he really was a fool. He had lost everything he owned.

18 November

The Foolish Farmer's Bet

So clever Joshua settled down in Candleford and started farming. Hedges, who was now a very poor man, went to complain to the mayor, but he just laughed at him. 'That sort of thing couldn't happen to me,' he said, puffing out his chest. Now Joshua heard about this, and he set off at once to introduce himself to the mayor. As soon as the door opened he began to make cunning compliments. 'I know *you* would never fall for the sort of thing Hedges fell for. You'd never get mixed up!' The mayor felt very pleased with himself, and he said, 'Why not have a bet? My office against the farm you have just won. You'll go away as poor as you came, you'll see!' 'Very well,' Joshua agreed. So they invited a few of the neighbours and Joshua began his questions. All went well until he got to the last of them: 'Will you state before these witnesses that from now on I am the mayor of Candleford?' 'Why, of course,' was the reply. 'You won't catch me out. From now on you are the mayor here!' 'Very well,' said Joshua. 'You win the farm, but now I shall be in charge of the whole village. You said so before witnesses and your word is your bond.' So the mayor had to give up his office. It was probably a good thing for everyone in the village.

19 November

The Solitary Traveller

Mr. Robbins lived a lonely sort of life. He would greet the neighbours on the stairs or in the corridor and then disappear behind his door, and that was all you ever saw of him. His next-door-neighbour, Mrs. Dawson the widow, was quite the opposite. She liked to stop and talk to everyone, liked to go visiting even better, and most of all liked people to tell her their troubles. After that she had something to talk about. She lay in wait for Mr. Robbins wherever she could, by the door of the house, at the dairy, at the shoe-shop, trying to get into conversation with him. But all her attempts failed. Mr. Robbins would only grunt 'good afternoon', and then be gone, almost at a run. He would neither stop for a talk, nor invite her to visit him, nor confide his troubles. Then it happened that Mrs. Dawson watched out for him for one week, then for another, and saw no sign of him at all. She summoned up her courage and went and rang his doorbell. There was no answer. She tried knocking and there was no answer again. 'Oh, Lord!' she cried. 'Something's happened to him!' She quickly called the police. They forced the lock, expecting the worst, but the flat was empty. The walls were covered in pictures, all of them landscapes.

20 November

The Solitary Traveller

The sergeant was just about to tell Mrs. Dawson off for wasting police time, when a notebook lying on the table caught his eye. It was open, and half filled with notes. He regarded the notebook as evidence and so he picked it up and read the last few lines. 'This time I shall go and have a look in the Rocky Mountains, because I have an idea there's a grizzly bear lurking behind one of the rocks. You can't see him, but I can feel he's there.' The sergeant flipped through the pages of the notebook, and then looked at the pictures on the wall in

amazement. Now he understood that Mr. Robbins was a traveller and a strange sort of traveller at that. For he explored the landscapes that were painted in the pictures hanging in his room. Sometimes he would wander off to an Arab mosque, sometimes to the jungle, or perhaps he would sit by the shores of the Mediterranean. He had always

returned safely, and recorded in his notebook what he had seen and experienced. This time he had set out for the Rocky Mountains. 'I don't believe it!' declared the sergeant. 'An ordinary person can't just step into a picture like that! There wouldn't be room for him!' Then he looked at the picture of the Rockies and froze to the spot. In front of a rock stood a huge grizzly bear, with a well-fed expression on his face.

21 November

The Solitary Traveller

The sergeant began to dictate notes. 'There is reason to believe that the missing person, Henry Robbins, disappeared while on a trip to the Rocky Mountains, where he was probably eaten by a bear. The evidence for this can be found in his notebook and painting which are enclosed.' And Mrs. Dawson began to say, 'And he was such a nice man. I was the only person in the world he trusted! He said to me, if anything should happen to me, I want you to have everything, Rosy...' 'That,' said the sergeant, cutting in sharply, 'is for the court to decide.' 'What court?' said a voice from the doorway. They all turned round. There stood Mr. Robbins in hunting gear, with a popgun in his hand. 'His ghost!' shrieked his next-door-neighbour, collapsing in a faint. The sergeant didn't faint, but asked the newcomer for his identity. It turned out to be Mr. Robbins in the flesh, just returned from a fortnight in the New Forest. 'But what about these pictures?' asked the sergeant, secretly tearing up his report. Mr. Robbins gave an apologetic smile. 'Everyone plays at something,' he said. 'I play at being a traveller. I look at the Rocky Mountains, then I go to the New Forest, and since I have a good imagination, I hunt for

wear yourself out, my lad. What if I were to try and cure your brother?' And he entered the house. He offered each of the youths a gold coin in return for a small service. One of them was to sew a button on his fur coat, the other to dust it. Hubert thought, 'What a crazy old man this is,' and at once reached for a needle in order to carry out the easier of the tasks. He sat down on the veranda with the coat, but he had not even threaded the needle when he dropped off to sleep. The fur coat was warmer than the stove he liked to laze beside. In a while Jaspar came along to perform the second task. Not knowing that his brother was underneath the coat he set to work at once, beating the fur with all his might. When Hubert's cries began to fill the house, the wayfarer said, 'That is what you should have done long ago, Jaspar!' And then he vanished. He didn't leave them their gold coins, but his advice was worth more than gold. After that Hubert was not quite so fond of sitting by the stove.

bears there.' He looked at the picture. 'Good Lord!' he said. 'But that grizzly bear in the picture really wasn't there before ...!'

22 November

The Wise Wayfarer

Two brothers called Jaspar and Hubert lived together under one roof. Their little house was neat and tidy, but thanks only to the efforts of Jaspar, the younger brother. Hubert would spend the whole day lounging in front of the stove. 'Why don't you help me?' Jaspar asked his brother. 'Can't you see I'm rushed off my feet?' But it was no use, Hubert took no notice. One day a wayfarer passed the cottage. He saw how things were and called out to Jaspar, 'You'll

23 November

The Poor Girl and the Robber

There was no one in the world whom Lizzie loved more than her mother, and her mother loved Lizzie just as well. They thought they would never part, but hard times came along, and there was no longer

215

The Poor Girl and the Robber

'I haven't got much in my bundle,' Lizzie told the dove. 'But I've learnt a lot in the world, and that's maybe worth more than a nugget of gold. I can sew clothes or bake bread at home now. I know a good deal about farming too, and I surely won't make such a bad wife.' As she thought of her homecoming Lizzie began to sing. Far across the hills and valleys Blaggard the robber heard her. He lay in wait for her, and it began to seem as though all her high hopes were soon to come to nothing. 'You shall become my wife, and work for me!' he shouted at Lizzie, stepping into her path not far from the village. The girl almost turned dumb with fright, and her knees began to shake. But the dove, hidden in a tree above her, whispered, 'Pretend to be willing to obey him. Go with him, but waste as much time as you can. I will fly to tell your mother. You must secretly put the lock of her hair in my beak. Then she will know you are in danger.' Lizzie did as the dove had told her and then let the robber lead her off

a living for both of them in their native village. The robber Blaggard had moved into the nearby woods. He robbed the poor and stole every last penny from the villagers. Lizzie decided that she had to go out into the world for a while to find herself some work and earn some money. When she was setting out, her mother gave Lizzie a lock of her grey hair as a good-luck charm, to protect her from danger. Lizzie strode off purposefully, promising to return in a year and a day. The first work she got was sewing from morning till night, and the only reward she received after weeks on end was a small piece of linen to make into a scarf. Then she worked for a gingerbread-maker, where she had to get up early in the morning and mix marzipan until she was ready to drop. After a month she had earned no more than a piece of gingerbread. She baked it herself and wrote her name on it in white icing. The last place she worked was at the house of a rich farmer. All she received in return for her back-breaking work was a single egg. A little dove hatched out of it and said to her, 'Go home now, it is time. A year has passed!'

through the brambles and bushes. She pretended that she was nearly too tired to walk. On the way she dropped first the gingerbread cake and then the white scarf.

25 November

The Poor Girl and the Robber

The dove flew off to get help, but he didn't even reach the village. Just beyond its edge he got caught in a net that had been placed there by Blaggard. As he was fluttering about there, Lizzie's mother felt a jab at her heart. 'Where is my daughter?' she sighed. 'The year is up, and she has not returned.' And as if she sensed some danger she left the cottage and walked out of the village. There she found the dove with the lock of her grey hair in his beak. As soon as she had set him free and found out what had happened, she hurried off into the woods. The dove showed her the way, and when he no longer knew where to go, the old woman found the way herself by the gingerbread cake with Lizzie's name on it and the white scarf. She caught up with the robber and her unfortunate daughter, but the

evil-hearted fellow wouldn't even let her hug Lizzie. He dragged the girl on towards his home in the woods. The sadder Lizzie and her mother became, the harder Blaggard's heart became, until in the end it turned to stone. The cliff that appeared in that spot had the shape of a heart, and it has always been known as Black Heart, or some say Blackguard, or Blaggard. Free again at last, Lizzie and her mother hurried home, wishing to be as far away as possible from that dark rock, and looking forward to a good breakfast.

26 November

How Latecomer Improved

Everyone just called him 'Latecomer', and no one knew what his real name was, neither his christian name nor his surname. He had never arrived on time for anything since the day he learned to walk. 'I'll be

home at six,' he would promise, as he went out to play with the lads. At eight o'clock his mother would find him still happily playing away. 'Is it as late as that?' he would always ask in surprise. He was regularly late for school, and it was no use sending him to the headmaster or having letters sent home to his parents. When he went out to work he arrived late every day of course, and after a number of warnings his boss gave him the sack. Then Latecomer got a job as an insurance agent, which meant that he had to travel round trying to persuade people to take out insurance against injury, fire, flood, and so on. The only trouble was that whenever he had an appointment with a customer, he turned up late. If he was supposed to be there at nine it would be ten before he arrived, and if he said ten then he wouldn't be there before eleven. He got later and later. If his appointments had all been in the same place, it wouldn't have been so bad, because he might still have arrived in time for the next one, or the one after. But he was never in the right place at the right time, and his customers began to complain to the insurance company. The manager called him to his office, and when Latecomer finally arrived, he was soon outside again, sacked once more.

27 November

How Latecomer Improved

Latecomer went back to the insurance company and said, 'I'd like to take out a policy against arriving late.' When the man behind the counter didn't seem to understand, he explained, 'If I'm an hour late for an appointment, I get a fiver from you.' 'What if you're two hours late?' the clerk asked. 'Then I get a tenner, of course,' retorted Latecomer. 'For every hour, a fiver.' Then his former colleagues all burst out laughing. 'The company would go bankrupt in no time,' the clerk told him. 'We'd be paying out all the time. There's no

chance of you getting such a policy.' 'We'll try another way,' said the manager, who had overheard what was going on. 'We won't insure you against arriving late, but against arriving on time.' This time it was Latecomer's turn not to understand. 'You get a fiver from us, if you bring us a signed statement from someone to say you arrived somewhere bang on time,' the manager explained. Latecomer thought about it, and then agreed. He bought two wristwatches, one for each wrist, and three alarm clocks, and from then on he arrived everywhere not only to the minute, but to the second. Then people started to call him by his real name at last which was Mr. Quick. And what about the insurance company? They thought they'd better take him on again, before he cost them too much money. But he turned down their kind offer and went on arriving places on time until the insurance company had to pay out so much money that Mr. Quick owned it himself.

28 November

The Three Painters

Once upon a time there were three brothers who were all painters. One of them was good at figures, another at faces, and the third was good at houses and trees. So they all painted together, and a lot of people bought their pictures. The brothers should have been content, but far from it. The first of them said, 'The figures are the most important thing in our paintings. Without them the picture wouldn't be worth a thing. I am the greatest artist of the three!' But the second painter said, 'It is the face that shows all the expression. The rest is only background! I really don't know why such a maestro as myself works to keep his brothers.' And the third brother looked at it another way and said, 'How come we divide

the money three ways, when I do most of the work? The other two just draw the people between them, but I have to do all the rest myself!' One day after work they looked at each other and all exclaimed at once, 'I've had enough!' So they each opened up studios of their own and began to paint their pictures separately. People came along to have a look, then shook their heads at the pictures and went away again. They never bought anything because they didn't like the paintings any more. Then the brothers realized that none of them could make a living on his own. They joined forces again and it was the last time any of them complained.

The Doughnut at School

Do you still remember the doughnut we left in October? Well, he travelled by train until he reached a familiar-looking town. Of course! He realized that he had arrived back in the place where he had met the tearful doughnut in front of the school, and where he had run away from the hungry dog. He went into the school, and from the corridor he stepped into a large room with two rows of benches. He crawled into the back one and went to sleep for by now he needed a good rest. When he woke up in the morning he could hear a woman saying, 'Two and two is four, three and three is six . . .' He peered out from the bench, and saw that the classroom was full of boys and girls. There was just one place empty. Maybe it was waiting for him. Hadn't he wanted Grandma Bailey to send him to school? He decided to stay there and learn his lessons with the children. Imagine! He stuck it out there for a whole month, which was a long time for a globetrotter like him. After lessons each day he had to hide away from the caretaker, so that he wouldn't get thrown in the bin as someone's unfinished elevenses. But it was worth it. He learned to read, write and count. Are you surprised that it only took a month? Well, he was a very gifted and bright sort of doughnut, you know. When he decided he had learned enough he went rolling on. December was waiting for him after all.

Cecilia and Her Shadows

Cecilia the witch had not been very good at school, but there was one thing she was especially good at, and that was bringing shadows to life. Whenever she met someone she would stare at his shadow and mumble some magic words, and the person would have a double in no time at all. One day she met the mayor, and his shadow was particularly attractive. It was small and plump, and hurried along beside his worship on its short legs. It wasn't long before there were two mayors striding along the pavement, arguing over which of them had the right to sit in the town hall. They couldn't agree, and out of curiosity, the next day, Cecilia, the bad pupil, brought both *their* shadows to life. She took such a liking to her new game that she would multiply the mayors every day, and watch gleefully from her hiding-place as they fought over which of them was real. When there were so many mayors around that they filled the town-square, the constable went up to the nearest of them and informed him that the town council had had to elect a new mayor, since whoever the mayor was hadn't been to a council meeting for so long. 'But what are we to do?' cried several hundred ex-mayors, all in tears. 'We can't do anything else but be mayor!' 'Of course you can,' the constable comforted them, 'only you don't know what it is yet.' And he led the mayors off to the place where a new school was to be built. Thus it was that, thanks to Cecilia, a new school grew up in the town of which the townspeople would proudly say, 'It was built by the mayor, you know. All by himself!'

December

1 December

The Tree that Wanted to Be a Memory

'The forest is very beautiful in winter,' said the wind elf out loud, as he flew quietly past the tall old spruce trees on his way to a clearing. On each of their branches they had a dollop of snow and tassels made of icicles. The snow protected the trees from the frost, just like the wind elf's cloak. Once upon a time that cloak had been like a wisp of evening mist, but in the course of the elf's long travels it had changed. It had become wrinkled, puffed out and bulging with the things that were stuffed in its pockets. If the wind elf had had a home, he would surely have got himself a chest of drawers long ago. As it was he had only his pockets. If you looked inside them you would find a little of the scent of summer, a dandelion seed, a four-leaf clover from the mole's sitting-room, a musical note lost at a concert, the tip of one of Julie's crayons, a cat's whisker, and a stamp from young Stephen. The wind elf called all these things his memories, and now he gave each of them a little stroke. A tiny spruce, growing out of a crack in the tree-stump the wind elf was standing on, saw this and said, 'I want to be a memory too! If you've got an empty pocket left, put me in it!' 'Very well,' the wind elf agreed, but he had no idea what would become of it. If we wait two weeks and four days, we'll find out.

2 December

The Porcelain Tale

In the window of an antique-shop stood a china girl and a china boy. They had been there a long time, and life was not the least bit boring for them, since all sorts of people passed by the window or stopped to look in. The two china figures would watch them and chat about them. 'Have you noticed the dark-haired girl in the old fur coat, my dear?' china boy asked china girl, and she replied, 'I noticed her a long time ago, but whenever she comes a young fellow in a sheepskin hat comes and stands beside her. They both look in the window, but neither of them says anything.' 'Maybe they don't know each other,' said china boy. China girl smiled and said, 'Of course they don't, but they like each other. Yet they daren't speak to one another.' 'Just what I think, my love,' said china boy, 'don't you think we should help them?' 'I think about it all the time, darling, but I don't know how.' Just then the girl in the battered old fur coat appeared in front of the shop. In a few moments the young man in the sheepskin hat was standing beside her. They stood there in silence, staring at the two china figures. You would have thought they were waiting for help. China boy winked at china girl, and then pretended to wobble and accidently fall off his stand. 'That figure . . .' exclaimed both the young people at once,

and looked into each other's eyes for the first time. Then they smiled. They walked away hand in hand, and soon forgot all about the antique-shop.

3 December

How Needy Earned an Ass

A poor lad worked as a groom in the stables of a certain king. They used to call him Needy because he owned nothing but the coarse linen shirt on his back. He was sometimes so hungry that he was glad to share the horses' oats. He had big sad eyes like the scrawny donkey that lived in the corner of the stables, and indeed the two of them made friends. When Needy had served in the royal stables for seven years, he begged to be allowed to take the donkey with him as his reward. The palace was glad to agree, since the donkey had only got in among the king's super stallions by mistake anyway. So Needy led the donkey out into the yard, and they set off together towards the nearest village. But the villagers drove them away, and some even set their dogs on the tattered pair. Only the kindhearted daughter of a watchman said to Needy, 'We have no room in the house, but there is a summer-house in the garden with a bench inside, and you may sleep there. The donkey would warm you with his breath.' But the watchman would not agree to that, so there

was nothing for it but for Needy and his donkey to sleep in the wintry forest. But they had scarcely passed the first of the trees when the donkey shook itself, and a number of gold pieces fell to the ground. 'You have nothing to worry about,' he told his new master. 'I am not just the ordinary ass you may think I am. Since you were never cruel to me once in seven whole years, and were my friend, I will reward you now.'

4 December

How Needy Earned an Ass

From then on Needy had everything he wanted. He had a donkey like a money-box, and there seemed to be no end to the supply of gold. The groom bought himself some fine clothes, rented a house in town, and became a respected citizen. There was nothing he lacked except a good wife, and he wanted to go to the village near the royal castle to find one. The girl he fancied was none other than the watchman's daughter. 'I shan't find anyone better,' said Needy to himself, as he went along the forest path. So as not to arrive empty-handed, he asked the donkey for a few gold pieces to warm the watchman's heart. But one of the gamekeepers saw him, and ran off at once to tell the king. 'We'll soon put that right!' cried the king. 'Before the sun sets, the ass shall be mine again!' So he called the guards and ordered them to lock Needy up and bring the ass to him in the palace. Needy found himself in the royal dungeons without even knowing why. 'I'll teach you a lesson for taking my most precious possession!' the king threatened Needy, and at once he ordered the donkey to shake itself. This it did, but instead of gold pieces heavily-armed soldiers fell from his mane, and there were so many of them that the royal guards were soon on the run. Then Needy rode to fetch his bride. He settled in the village and worked for a living

8 December

The Book of Spells

The next day Susie learned a spell to change her teacher back from being a singer into a teacher again. After she had sung *Jingle Bells,* the teacher coughed and said, 'We've got rather behind, girls, I'm afraid. We'll have to get back to subtraction now. I just wanted to show you how much time you can waste on this silly music.' So now Susie had found out that the book of spells really did show the way to put spells on and take them off again. When she got home she decided she ought to try conjuring something up for a change. Why not a friend? If she didn't like her, she could always send her back where she came from. So she read aloud a long spell that was supposed to make a little girl the same age as herself appear. Ooops! Scarcely had she said the last of the words, when there beside

her stood a ginger-haired and freckled little girl who said, 'It took you long enough to remember me!' Susie thought she wasn't too keen on this rather unpleasant little girl, so she reached for the spell book and tried to find out how to get rid of her again. But the redhead grabbed the book from her hands and threw it on the fire. 'You'll be lucky,' she said, 'I've been waiting such a long time to be conjured up, and now you think I'll let you send me back to the waiting room!' 'But . . . but the book!' said Susie, sadly. The redhead stuck out her tongue. 'Let it burn!' she said. 'The main thing is that *I'm* here.'

9 December

The Book of Spells

'I'm Ginny Ginger,' said the freckled girl. 'And now you must do everything I tell you. If you refuse, then I shall bash you!' Susie tried to persuade Ginny that she was the boss, but the redhead gave her such a slap in the face that it made her head spin. 'Now we'll go down to the sweet shop,' she said, 'and while I keep the shop assistant talking, you'll pinch a bag of chocolate raisins, they're my favourites.' Susie suggested they should buy the chocolate raisins with the money from her piggy bank, but Ginny snapped at her, 'They don't taste the same if they're not stolen!' And she dragged Susie off to the sweet shop. The next day she made her go to see a horror film instead of

going to school, and when they got home she ate Susie's supper without leaving her so much as a potato. Susie was terribly unhappy, and she got more and more miserable as Ginny thought up one thing after another to annoy her with. And she hid herself from Susie's parents so cunningly that no one noticed anything. 'Why ever did I conjure up a friend like her?' she thought. 'Now I'll never get rid of her . . . I daresay it was no accident, either. It must have been Ginny hiding behind the curtains in the dining-room, and she must have put the book in my satchel!'

10 December

The Book of Spells

'I'm staying in bed today,' declared Ginny after a day or two. 'I'm feeling lazy. You'll have to go to school, but come home straight after lunch, because I want to go to the zoo. I'm going to shove you in the cage with the monkeys.' 'But why?' asked Susie. 'Just so's I can laugh when they chase you round the cage,' Ginny explained with a mischievous grin. Susie walked to school with her head hung low. She told the teacher she had been poorly. 'You don't look very well,' the teacher agreed. 'If you like you can read under the desk today, just this once.' Since Ginny had come along, Susie hadn't read a single line. And now she didn't feel a bit like reading, because she was thinking about how Ginny was going to push her into the monkeys' cage. 'Is there anything I can do for you?' asked her neighbour, Angie, at break time. It was only now that Susie realized just what a kind little girl Angie really was. 'No one can help me,' sighed Susie. 'Not even a friend?' asked Angie. Susie couldn't believe her ears. 'Are you my friend?' she asked in surprise. 'If you

like I'll be your best friend in the whole wide world,' Angie promised. 'All right,' Susie agreed, 'and I'll be yours.'

11 December

The Book of Spells

Susie told Angie everything that had happened to her. Angie's eyes almost popped out of her head when she heard about the book of spells and about Ginny Ginger. 'Never mind, we'll think of something together,' she said at last. They whispered to each other on the way home from school, and they must have thought of something, because Susie was looking quite brave by the time she got home and Ginny

greeted her with, 'Off we go to the zoo!' Ginny was expecting her to cry and plead, but she didn't say a word. 'Just you wait till we get to the monkeys!' the redhead warned her. On the way to the monkeys they came across a litttle girl staring into an empty cage. 'What are you looking at?' Ginny asked her, for she was terribly inquisitive. 'They say there's an invisible animal in there,' the girl replied, 'and anyone who touches it will see it. But I'm afraid to go inside.' 'Huh!' laughed Ginny, scornfully. 'You're just the same as her.' And she pointed at Susie. 'Spineless! That's what you are! But I'm not afraid of anything!' And Ginny went into the cage to touch the invisible animal. Angie, for that's who the little girl was, quickly shut the door of the cage, hung the padlock on it, and snapped it shut. Then she put a notice on the cage saying: 'Ginny Ginger, a wild creature from Spellland. Do not feed!' They thought the three l's in Spellland looked a bit funny, but how else could it be written? Then Susie put out her tongue at the startled Ginny, and she and her new friend went off to see the monkeys.

12 December

The Frost Flowers

One day Jack Frost visited the village where the storyteller lived, and painted silvery-white flowers on all the windows. He drew the most beautiful ones of all on the window of the storyteller's cottage, under which his typewriter stood. The storyteller liked the flowers very much, and the frost flowers too were glad to blossom on a window that looked in on the birth of fairy tales. But then the sun came out, and began devouring frost like a greedy child eating ice-cream. The flowers were afraid they would disappear altogether beneath the harsh glare. 'We don't want to die,' they told the storyteller. 'We want to hear lots more stories first.' 'But I haven't the power

to save you from the sun,' the storyteller replied, sadly. 'Hasn't anyone?' the flowers asked, and then the storyteller remembered the fairy and asked her to save the silver blossoms on the window. Did she hear him, or didn't she? She can't have done, for the next day the window was clear and all the flowers were gone. But afterwards, in early summer, when the pansies, tulips, roses and peonies bloomed in the flower-bed beneath the window, there was among them a strange silver flower, that seemed to have been drawn with a frosty brush. So maybe the fairy had heard the storyteller after all.

13 December

The End of the Tale of a Cupboard

In a mysterious room in a mysterious house, there once stood a mysterious cupboard. It was positively the only thing in the room. There were no chairs and no tables, not even a settee. And no one lived in the house. It was empty, except for that one mysterious cupboard. What do you suppose was in that cupboard? That was just what a certain robber was anxious to find out. He put on his mask so that no one would recognize him, took with him his skeleton keys and his torch, and made for the mysterious house at night. How surprised he was to find that the house wasn't even locked and nor was the room, nor the cupboard. He opened all the doors and pulled out all the drawers, but couldn't find anything at all. Finally in the very bottom drawer he came across a little mouse. 'Mouse, can you tell me how you came to be in this mysterious cupboard?' asked the curious robber. 'Very simple,' replied the mouse. 'When Sir Soggybeard moved out of the house, he left the cupboard here so that I should have somewhere to live. Wasn't that kind of him?' 'Maybe it was,' mumbled the robber, 'but he needn't have kept me in suspense for so long . . .'

14 December

The Twelve Wolves

'Christmas is coming,' said Purple Riding Hood's mother. 'Pop along to Granny's. Take her the usual basket of goodies, and give her our regards. Tell her I'm rushed off my feet and invite her round to supper on Christmas Eve.' So Purple Riding Hood took the basket containing a sponge cake,

a bottle of sweet wine and a good-sized piece of ham, and off she went. The snow crunched beneath her feet. The forest was silent and peaceful. But appearances can be deceptive, and suddenly, from out of nowhere, a pack of wolves appeared and stood around the little girl. There were twelve of them, like the twelve months, and they looked as though butter wouldn't have melted in their mouths. 'May I carry your basket for you?' asked the first, politely. 'I'll show you the way, so that you don't get lost,' offered a second. 'And in the meantime I'll run along and scoff your granny,' said a third, but he corrected himself at once, saying, 'What I mean to say is, I'll run along to your granny's and get her ready for your visit.' And he would have gone, only the rest of the wolves growled at him to stay where he was. Purple Riding Hood saw that she was in a mess, but she didn't lose her head. She said to the first wolf, 'He wanted to eat Granny up himself, and he wouldn't have left any for you. But you wanted to eat me all by yourself, and these other poor wolves would have gone hungry!' That was enough. The wolves began to accuse each other of being greedy and selfish, and before long they laid into each other and fought until they had torn each other's throats out. Then Purple Riding Hood was able to carry on to her granny's house in peace.

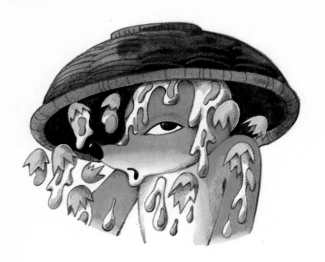

a few bits of fur were all that was left of Reynard the fox and the cock was promised that he would never be made into chicken pie. He remained ruler of the hen-house for the rest of his life.

16 December

The Clever Cockerel

Farmer Lockwood's cockerel, the one who captured Reynard the fox, was so proud of what he had done that he thought he could have a say in everything from then on. He wanted to comment on what to feed the hens, and on subjects such as which television programmes the farmer was to watch and which not. At first Lockwood put up with the cock's advice, saying to himself, 'After all, he is the brave cock who caught the fox.' Well, he was in love with the daughter of his neighbour, Woolley, and wanted to marry her as soon as possible, but the cock refused to agree to the wedding. 'Look here, old son,' he kept saying to the farmer, 'why don't you marry Wilkins' daughter instead? She's a good deal prettier and has a sweeter character. And what a way she has with poultry! I think you should know that the girl next door has a number of bad qualities.' The farmer wasn't going to put up with that sort of thing. He threatened to go back on his word

15 December

The Clever Cockerel

Reynard the fox was hungry. True, the weather was like spring, but it was December, and the fox didn't feel like running about the woods in search of food. Just before dawn he crept into the yard of Lockwood's farm, grabbed the nearest hen, and was gone. The cockerel blinked at him sleepily. The next day Reynard carried off another hen, and the third day yet another. The rest of the hens looked at the cock reproachfully, as if they were saying, 'Why don't you do something about it?' The farmer set traps all over the place, but they're not a great deal of use against a fox! But on the fourth night the cock made ready for the unwelcome visitor. He set up a basket of eggs on the perch and waited. The moment the fox appeared and snapped his teeth, the cock pushed the basket over. The eggs smashed on Reynard's snout, and the basket fell on his head. Before the fox could get himself out of the basket, the cock began crowing like mad. 'What do you want to go waking me up so early for?' grumbled the farmer, as he crawled out of bed. But he soon changed his tune when he caught sight of the fox struggling to get the basket off his head, blinded by egg yolk. Soon after,

and turn the cock into stew, if he didn't hold his tongue. But the cock wasn't afraid and continued, 'She's not much of a housekeeper either, and not the brightest girl in the village . . .' He would probably have gone on for ever, but Lockwood eventually promised to marry Patty Wilkins instead. So the wedding took place, and the farmer and his new wife lived in such happiness and contentment, and had such a high regard for the clever cockerel, that from that time there was no end to his pride at all.

17 December

Frances and the Squirrel's Hair

A new squirrel had arrived in the neighbourhood. She had a fine coat, and every month she would comb out of it a few tufts of hair and swap them for nuts down in the village. One day before Christmas, she knocked on the door of a cottage where there were five girls knitting away busily. Four of them were already good at their work while the fifth, Frances, was only just learning, and naturally not as nimble as the rest. This time the squirrel offered the girls bundles of her hair without asking anything in return. She said she would give them to the girl who knitted the nicest thing of all. The first of the girls said flatteringly, 'I shall knit myself a cap with two bobbles, as pretty as your two ears.' The second girl decided to make a muff, the third a cardigan with a pocket, the fourth a fringed shawl. She said she would decorate it with beads as shiny as the squirrel's eyes. Only Frances didn't dare suggest anything. But when the squirrel kept asking her, she finally whispered, 'I'll knit the wool into decorative cords.' The other girls laughed at her, but when she added that she would use them to hang up presents for her dear ones, they

were ashamed. And the squirrel knew at once to whom she should give her hairs.

18 December

The Ungrateful Prince

Prince Goldenlock had a nurse called Biddy. She rocked him in his cradle, sang to him, carried him in her arms, and combed his lovely golden hair. She taught him his first words and songs, took him out in the garden, and showed him how to play the most wonderful games. They were fond of each other, but when Goldenlock grew a bit older and became a young man, the king decided that his education should be completed by learned professors. Biddy could go where she wanted, but she wasn't required at the palace any more. It was true that the nurse was not as young as she once was, and not as sprightly any more, but her heart was still open to all the troubles which the young lad might bring along to her. She was able to advise him and comfort him. But Goldenlock seemed to forget her kindness overnight. Suddenly he wanted to be grown up, and he never said a word to try to persuade the king to let her stay. They turned her out into the cold and savage weather. She did not get further than the lake beyond the royal gardens, and there she turned into a sad and crooked willow tree. By and by the prince felt that something was missing, that he yearned for

someone close to him. He ran out to look for the old nurse, but he couldn't find her. But from then on he confided all his troubles to the willow tree. And it always seemed to him that the bent old tree was the only one in the world who really understood him.

19 December

The Wind Elf, the Tree and the Storyteller

Two weeks and four days ago, the little tree from the big forest was crouching in a pocket of the wind elf's cloak. But no sooner had he warmed himself in there, and smelt the scent of summer coming from the wind elf's memories, than two new little branches, full of light-green needles, sprouted out. They weren't the last to grow either. The tree grew and grew, until the sky traveller said, a little shocked, 'You'll be bigger than me soon!' 'What of it?' asked the tree in surprise. 'You should be glad. Don't you know I'm meant to go on growing and growing?' But the wind elf was a bit annoyed. 'Then you might as well have stayed in the forest among the tall spruces, and you could have tried to catch them up. But you insisted on getting into my pocket, because you said you wanted to be a soft little memory. What am I going to do with you now? The ground is frozen and you can't go back home. If you keep on growing like that my pocket will tear open and you'll fall out somewhere or other, and what then?' But he had scarcely finished speaking, when his pocket really did start to tear. 'We'll have to land!' cried the sky traveller. 'Hold tight!' And they plunged headlong at a dizzy speed towards the ground. They pulled up just behind the collar of the storyteller's winter coat. He was walking through the village to the school, where he was going to give a little talk to the children.

surrounding countryside was lit up all night long. But that was not all. The bell tinkled so delightfully that people would stop when they heard it, look at each other kindly, forget all their troubles, and give each other presents. But Princess Alba said that gifts and celebrations mustn't be everyday things, and after a few days she put the bell away in a casket. She used to take it out again once a year, and that's how Christmas started.' 'That's not the end of the story already, is it?' asked young Billy in the front row. 'Don't worry,' said the storyteller, 'there's a little surprise to come yet.'

21 December

The Wind Elf, the Tree and the Storyteller

'Just outside the silver kingdom lived Melaina the wicked witch. Light and happiness and kind smiles were all things she hated. So she dressed up as a merchant, sought out Princess Alba, and offered her all manner of beautiful things in return for the casket containing the silver bell. Alba didn't want to give it her, but she gladly accepted an apple when she was offered one. The moment she had swallowed the

20 December

The Wind Elf, the Tree and the Storyteller

The teacher, Mrs. Pritchard, who was well-known for being strict, led the storyteller into the classroom, and before the children could shout 'hurrah' she said, 'You can have a little chat now, but the moment the bell rings for the end of the lesson the talk will have to finish, and we'll get on with some work.' 'Of course,' smiled the storyteller, and he hung up his coat (with the wind elf and the tree hiding on its collar), sat down, and began to tell a story. 'Once upon a time in a far-off silver kingdom a blacksmith made a bell. The goldsmith covered it with silver, and they sent it up to the royal castle as a present for the princess. As soon as she hung it up over the table, such a glow came off it that the

last mouthful, she forgot everything that she had done a year before, and so she also forgot about the bell inside the casket.' The children breathed out 'ooooh!' loudly, but they were soon quiet again when they looked up at their stern teacher. 'And now it's time to follow Melaina the witch, give Princess Alba her memory back, and set Christmas free again,' the storyteller went on. 'Yes, yes!' the children began to call, but they soon fell silent again. Mrs. Pritchard was looking just like Melaina the witch. The storyteller was quiet for a moment. He looked as if he was working out the end of the story, and the children watched him eagerly. But at that moment the school bell rang. 'It can't be helped,' the teacher announced. 'We'll have to get on with our lessons now. We look forward to seeing you again next year.' And she handed the storyteller his coat and nudged him towards the door.

22 December

The Wind Elf, the Tree and the Storyteller

The tree in the wind elf's pocket was so upset at not hearing the end of the story

that he forgot his promise and started growing again. He had got nice and warm under the coat collar in the classroom, and now he spread upwards and outwards all at once. 'Stop it!' the wind elf warned him. 'I can hardly carry you as it is!' The storyteller didn't hear him, because he was too busy thinking about what he should have done. Why couldn't he have got on with it, and slipped in a happy ending before the bell rang? 'No use crying over spilt milk,' he said, as he opened his cottage door. But just then his next-door-neighbour pulled at his coat. 'In case you don't know,' she said. 'There's a spruce growing out of your collar. But you do know, don't you! You have to keep on proving that you're mixed up in magic. You can't go and buy a Christmas tree in the market like everyone else. Oh no! You have to get one to grow out of the collar of your coat!' At first the storyteller thought his neighbour had gone off her head, and he hurriedly closed the door. But when he took his coat off, he saw that there really was a spruce sticking out of its collar. When he looked more closely, he saw that the tree was growing out of some sort of pocket, that the pocket belonged to some sort of cloak, and that the cloak was being worn by some sort of little creature whose hair was as white as dandelion fluff.

23 December

The Wind Elf, the Tree and the Storyteller

The storyteller was so confused by the whole business that he forgot to have any tea. He couldn't have had any anyway, since he hadn't remembered to buy any on the way back from the school. 'I'm getting like Princess Alba,' he thought. But there was one thing, luckily, which he didn't forget to do. He planted the restless tree from the

it was Mrs. Pritchard on her way to see the storyteller. When she arrived she banged on his door. The moment the storyteller opened it, she thrust thirty exercise-books into his hands. 'I insist that you . . .' she started to say, but she didn't get to the end of the sentence, because a voice from inside the cottage said, 'Good evening, and welcome!' It was the wind elf, who was swinging on the branch of the spruce like a little bell. Mrs. Pritchard was just about to say, 'Shhh,' in her sternest schoolteacher voice, but somehow, inside that pleasantly-scented, fairytale room she

wind elf's pocket in a big flower-pot. He hung the elf on one of the tree's fresh green branches like an ornament. How? By the hanger of his crumpled and torn old cloak that smelled of mist and air and night, and heaven knows what else. 'I don't have to worry about Christmas now,' the storyteller said thankfully, but then he suddenly grew anxious, as he wondered if there would be any Christmas at all that year, when he hadn't finished the story at the school. The children were worried about the same thing, so during the last lesson, instead of a composition about 'Our Village in Winter', they wrote thirty different endings to the story of the silver kingdom. Their teacher found out that evening as she started to mark the compositions. 'What is the meaning of this?' she said, with a stamp of her foot that made the table jump. She grabbed all thirty of the exercise-books and hurried across the village to the storyteller's cottage.

24 December

The Wind Elf, the Tree and the Storyteller

Everyone in the village thought a blizzard had passed their way that night, but actually

began to melt like a lump of ice. Meanwhile the storyteller opened one exercise-book after another, and read how Melaina had been captured by soldiers, how the king had thrown her in the dungeon, how she had been washed away by water and buried by rocks . . . But none of the endings was quite what he wanted, and he already had the twenty-ninth composition in his hand! He read the last one, which little Billy had written, out loud: '. . . and Melaina accidently ate one of the apples that make you forget what you've done before, and she forgot she had been evil, and everything turned out all right.' So Mrs. Pritchard took out her red pencil and wrote a big figure 'one' under the homework, the storyteller underlined it twice, and Christmas could begin.

25 December

The Doughnut's Christmas

Do you remember the doughnut we last met in November? Well, he rolled along the snow-covered path towards his home, singing a little song:

'This doughnut's a singer, a singer is he,
He's more nutty than doughy, 'tis plain to
see,
But after all his to-ing and fro-ing,
Today he knows just where he is going.
At Christmas time he makes his way gaily
To see a great-grandma called Grandma
Bailey.'

And in the meantime Grandma Bailey had indeed become a great-grandma, and now that Christmas was here her sons and daughters and grandchildren and great-grandchildren were all coming to see her. Though she was busy baking and roasting and boiling and frying, strangely enough she remembered the doughnut.

'I wonder what he's doing? Perhaps he got lost in the wide world. I suppose I should have sent him to school, since he wanted to go so much . . .' 'If you're talking about me then I've had my schooling,' said a voice from the door. The old woman threw up her hands. 'Wherever did you come from, doughnut?' 'Everyone should come home at Christmas, shouldn't they?' replied the doughnut. And on Christmas Eve he sat at the festive table and told them all the story of his adventures. 'Are you going to stay with me now?' asked Grandma Bailey. 'If you promise not to eat me,' the doughnut told her. Everyone laughed. 'Do you think anyone could eat you after all this time?' 'Well, well,' thought the doughnut, 'I'm out of danger now.'

26 December

The Jumping Christmas Present

Christine knew that her daddy always liked the presents she made herself best of all, so she cut him a pair of insoles for his shoes from an old box-top. She painted a kangeroo on each of them because she knew that he liked animals. She got a kiss for her clever present, and she was glad when her daddy put the insoles into his new slippers. But he had scarcely taken a step in them when he leapt off the ground, flew over the Christmas tree and the

236

prettily-decorated table, and ended up on the refrigerator in the kitchen. Christine and her mother looked on with their mouths wide open. Then they tried to get daddy down again, but he jumped down himself and bounced out of the window into the street. He landed on top of a taxi, and the taxi-driver said a little sourly, 'I'll be happy to take you anywhere you like chum, but first you'll have to sit inside!' But his strange customer probably didn't hear him, because he jumped up onto a street lamp, and from there onto the back of the dignified-looking statue in the middle of the town square. But when he started jumping over the people he met the fire-brigade were called out. Christine's daddy was lucky he landed in a snowdrift, where his slippers got stuck. He left them where they were and ran away. If anyone else found them and put them on — well you know what must have happened.

the fishpond. As a reward the carp gave them seven of its scales. Pleased as Punch the boys carried them home in the palms of their hands. The moon in the sky saw them, and turned those ordinary fish scales silver. When they got home, they found that their silver scales were worth a lot of money, enough to keep them all until spring came. The neighbours heard about it, and they too tried walking around on moonlit nights with fish-scales in their hands, but it was no use. They must have been different to the seven lads in Aunt Wilma's old house.

27 December

A Silver Reward

Heaven knows what all those boys who lived in Aunt Wilma's old house were called. There were seven of them like the days of the week. The roof above their heads was full of holes and the larder was usually empty, but they were always in a good mood. However when Christmas Eve came along and Auntie had nothing to give the children, she started to feel sad. So she hurried down to the market and swapped her woollen shawl for a big carp fish. 'I'll make them a nice soup out of it,' she thought, but the moment she showed the fish to the boys they felt sorry for it, and not one of them would hear of having it for supper. So instead they went and put it in

28 December

Chips the Cat and the New Television

Since Christmas Eve the Millers had had a new television, the biggest and most coloured one you've ever seen. They nearly never turned it off, because there was almost always someone sitting in front of it, most often Grandma and the twins Monty and Mike, or at least Chips the cat. The cat's favourite programmes were children's cartoons. One day she was lying in the

237

armchair, when she started to purr with delight to see that the next film was going to be about a cat and a mouse. She thought to herself that it would be great fun watching the clever cat catch the silly mouse. Only it turned out to be more or less the other way round! That sly mouse always managed to get the poor cat to do something that made a frying-pan fall on his head or left him dripping with paint or something. Chips started to frisk her tail angrily. When the cat got his foot caught in a mousetrap, Chips couldn't take any more, and she leapt off the armchair and bit through the aerial cable. The picture went off. Grandma and the twins were just arriving, and they were really surprised that there was nothing to see. 'They're probably having a rest, Granny,' said Monty. 'It doesn't matter though, 'cos you can tell us a story, can't you?' And so she did, about Red Riding Hood, Snow White, Cinderella and so on, and the children sat stock still. They all remembered that nice evening for a long time, even Chips the cat.

29 December

The Christmas Lollipop

Derek always looked forward to Christmas simply because it smelt of vanilla, raisins,

and marzipan. He wasn't interested in anything else. It upset his mother because, as you can imagine, it's not much use having a little boy who wants the whole world to be made of chocolate and gingerbread. One year she decided it was time to put a stop to Derek's greediness, so she didn't bake a thing for Christmas. The only things on the Christmas tree were glass ornaments. But Grandma, who had come for Christmas, was so sorry for the youngster that she slipped just one little lollipop wrapped in cellophane in among the presents. As usual Derek didn't take any notice of anything else, and stuck the lollipop in his mouth at once, wishing it could last for ever. But just fancy! It really didn't get sucked away, and Derek had the lollipop in his mouth all day, and then the next day, and for five whole days, and he couldn't stop sucking it!

30 December

The Christmas Lollipop

At first Grandma was delighted that Derek liked her present best of all, but she soon

238

began to think differently, as her darling grandson started to turn into a lollipop himself. He was sweet and sugary inside and out, and began to look like a candied stalagmite. When he spoke, marshmallows tumbled out of his mouth, and Grandma could have taken his honeyed voice and poured it over bottled fruit or put it in syrup bottles. She was beginning to think the lad might be quite useful in the kitchen, when his mother took a hand. Maybe she remembered the story of the pot that kept

on making stew until everything in the village was covered in the stuff. Anyway she suddenly shouted 'Enough!' Then she took the lollipop out of his mouth and threw it on the fire. At that moment Derek leapt out of his chair, gave his mother a big kiss, and thanked her for saving him. 'I thought it was never going to end,' he said. He went to wash his sticky fingers, and started reading the books which were still lying untouched under the Christmas tree. After that he was just a normal boy, except that he didn't like sweets at all.

31 December

Adam and the Wind Elf

'I can never stay in one place for very long,' the wind elf told the storyteller, when Christmas was over. 'After all, I *am* a sky traveller!' So they said goodbye, but the wind elf had scarcely taken off when he realized just how tired he was. He thought he had better slip into an attic and go to sleep. He was woken up by the crying of a child. 'What's going on?' asked the wind elf, and then he saw little Adam rubbing tears the size of marbles all over his face. 'I'm sulking,' replied Adam, looking over at the beam the wind elf was lying on. 'Huh!' the wind elf said to him. 'That's about the silliest thing you could do in all the world. You can believe me! I'm a hundred and twenty years old, and there's not a lot I haven't seen in my time. Anyway, what happened?' 'Nothing really!' Adam replied. 'It's just that I'm cross 'cos it's gone and got warm and I can't go sledging, and I've got nothing to do.' The wind elf nearly got cross too, but then he remembered that he used to be pretty silly himself. 'Try dreaming!' he said, instead of telling Adam off again. 'Attics are good places for dreaming, and it's much more fun than sulking.' 'I expect you're right,' said Adam, and he blew his nose. Just then they both saw out of the skylight that it was beginning to snow again outside. 'Hurrah!' shouted Adam, leaping up, and he went into the boxroom to get his sledge. When he came back into the attic the wise wind elf was gone. He had flown out into the snowstorm, where his white hair and tattered, misty cloak were quite lost from sight among the falling snow-flakes.